SHADOWCRY

JENNA BURTENSHAW

SHADOWCRY

⇥ THE SECRETS OF WINTERCRAFT ⇤

GREENWILLOW BOOKS
An Imprint of HarperCollinsPublishers

Shadowcry
Copyright © 2011 by Jenna Burtenshaw
First published in 2010 in Great Britain by Headline Publishing, an imprint of Hachette Livre UK; as *Wintercraft*. First published in 2011 in the United States by Greenwillow Books.
The right of Jenna Burtenshaw to be identified as the author of this work has been asserted by her.

Library of Congress Cataloging-in-Publication Data

Burtenshaw, Jenna.
[Wintercraft]
Shadowcry / by Jenna Burtenshaw.
p. cm. — (The secrets of Wintercraft)
"Greenwillow Books."
Summary: Pursued by two ruthless members of the High Council of Albion, fifteen-year-old Kate Winters discovers that she is one of the Skilled, a rare person who can see through the veil between the living and the dead.
ISBN 978-0-06-202642-2 (trade bdg.) [1. Fantasy. 2. Dead—Fiction.] I. Title.
PZ7.B94569Ni 2011   [Fic]—dc22   2010025823

11 12 13 14 15 LP/RRDB 10 9 8 7 6 5 4 3 2 1
First Edition

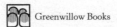

Greenwillow Books

For my mother, Janette,
for all of your help and inspiration.
You are a wonderful mum and will always be
my most precious friend.

CONTENTS

PROLOGUE

At the southern edge of a moonlit city, a woman stood over an open grave. The blue edge of a tower's long shadow sliced across the ground beside her feet and the grave yawned like an open throat, its headstone cracked in two, leaving only a broken piece of stone to mark the place where the dead still lay.

The lamp in her hand was hooded against the wind, and the ruby beads sewn along her sleeves shone and sparkled in its light. Shovelfuls of earth arched up through the air and she leaned out farther, watching her companion slice into the ground, clearing the way to the coffin she knew would be waiting deep down in the dark.

"Faster," she commanded.

The man obeyed, muddying his black robes as he worked.

A few late carriages rattled along a road in the distance, but they were too far away to see anything but the lantern's tiny light, and when the sharp crack of metal striking wood sounded through the night, only the woman could sense the spirits of the dead that gathered close around their digging place.

"Open it," she said.

The man knelt to clear the last patch of earth from the coffin's face, then he snatched his hands away and stared in horror. "I don't think ya wanna do that," he said. "Take a look at this."

He moved back, letting the lantern light spread all the way down to where a large symbol was burned deeply into the wood. It was a perfect circle, almost as wide as the coffin itself, and scorched into the very center of it was a large snowflake, burned down to a finger's width deep.

"That is the mark of the Winters family," said the woman. "We are close. Now, open it!"

She glared at Kalen when he hesitated. The dead were close by—that mark meant that the coffin was protected by more than the eye could see—but she had waited too long for this moment to turn back now. "I have no time for superstition, Kalen," she said. "Get out of my way."

"My lady?"

"Out!"

The man clambered up onto the ground as the woman lowered herself into the grave, staining her dress with streaks of grass and moss. She did not care. She lifted the spade and smashed it straight into the center of the symbol, releasing an invisible energy that spread out across the ground, making the hairs on Kalen's neck bristle and forcing the spirits that had gathered around them to retreat at once.

Kalen stood warily over the hole as the lid of the coffin crunched and split beneath his mistress's hands. The ruby beads on her sleeves alone could buy her ten teams of carriage horses, but she dropped to her knees and reached down into the dark void she had uncovered, scraping them carelessly against the broken wood and snapping them from their threads as if they were made of glass. The grave was old, the coffin lined with yellowing bones, and in the very center—where it had remained for more than a hundred years—was the object the woman had come to find.

She slid it out into the open air: a small black box barely ten inches wide, made from gnarled wood and sealed with a silver clasp.

"Give me your dagger," she said.

The clasp snapped easily with a twist of the blade, and beneath the lid, which creaked and split when she lifted it, was a small leather-bound book.

The woman snatched it up, desperate to possess it at last, and inspected the edges of its discolored pages as if they were the only ones left in the world. It was small, but the pages were packed tight—as thick as a fist—and folded inside its cover was an ancient document bearing a warning that had been ignored many times. There, in the hands of its discoverer, it was about to be ignored again.

Kalen held out a hand to help her climb out of the grave, where she read its words with eager eyes.

⤝⟶ ❉ ⟶⤞

THE *ways of* Wintercraft *are not for the careless, the arrogant, nor the unwise.*

You hold now a book of instructions that, if followed, shall allow the fearless mind to go beyond the boundaries of this world and step without restraint into the mysteries of another.

Keep it safe. Keep it secret. And follow its words with care. This path is more dangerous than you can know.

The woman smiled. After years of searching, she had found it. She opened the book to the first page, where a further warning was written in sharp black ink.

Those Who Wish to See the Dark, Be Ready to Pay Your Price.

She nodded slowly, as if the book had spoken those thirteen words out loud. Whatever price was required, she would pay it gladly.

Kalen looked around warily as the woman ran her fingers along the title on the front of the book, its silver-leafed letters glinting in the moonlight.

WINTERCRAFT

"This is only the beginning," she said.

⤜ 1 ⤝

MARKET
DAY

For ten years the town of Morvane had been left alone. Its people had lived safely behind its high walls and watched as other towns around them died one by one. The country of Albion was at war, but most people had never seen an enemy come close to their gates. The only threat they knew came from within their own lands; from the High Council seated within the distant capital city of Fume and from the wardens sent to harvest the towns for anyone strong enough to fight.

There was never any warning before the wardens came. When soldiers were scarce, ordinary people were forced to take their place in battle and anyone who refused the call to fight was put to death. In five decades of war, Morvane's citizens had been harvested twice. Children had grown up hearing stories of missing parents they would never know; people had built hiding places and dug secret paths beneath the ground to escape the wardens; and many buildings stood bare as people

---

gradually left the town to live in the wilder villages instead, where harvesting rarely happened.

Kate Winters had been five years old when the wardens last came. That was the day when everything changed. The day her parents were taken away and she had first learned what it meant to have an enemy.

Since that day, she had grown up with her uncle, Artemis Winters, living and working in his bookshop on the edge of Morvane's market square. Morvane was one of the last few great towns in the northern counties, almost three miles wide from wall to wall and divided into quarters by four stone arches left behind from an age long before the wardens and the war. The market square stood in the very heart of the town, but instead of trading in luxuries and curiosities alongside the usual market fare, the traders sold only what they could grow, stitch, or build themselves, concentrating on the basic items Morvane's people needed to survive.

Books were not one of Morvane's main priorities anymore, but since Artemis and Kate's bookshop was the only one left in the town, there was still enough trade to justify keeping it open. Every book they had for sale was at least secondhand and every spine was cracked and worn. They repaired them whenever they could, taking tattered old books and selling them for a small profit, and the shop earned just enough silver to be able to support them comfortably, as well as paying a small wage to a third member of staff who could repair two books in the time it took Kate to fix one. The bookshop had been passed down through the Winters family for generations, and Kate hoped that one day it would be hers.

Artemis had taught Kate to be cautious and alert in case the wardens ever decided to return to Morvane, and theirs was the only shop on the market square to keep a dagger hidden beneath the counter and bolts locked on every window, even during the day. Precautions, Artemis had said, that could one day save their lives.

The rest of the townspeople had become complacent, preferring to live with the pretense of freedom rather than living in fear. They no longer checked their escape routes as often as they should, or kept horses bridled by their doors at night. Soon only the two quiet owners of the dusty old bookshop had been left with their suspicions. Morvane had begun to relax. The townspeople's lives went on. And so, on the day the wardens finally did return, only the Winters family was ready.

Kate woke at sunrise to a soft tap on her bedroom door. She grumbled at the unwanted noise and pulled her blanket over her head.

"Kate, are you awake?"

"No."

"Breakfast's ready."

"I'll be out in a minute."

Artemis Winters was a great believer in early mornings. Kate definitely was not. Normally, she would have tried to grab a few extra minutes of sleep before he came to wake her again, but then she remembered what day it was and forced herself to sit up. Rattling sounds were coming from the kitchen, and the smell of hot porridge crept under her bedroom door. She slid her feet into her slippers and shuffled over to the mirror.

It was market day—the last market day before the Night of Souls—and the bookshop could expect to see a lot more customers than the handful that usually came through the door. The Night of Souls was Albion's biggest celebration, when everyone dressed up and threw parties in the streets to honor their ancestors and remember the dead. Each year, Kate would defy her uncle and climb up onto the bookshop roof to hang colorful banners in memory of her parents, adding them to hundreds of others scattered around the town. Crates of fireworks had been arriving in the market square for weeks, ready to mark the stroke of midnight in four days' time, when the spirits of the dead were said to walk the streets and speak to the living. Not that Kate really believed in any of that.

To most people the Night of Souls was all about dressing up, planning parties, and exchanging gifts. It was a time for drinking and feasting and celebrating. Raising a glass to the dead was just one old tradition hidden among the new. Far more important was the gift giving. Even the quietest shops were at their busiest that time of year, and the bookshop would have to open early to make the best of it.

Kate tied her black hair into a braid and glared at her reflection. Her eyes were wide and feline, her nose was small, and her skin was pale, thanks to the long hours she spent in the shop. Artemis insisted she looked like her mother. Kate thought she looked more like a skinny cat. Her hand went to her throat, where a small pendant hung on a silver chain: a delicate circle of precious metal holding an oval gemstone that matched perfectly the vivid blue brightness of her eyes. Her mother had worn that necklace every day and, apart from the bookshop, it was all she had left of her.

Kate closed her tired eyes against the tears that were already starting to gather there. It had been ten years, but the Night of Souls always made the bad memories come creeping back. She let them settle in her mind for a few moments and polished the surface of the stone with her thumb, making it shine a little brighter than before.

"Kate?" Artemis's voice carried down the corridor again.

"I'm coming."

"Get dressed. Quick as you can."

Kate turned away from the mirror, letting the stone fall back against her skin. Then she dragged on her clothes, fought her boots out of the mess lurking under her bed, and shuffled sleepily down the corridor to the kitchen, letting her nose lead the way.

"I've heard something new," said Artemis, pouring her a

cup of hot milk from a steaming pan. His brow was tense; an open letter lay upon the table, bearing a black wax seal that Kate had seen many times before.

She dropped onto her chair and tried to wake up.

"As you know, the wardens haven't taken anyone from the northern counties for some time," said Artemis. "I contacted a few friends in the south and it turns out things have been just as quiet all over Albion."

"That's good, isn't it?" asked Kate, resigning herself to yet another early morning warden conversation.

"I'm not sure. The last I heard, Continental soldiers had tried to land boats on the southern coast and Albion soldiers burned every one of them with fire arrows before they even reached the shore. The war could be going well for once. Or the wardens might just have new orders."

"I don't suppose they'll leave people alone for very long," said Kate, eating as she talked. "What else did your friends say?"

"They told us to be careful, "said Artemis. "Without a pattern to follow, no one knows where the wardens are likely to go next. Morvane is doing well. We have more people here than any of the smaller towns nearby. In the High Council's eyes we could afford to lose a few hundred to the war effort. A harvest here could well be overdue."

"You think they're coming back," said Kate, her face serious.

"I think we need to be prepared." Artemis pushed his bowl aside and stood up. "We won't be opening the shop today," he said. "I've sent a note to Edgar telling him not to bother coming in to work. Find a bag and pack whatever you will need for the next few days."

"We're leaving Morvane?"

"Just for a while."

"But if the wardens are coming, we have to warn people. We have to tell them! We can't just leave!"

"Yes, we can," said Artemis. "Two of us might pass unnoticed on our way out of the town gates. Any more than that will certainly be seen and stopped."

"What about Edgar? He can come with us. One more won't—"

"No," said Artemis. "Not even him. We can't take that risk. You'll just have to trust me, Kate. We're leaving today."

Kate had never seen Artemis as worried as he was that morning. She packed a small bag as quickly as she could and dragged it downstairs to wait for him on the bookshop floor. She looked out of the front window and across the market square. The sun had started to rise over Morvane's frosty streets and the market traders had already set up their stalls on the cobbles, welcoming their first customers with red cheeks, hugging themselves against the cold. Two would-be book buyers tested the bookshop's door and Kate hid behind a curtain, not wanting to explain why she couldn't let them in.

11

"Good idea," said Artemis, lugging his traveling bag down the stairs. "The last thing we need is customers trying to fight their way in. We'll make our way out of town on foot and follow one of the old roads out to the west. No one will know us there. We'll walk to the next town, find a good place to stay and after a few days . . . Well . . . We'll be back before you know it."

"This is the best trading day of the year," said Kate, who had never known her uncle to take a day off work, never mind actually close up the shop. "Why do we have to go today?"

Artemis pulled on his coat and gloves and slid the dagger from its hiding place beneath the desk. "There are far more important things in this world than money," he said.

Thud.

Kate turned.

Something had just struck the window.

"What was that?" Kate asked.

"Whatever it was, it's not important," said Artemis. "We have to go."

Kate picked up her bag while he unlocked the door and when they stepped out into the icy square she almost trod on something small and black lying upon the cobbles.

"It's a bird," she said, picking up the limp body and cupping it in her hands. "It must have flown into the window."

Artemis's eyes went immediately to the sky.

"I thought blackbirds didn't nest here in Albion

anymore," said Kate. "I've never seen one in town before."

"Kate. Get inside."

"What? Why?"

Before Artemis could answer, a second bird speared down past his head and struck the shop door with a sharp crack. And it was not alone.

Kate looked up and saw a huge flock of blackbirds swooping over the square. Hundreds of them, screeching to one another and thumping down at the buildings, two or three at a time. People ran for cover, huddling together in doorways as the flock shifted and dived. Artemis grabbed Kate's arm and pulled her back into the shop.

"We're too late," he said.

Thud-thud.

"What's happening?"

"It's a hording! Get in! Don't let them into the shop."

"What's a—? *Ahh!*"

Kate ducked away from a blackbird that speared down at the door on a collision course, its bright eyes wild and unnatural. Artemis swung the door shut, ignoring Kate's shriek of horror as a flurry of black feathers bounced off the glass and flopped lifeless to the ground. He dragged the bolt across and pulled her away from the window.

"Go down into the cellar," he said, throwing their bags into the darkness at the back of the shop. "Stay there and hide. It'll be all right."

Thud-thud.

"What are you going to do?"

"I—I don't know. Just stay down there."

Bang-bang-bang.

A fist pounded on the front door and Artemis jumped.

"Everyone all right in there?" A young man was outside, braving the mad birds with his nose pressed to the glass.

"Edgar!" Kate yelled. "Edgar's out there!"

Edgar waved at her through the door. "Bloody birds! "he shouted, his voice muffled by the glass.

"We have to let him in!"

"No. Get down to the cellar. Please, Kate!"

"We can't just leave him out there!"

Edgar squealed as one of the birds flapped down onto his head, tangling its claws in his mess of dark hair. He reached up and grabbed it, tugging it loose and pinning its wings to its sides so it couldn't get away. "Steady there!" he said, trying to calm it down.

The bird pecked at its reflection in the glass and freed one of its wings, fluttering hard. Edgar's boots slid on an icy cobblestone and he fell onto his back, keeping tight hold of the bird until its other wing flapped loose, smacking him full in the face.

Kate wasn't about to stand and watch her best friend wrestling on the ground. She dropped the dead blackbird into her coat pocket and pushed past her uncle, ignoring his shouts as she threw back the bolt and swung open the door. "Edgar, come on!"

"Look out!" cried Artemis.

The bird flapped hard and Edgar let go, sending it fluttering up past Kate's face to join the others in the air. Kate helped Edgar up and pulled him into the shop.

"Now that's something you don't see every day," he said, holding out his arms as if his coat sleeves might bite. A sticky green residue had stained one of the cuffs. "I rubbed that off its beak," he said. "Bloodbane. Very poisonous. If I was a bird, I wouldn't want to eat any of that." He sniffed it experimentally. "And it's fresh."

"The wardens are responsible for this," said Artemis. "Both of you, get down into the cellar."

"Are you nuts?" said Edgar, taking off his coat and kicking it across the floor. "If there are wardens about, we have to run. Hiding won't do us any good."

"Did you see any of them out there?" asked Kate.

"No, but they're not exactly going to walk up and start a conversation, are they? Hey! What are you doing?"

Artemis had grabbed hold of Edgar's arm and was marching him and Kate over to the cellar door. The three of them squeezed onto the cellar steps, and Artemis locked them in. A flame flickered in the darkness as he lit a match from his pocket and fed it to an oil lamp that swelled with light, revealing an underground room packed with shelves, books, and dozens of storage boxes.

"Down to the bottom," he said.

Kate and Edgar followed him into the middle of the cellar and stood there listening to thud after thud as the birds slammed into the windows above.

"Those birds are here as a test," he said, in as loud a whisper as he could manage. "We can't let them in. We can't even look at them. Do you understand?"

"A test for what?" asked Kate.

"You wanted to know what else my friends told me? They told me about this. This exact same thing has happened many times in the south over the last few years. Hordings were witnessed in six towns in just six days right before the wardens went quiet. It seems the High Council aren't happy collecting just anyone anymore. They want a specific kind of person. I think they're looking for the Skilled." Artemis was trying his best to put on a brave face, but his hands were shaking and his fear was infectious.

Kate gently lifted the blackbird's body out of her pocket. She only knew a little about the Skilled, from rumors, mostly. They were people with abilities that most ordinary people did not possess. No one knew exactly what they could do, but most of them were healers, or seers who believed they could see into the future or communicate with the dead. Many of them lived in hiding, and by the time anyone realized they had met one of the Skilled, they would already be gone, never to be heard from again.

"Those birds will have been bred for this," said Artemis. "The wardens have used the same technique for years. Whenever they want to find the Skilled, they poison hundreds of blackbirds and set them loose. The birds die, the wardens make their move, and when a Skilled eventually comes into contact with one, the bird is healed. No one knows how. All the wardens have to do is find one of their birds alive and hunt close by for the person who healed it. Most of the Skilled are wise to the trap, but there are always some who don't yet know that they have the ability. Those are the ones in real danger."

Kate felt a small stirring in her hands. Had she imagined it? Had the bird moved?

"If there are wardens here, there will be very little left of this town by nightfall," said Artemis. "The hording is only the beginning. I'm sorry, Kate. I should have taken you away from here sooner."

Kate looked down at her hands. The bird's leg had definitely twitched. "I think we have a bigger problem than that," she said, staring in disbelief as the dead blackbird suddenly blinked, fluttered one wing, and struggled drunkenly to its feet. Once up, it teetered a little and then flapped into the air to land expertly on one of the shelves.

"That bird . . ." said Edgar. "It was just stunned, right?"

"No, it wasn't," said Artemis. "Its neck was broken."

"It couldn't have been. How could it fly up there with a broken neck?"

Artemis's lamp was shaking now. "Kate," he said. "You're the right age. And they say when it happens, it happens suddenly. Often under stress."

"No," said Kate, staring at her hands as if they were no longer a part of her. "It . . . it couldn't have been me."

"Did Kate do something to that bird?" Edgar looked around stupidly, as if everyone had gone crazy except him. "It looks pretty perky to me."

Artemis lowered the lamp, making his eye sockets look deep and dark in the shadows. "This changes everything," he said. "I think . . . I think she just brought it back to life."

2
THE
COLLECTOR

Outside, the market square was in chaos, and high above it, a tall, dark figure stood alone upon a rooftop, his wide shoulders silhouetted against the sky.

Silas Dane was the last man any town wanted to see. He stood there in silence, watching events unfolding exactly as he had planned. His clothes were deliberately dark and plain, but that was where his ordinariness ended. Silas had the presence of ten men. Power and threat exuded from him as clearly as fear leaked from the people down below, and his eyes shone with faint light, their irises bleached gray: the washed-out empty gray of death.

Even in their madness the birds stayed clear of him, sensing the unnatural essence that made him what he was: neither fully dead nor completely alive, but unimaginably dangerous. Only one bird stayed close, one that had been with Silas since before his second life had begun: his own black crow, perched upon his shoulder, ignoring the mass of feathers and death swooping down around them.

Silas rested a scarred hand against a chimneystack and cast his eyes around the market square. The wardens were not far away. From his viewing point he could see three of their black robes lurking nearby, daggers already drawn, blades shining in the rising sunlight. Those three were only the beginning. He had over a hundred more men stationed around the town, all waiting to make their move.

The last of the dying birds plunged into one of the market stalls and Silas watched the traders step out of their hiding places, each one nervously checking the sky for more birds. He sighed, wishing for once to face some kind of challenge . . . some form of resistance. Then the streets fell quiet, as if the entire town was holding its breath, and an unexpected sound carried to him on the wind. A flapping sound, like two strips of leather being clapped together. He looked up, his eyes darting straight to the roof of the little bookshop he had been told to watch more closely than the rest, and then he saw it.

His muscles tensed. There, rising from the bookshop's chimney, was a black fluttering shape, trailing soot behind it as it awkwardly took flight.

Bird or bat? He had to be sure.

Bird or bat?

The flying creature turned in the air, rode upon an updraft and soared across the market square, over the heads of the traders and right past Silas, so close that he could have snatched it out of the air if he had tried.

"Bird," he said, with a cruel smile.

The wardens were looking to him, waiting for instructions. Silas raised a hand and signaled the order they were all waiting for. The order to move in.

"The chimney!" cried Artemis. "Grab the bird. Quick!"

Edgar lunged forward but Artemis was already ahead of him, climbing up the shelves like a ladder. The blackbird watched them warily. Artemis made a wild grab for it, but he was too slow. The bird took flight, headed straight for the old cellar fireplace and fluttered up the chimney, searching for the sky. Edgar ducked in after it, waving his arms around blindly in the dark. When he re-emerged his face and hair were thick with soot, but his hands were empty.

Artemis stared at him. "If a warden sees that bird they'll find us in a second," he said.

Edgar sneezed and wiped his nose along a filthy sleeve. "Best start running then," he said. "Better that than be trapped down here. Right, Kate?"

Kate didn't know what to think.

"I'm not giving either of you a choice," said Artemis, swinging the lamp as he headed toward the back of the cellar. "We have to hide. The wardens can't take what they can't see."

Artemis heaved aside two boxes of old books that were

stacked in the corner furthest from the door. He held the light up to the wall, revealing a tiny door sunk into the stone, just wide enough for a person to crawl into. He scraped his fingers around the dusty edges and searched his pockets for the key. Kate knew that place. She had hidden behind that little door before and she never wanted to go near it again.

"I—I can't," she said.

Something clicked and creaked above them.

Slow footsteps crossed the shop floor.

"Come on, Kate." Edgar held out his hand, and Artemis blew out the lamp, unsticking the old door as quickly as he could.

Kate knew she had no choice. She crept forward through a cloud of dust knocked down from the floorboards above and crawled into the secret hiding place. An old blanket was bunched on the floor, giving a soft place for her knees to rest, but the little hollow behind the wall was a lot smaller than she remembered. She shuffled forward a few knee-steps and scrabbled around, making room for Edgar to squeeze in behind her.

"Move up," he whispered.

"There's no more room."

"What about Artemis?"

But Artemis had already tucked the blown-out lamp behind the door and he made no attempt to follow them inside. "Whatever happens, you two stay in here until they are gone," he said. "After that, I want you both to leave Morvane, and don't look back. Do you understand?"

"But—"

"It'll be all right, Kate. Do you remember how to get out?"

Kate nodded nervously.

"Good. When it is safe, go. Don't worry about me. Nothing is going to happen to you. I promise."

Kate could not see Artemis's face when he closed the door, but she heard the scratchy sound of a key turning in the lock and suddenly she was afraid. The tiny room felt a lot smaller, its walls pressing closer around her body as she knelt in the dark. She was touching the wall in front of her, reassuring herself that there was still plenty of air to breathe, when a quiet whimpering sound started beside her.

"Edgar? What's wrong?"

"We're locked in," said Edgar, sounding even more terrified than Kate felt. "I don't like this. We have to get out. We have to. Artemis!"

Edgar thumped his fist against the door and Kate grabbed his hands, forcing her own fear aside as she tried to calm him down. "It's okay," she whispered. "Listen to me. You have to be quiet. If they hear us—"

"I can't breathe. Kate . . . I can't . . ."

"Shh. Yes, you can." She held his hand and pressed it against her chest. "You feel that? I'm breathing. You're breathing. We're going to be all right."

Edgar fell quiet and small scraping noises bumped against the door as Artemis quickly stacked boxes against it. Then Kate heard the sound of metal rattling against stone and a cold key fell into her hands. The eyeholes! Her fingers reached up to feel out the thin spaces in the wall. How could she have forgotten the eyeholes?

"Stay quiet and don't come out," said Artemis. "I love you, Kate. Remember that."

Kate walked her fingers along the stones and found a flap of leather pinned a little way below the ceiling. It was dry and curled with age, but when she pushed it aside, she could see through a carefully cut slit between the mortar of the wall and one of the old stones. She moved Edgar's hand up to a second leather strip and together they looked out.

At first they couldn't see anything, just deep darkness. Then there were voices, quick footsteps, and a loud slam as someone forced open the cellar door. Two black-robed men burst onto the staircase, flooding the room with light from a lantern that cracked hard against the wall.

One of the men had a crossbow trained carefully down the cellar steps and the other held the lantern high, straining to keep hold of a long leather leash with a vicious dog panting at the end of it. Kate's mind threw up visions of the great beast sniffing them out, snuffling its jaws into their hiding place and dragging them out with its sharp yellow teeth, but those terrors were soon buried under something far more important.

Where was Artemis?

"Search it," said the bowman, and the warden with the dog scuttled down the steps, letting its nose investigate, hunting its prey.

The dogman dragged full boxes aside as if they were empty, scouring every cranny for signs of life. He pulled handfuls of paper out of the storage chests, rapped his knuckles on the walls, and dug his long fingers into every crack, leaving nothing unchecked. Closer and closer he came to the little door, until a sudden scrabbling noise in the wall made the dog lower its head and snarl.

"Here," the bowman said. "What's that in there?"

Kate froze, but the wardens were not looking in her direction. They were looking toward the fireplace, where a trickle of soot was falling into the room. Artemis was hiding in the chimney. The wardens had found him.

"Come out of there!" demanded the dogman, mashing his fist against the chimney breast. "Now!"

The dog's ears pressed back against its skull as Artemis's feet thumped down into the hearth. "Wait!" he said, holding his hands out. He stepped into the room, dropping his useless dagger on the floor. "Please."

The bowman raised his weapon to Artemis's chest. Kate wanted to shout out, to distract them, stop them, but fear was gripping her throat so tightly it was a struggle even to breathe.

"Name."

"Winters. Artemis Winters. I—I own the shop upstairs."

"Who else is in here?"

"No one."

The glinting point of the arrow moved up to Artemis's throat. "Who *else?*"

"I already told you . . . *ooof!*"

Artemis's lip dripped with blood. The dogman had struck him with a meaty fist, knocking him to the floor.

"There's no one here!" said Artemis, trying to stand up again. "I told you . . . *ahh!*"

The dogman's boot kicked hard into Artemis's ankle and he dragged Artemis up by the shoulders.

Tears stung in Kate's eyes. She couldn't bear to watch.

Edgar squeezed her hand gently as a shadow spread from the cellar door. The dog crouched low, head down, turning its eyes away from a man who was standing at the top of the stairs. All Kate saw was his shadow, and she heard the flutter of feathers as a large bird shuffled upon his shoulder.

"What do you have down there?"

The dog whimpered at the sound of the man's voice and pressed its body against its master's legs.

"A bookseller," said the dogman, grinning. "Only one here. It must have been him."

"Are you certain of that?" The man stepped down the stairs into the lantern's glow, and Kate saw him clearly for the first time. He didn't dress like a warden, he didn't even speak like a warden. Instead of robes he wore a long coat that hissed across the floor as he walked, and his voice was dark and eloquent, demanding the attention of anyone who could hear it. His black hair was long enough to touch his shoulders. He was younger than Artemis and walked with the strides of a man used to being in control, but the strangest thing about him was his eyes. Dead eyes, Kate thought. Eyes without a soul. She watched him closely, waiting for those eyes to look in her direction, and when they did, pausing for only the smallest moment before moving on, her body felt cold with fear.

"His name?"

"Winters, "said the bowman.

The man towered over Artemis, at least a head and shoulders taller than him. "He is not the one we have come for," he said, taking one last look around. "There is someone else here."

"No," insisted Artemis, his voice unusually strong. "There's no one. Only me."

"The girl. Where is she?"

"W-what girl?"

Kate shrank back in the darkness. He knew about the blackbird. He knew that it was her.

"Lies will not keep me from her for long." The man turned to his wardens. "You, take him outside and put him with the others. And you, check the upper floor. If the girl is not found here, I will burn this place down."

"Yes, sir."

"No!" cried Artemis, looking back at the hiding place, his face pale with desperation. "My shop! M-my work!"

"None of that matters to you now," said the man. "If you are one of the Skilled, as these men think you are, then your life as you know it is over. If not . . . the same applies, only in a much more final way. Take him."

Artemis struggled all the way up the cellar steps, limping whenever his bruised ankle was put to use. He barely made it halfway before his leg gave way altogether and the dogman had to leave his lantern on the floor and drag him up into the shop, with his dog and the bowman close behind.

Soon only the gray-eyed man was left in the cellar, and he stood there, motionless, staring at the wall as if he could see Kate and Edgar cowering behind it. The bird on his shoulder cocked its head to one side, and Kate pressed her nose right up to the stone beneath the eyehole, watching. She wanted to move back, but any movement might give her away. Edgar's chest was wheezing with each nervous breath, and she squeezed his hand, desperate for him to be quiet.

"We're ready, sir," came the bowman's voice from the floor above. "There is a girl's room on the top floor, but the rest of the house is clear."

"Very well," said the man. "Return to the square."

With the wardens gone, the gray-eyed man opened the lantern and slid a small book from a storage shelf beside him.

He cracked the book open with one hand, touching its pages to the lantern's exposed flame. They caught at once. The book smoldered and burned with growing fire, and he carried it up the cellar steps to begin his work.

"He's going to burn the shop," whispered Kate, as heavy footsteps crossed overhead.

"Maybe he's just trying to scare Artemis," said Edgar. "To make him tell him where you are."

The hot smell of burning paper crept in around them, and Kate pressed the key into Edgar's hand.

"He's doing it!" she whispered. "Open the door. We have to get out."

Edgar fumbled with the key, dropping it in his panic. "Kate, that man . . ."

"I know," said Kate. "Just get us out."

"No, you don't understand . . ."

Something thumped nearby. A door, slamming open.

"What was that?" Kate twisted back to the eyehole. The man had returned, his face glowing in the light of a flaming torch that blazed in front of him as he walked down the cellar steps. He stopped for a moment at the bottom, looked along the shelves one last time and then rammed the head of the lit torch into the box nearest to him, letting the flames catch, crackle, and spread.

"Oh no," said Edgar, desperately searching for the fallen key.

The man moved to the next shelf, then another and another, until one side of the cellar was a rising wall of flame. Edgar found the key and felt around for the keyhole, but Kate held him back, pulling on his arm with all her strength. The man did not hear the scuffle above the crackling noise of the flames. He threw the torch into the center of the room, watched it splutter against the stone, and then climbed back up to the doomed shop floor, leaving his deadly fire to spread and grow.

Edgar struggled and scratched the little key into place, fighting to make it turn.

"Stop! It's too late," said Kate. "Listen to me!"

Firelight seeped in through the open eyeholes, reflecting in Edgar's frightened eyes as he turned to her. "The shop is on fire!" he said. "We have to get out!"

"Yes, but not that way. Give me the key."

"What? No! You said . . ."

"Edgar, please."

"We're going to die in here, Kate!"

"No, we're not." Kate tugged up a corner of the floor blanket and rapped her knuckles on what sounded like hollow wood where stone should have been. Edgar looked at her, confused.

"Artemis knew what he was doing, putting us in here," she said. "There's another way out. Please, Edgar. Trust me."

3

THE
WARRENS

Thick smoke swirled around the cellar, creeping along the stairs, up the chimney, and under the door of the little hiding place. It crawled up Kate's and Edgar's noses like ghostly worms, making them cough and choke as the air around them was churned into a deadly soup.

"Here." Edgar thrust the key into Kate's hand, and she wrestled the blanket out from under her knees, flapping it back to uncover a circular trapdoor with a sunken handle. Her fingers felt for the keyhole, pushed the key in, and turned it, sending a deep clunk echoing from under the floor.

"Open it. Open it!"

The rusted hinges cracked and moaned as Kate lifted the hatch, sending a gush of dead air swirling up to fill the smoky space. A match flared as Edgar relit Artemis's lamp and held it out over the deep narrow shaft. There was just enough light to make out a passage at the bottom and a long wooden ladder nailed down the side.

Kate went first, leaving Edgar struggling to keep his eyes open, they were so sore with the smoke.

"It's not far," she said, dropping onto hard earth. "Come on."

Edgar swung himself down the hole and descended the ladder as fast as he could, closing the trapdoor as he went. He jumped the last two rungs and looked back up the shaft, half expecting a warden to come slithering behind them. "Where are we?" he asked.

Kate could hear the worry in his voice and he clung to her wrist. They were standing at the end of a low tunnel built of small gray stones, not far from a shadowy crossroad where it linked with two wider tunnels that split off at sharp angles.

"I'm going to take a look up ahead," she whispered. "You stay here. Watch the door."

"Me? Why? Hey, wait!"

Kate ignored him and headed off down the tunnel, taking their only light with her.

Even with the lamp, the tunnel felt tight and claustrophobic. The walls were rough and uneven, and narrow enough at some points to rub against her shoulders unless she turned to the side. The little flame flickered, burning dangerously low as she drew close to the junction up ahead. She ran her fingers along the wall and was trying not to think about the fires tearing through her home above her, when something crunched under her feet.

Kate stopped and stepped back, worried that the old floor might collapse into a tunnel below. She shone the light toward her feet. The ground felt sturdy enough, but there were tiny brown things scattered over it: things that crunched and clicked under her boots. And they were moving.

The little shapes clambered over one another, writhing across the floor, making it wriggle and shine as if the entire place was alive. Artemis had complained for months about hide beetles attacking the leather-bound books in the cellar; now Kate knew where they had been coming from. She stepped straight through them, reached the junction, and pressed her back against the wall, summoning the courage to look out.

The left-hand tunnel sloped downward and turned a corner some way along, where a torch was burning on a hook in the wall. Maybe someone else had found their way into the tunnels: a neighbor, perhaps, someone who might help her save Artemis from the wardens. Then she looked to the right, where the second tunnel had a torch of its own much farther away, linking on one side with another branching path.

Footsteps echoed slowly in the distance and a third torch moved into sight, carried by a hunched figure walking with slow, shuffling steps. It was a man, his face lit by the flames while his eyes stared hard at the ground.

Kate stayed still.

The man stopped, straightened his back with great effort, and raised his nose to the air. Then he turned, his bloodshot eyes suddenly looking right into hers. She ducked out of sight, pulling her coat over the lamp, her heart pounding in her chest.

"Hello?" the man called down the tunnel, making that one word sound dangerous and threatening. He definitely was not a neighbor.

"Who's there?" he shouted again.

"Kate?" Edgar called her name from the ladder, and she turned back, gesturing for him to be quiet. "What's wrong?" he whispered.

"Hello?"

Kate squeezed along the tunnel as fast as she could and pounced on Edgar, clamping a hand over his mouth. "Shut up!" she hissed, pulling him down into a crouch and blowing out the lamp. "There's someone else down here."

"Better come out," came the man's creeping voice. "Come on out, now." A scratching sound scraped the walls: the sound of a blade being dragged slowly along uneven stones. "Yer trespassin'! You got no business bein' in my place. Come on, now. Show yerself and yer sweet young bones. Let old Kalen pick 'em clean."

Kate and Edgar waited as the footsteps drew closer, trying to make themselves as small as possible in the space next to the ladder. There was nowhere to go, and smoke was seeping down through the trapdoor as the fire made quick work of the cellar.

"Where are ya, eh? Don't think I didn't see you up here, girly."

The man's torch swelled the tunnel junction with a wash of light, and he shuffled in after it. He was dressed in the long black robes of a warden, but he looked much older than any wardens Kate had seen. His robes were shabby and worn, he had strips of rags wrapped around his feet instead of boots, and every piece of uncovered skin was streaked with pale mud, making him look grim and skeletal in the half-light.

He raised his torch, turned a grimy dagger in his hand, and looked down the bookshop's tunnel. Kate and Edgar stared back, not knowing what to do. The man's light did not stretch all the way along the tunnel. Maybe the shadows would keep them safe. Kate looked up the shaft. The hatch was starting to crackle now. The fire had made its way into the hiding place and the trapdoor was smoldering, sending small sparks fizzling through cracks in the wood.

Something snapped above them, and a handful of hot sparks rained down from the trapdoor into Edgar's hair. Kate brushed them out before he could notice, but the edges of the door were glowing and curling in the heat. A few minutes more and they would be getting more than sparks dropping on their heads.

The old man showed no sign of moving.

More sparks sprinkled down. The trapdoor began to buckle.

It was time to go.

Kate grabbed Edgar's arm, pulling him awkwardly behind her, and together they ran for it. The man looked up, spotted Kate's frightened face heading his way, and grinned.

"Ha!" He lifted his blade, but Kate kept running. She had just one chance. Dozens of shiny beetlebacks were glistening on the floor and some were creeping their way steadily up the tunnel walls. As soon as she was close enough, Kate scraped a handful of squirming beetles from the stones and threw them into the old man's face. He yelped with surprise, trying to scratch them off with his fingernails, and Kate collided with him, struggling to keep her balance as he fell to the floor.

"Keep going!" shouted Edgar, holding her steady as they clambered out of reach of the old man's slashing blade. A fist-sized chunk of burning wood bounced down the bookshop's ladder, sending fiery splinters spearing toward them from the dark, and the man cried out, shielding himself from the sudden burst of flame. Kate and Edgar didn't wait to see what would happen next. They were already past him, hurtling as fast as they could along the right-hand tunnel, hoping to find a way out— but instead of heading upward, the tunnel dipped steeply down. Edgar grabbed a flaming torch from the wall and tried to keep up.

The tunnel walls whipped past them in a flicker of stones and damp slime, widening slightly the deeper they went. It was like running through a dirty alleyway closed off from the sky. Rotten food spilled out of paper bags stacked against the walls, old blankets were piled up high, wrapped around pieces of rusted metal left leaning against each other, and there were rats: dozens of brown, furry bodies scuttling through it all, carrying off whatever they could salvage from the mess.

At last the tunnel sloped upward and Kate checked the ceiling as they ran, hunting for another trapdoor, a ladder, anything that would take them back up into the world outside before the old man caught up. She could hear him in the tunnel behind them, shuffling along like a vicious crab, gaining on them all the time.

"What's this?" said Edgar, stopping suddenly. "Look! A door!"

Kate doubled back and found him tugging frantically at a curled handle jutting out of the wall.

"It won't open," he said, trying to push it instead. "It won't . . . Got it!" With one good shove the door scraped open through a mess of food spilled over a hard stone floor. They squeezed in as soon as there was room, bolted the door, and backed away from it, listening for any sign of their pursuer on the other side. He was definitely faster than he looked. He reached the door less than a minute after they did. They could hear him moving in the tunnel, talking to himself.

A sharp scratching noise traced the door's frame, the handle rattled suddenly, and Kate stepped farther back. The bolt was small. One good kick and it would snap from its screws in a second. "We have to get out," she whispered. "Where do you think we are?"

The torch shone around a large underground room lined with shelves, each one holding rows of different colored bottles and rough sacks, but for every bottle and sack lined up along the walls, at least two lay smashed or torn open on the floor. Dark brown liquid seeped through islands of bread rolls, fresh meat, and squashed vegetables, and the warm tang of alcohol thickened the air.

"Smells like ale," said Edgar, crunching through a scattering of broken glass. "I think we're under an inn."

"It looks like the wardens have already been here," said Kate. "We should be all right, so long as they've gone."

Kate made her way over to a wooden staircase at the back of the cellar and listened for any sound coming from above.

"Hear anything?" asked Edgar.

"No. I think we can risk it."

The tunnel door rattled hard with a loud bang, sending one of the bolt's screws bouncing across the floor.

"You first," said Edgar. "Better he gets me than you."

Kate didn't have time to argue. She grabbed the handrail and threw herself up the staircase, heading for the sunlight that was seeping in under a door. She flung it open and burst through, emerging in the main room of the inn behind a long thin bar. Sunlight streamed in through a row of small arched windows decorated with stained-glass shooting stars.

"We're in the Falling Star," said Edgar, panting up behind her. "We're on the other side of the market square."

"So where is everyone?"

The inn was deserted. Most of the tables were crushed or upturned and some of the spindles were snapped on the banister of the staircase leading to the rented rooms above. They could still hear the *thump-thump* of the old man smashing something against the cellar door, but other than that, the whole place was horribly silent.

"All right," said Edgar. "We've got wardens on the loose and a creepy old guy in the cellar. Now are you ready to run?"

"I'm not going anywhere without Artemis."

"They think he's one of the Skilled, Kate! They think he was the one who brought that bird to life. They're not going to just hand him over. You know what that means, right?"

Kate didn't want to think about what it meant. All she knew was that her uncle was in trouble because of her. She was not going to leave him behind.

"That man we saw back at the shop, he's trouble," said Edgar. "Have you ever heard of Silas Dane?"

Kate shook her head.

"He's a collector. One of the best. Whatever the High Council wants, he goes out and gets it for them. And if he's got your uncle—"

A shout from outside cut him off, and Kate ran to the window, rubbing grime away from a blue pane to look out across the square.

The market square was not a market any longer. Clustered

among the squat wooden stalls were dozens of metal cages, each one mounted on wheels, with two horses at the front and big enough for four or five people to be squeezed inside. There were wardens out there. Kate counted at least thirty, with more arriving all the time, all pacing around the square in their black robes, surrounding groups of people like vultures circling a kill.

The wardens shouted orders as they walked, dragging people out of the crowd and forcing them into the cages, ready to be sent off to war. Every one of the wardens was armed, but the town had been taken by surprise and there had been no resistance strong enough to require bloodshed yet. The town would be harvested, and the wardens would be gone as suddenly as they had arrived. Everyone knew what to expect. Morvane was beaten, and there was nothing anybody could do.

The sun was shining brightly now and the air was crisp and cold, tainted by the smell of smoke. Kate looked across the square to the bookshop. The little building was completely ablaze. Its windows were smashed, the lower floor was engulfed in flames, and smoke was pouring from the upstairs rooms, snaking up into the sky, taking everything she had ever known with it.

"Look," said Edgar. "Over there."

Something was going on in the northeastern corner of the square, where a tall man was standing next to the town's memorial stone. Kate recognized him at once. The man with gray eyes. Silas Dane.

She pressed her cheek against the window to get a better

view and saw a group of prisoners standing near him with their hands tied. One of them was being supported by one of the others, unable to put his weight upon an injured ankle. "Artemis," said Kate, pushing away from the window and making a sudden run for the door, all fear of the wardens forgotten.

"Kate! Look out!"

Something sharp and silver cut through the air, narrowly missing Kate's arm, and Edgar ran to her, fleeing from a face that had appeared on the other side of the bar.

The old man from the tunnels looked even more terrifying in the sunlight. Everything about him looked pointed and vicious. His nose was short and sharp, his cheekbones jutted out, and his mouth looked more like a beak, with a pointed top lip spiking down over a thin scar where the lower lip used to be. He crept forward and drew a second dagger from his rat-eaten belt, a smile squirming across his lips.

"Gotcha now, girly." He raised his hand to throw another blade, and the bright glint of metal flashed again.

Kate ducked. The dagger flew over her head and thrummed into the door. Then Kalen was in front of her. He reached out and clamped his cold hands around her neck, pinning her back hard against the door handle.

"Such a pretty girl." He grinned, breathing out a cloud of stinking breath. "I'll teach ya to go pokin' around in other people's business."

Kate kicked out, stamping hard on the man's ragged feet.

"Arrrgh!" he snarled and tightened his grip.

Kate stamped again and scratched his arms with her fingernails, fighting him off so she could catch a breath.

"Let go of her!" There was a loud crack. Kalen's eyes bulged, his knees buckled, and Edgar stood behind him with one of the bar stools raised high, ready to hit him again.

Kate clutched at her throat, coughing her lungs back into life as the old man arched an arm across his face for protection. Only he didn't look afraid. He was *smiling*.

"J-just leave us alone!" said Edgar, switching his gaze nervously between Kate and the old man, and in that moment, Kate saw something odd in her friend's eyes. There was fear there, but there was anger too. Deep anger that she had never seen in Edgar before. It looked like he wanted to hurt that man. *Really* hurt him. And he was more than ready to do it.

"Edgar," she said carefully. "Don't."

The atmosphere in the inn bristled. Edgar's fingers clasped tightly around the leg of the stool and his hands shook a little, betraying the uncertainty behind his rage. He bit his lip and forced his muscles to relax.

"Leave. Us. Alone," he said, lowering the stool. "We haven't done anything to you."

Kalen glared back at him and shook his head. "What're ya doin'?" he bellowed, spraying globs of brown spittle into the air. "You know better than that. Don't ya, boy? *Never* yield to an enemy. *Never* give 'em a chance. Do it, why don't ya? Finish me off!"

Edgar faltered under Kalen's stare, and the old man laughed.

"You won't last five heartbeats out there," he said. "The world is changin'. You know what's happenin'. You know what that little wench is. You've seen 'er kind before. Nothin' but trouble. Just hand 'er over an' maybe I'll forget I saw you 'ere, eh? You know what Silas'll do if 'e catches up with ya."

"Shut up!" said Edgar.

"There's those who'd pay fine gold to 'ave this little bird locked up, good and tight. What's she worth to a fine young man like yerself? Bet you could do with a few coins in yer pocket. And 'oo knows? Hand 'er over quick and the council might even be willin' to forget a few things. Make yer life a bit simpler, wouldn't it?" Kalen smiled deviously. "Every man 'as 'is plan," he said. "What's yours, eh? How's it goin' so far? What's that little voice inside yer 'ead tellin' ya to do next?"

"Edgar? What's going on?" asked Kate.

"Nothing. The stupid old guy's crazy, that's all."

"Not so crazy that I forget a face, boy. And I've seen yours before. If you 'ad any sense, you'd let me do it. You'd let me snap that girl's sweet little neck right 'ere and save Silas the trouble. Or maybe ya want to do it yerself? Please, be my guest. I won't stand in yer way."

Edgar's foot kicked out and slammed hard into Kalen's

chest, sending him sprawling back. "I said, *shut up!*"

"That's better! Ha! Much better," coughed Kalen, wheezing and chuckling on the floor. "Makin' it look real. Wouldn't want 'er to know what you really are, now would we? Careful, boy. Think! The life of a traitor's 'ard enough, but when they catch ya the dyin's always slow and cruel. Do ya want to know what hell looks like? Silas'll show ya things that'll make my life 'ere look like a rich man's blessing. You mark my words."

"Edgar, just leave him," said Kate. "We have to get out of here."

Kalen turned toward her. "It's too late for that," he said. "Silas won't let ya. You've got something he needs. That spark inside ya. You think he won't see it? You think he won't know what you are? Silas is the kind of man ya don't ever want to meet. He'll walk around inside yer pretty little mind leavin' footprints that'll never go away. He's a devil, see. Just . . . like . . . me."

Kalen's hand whipped down to his belt where the hilt of a third dagger jutted from the cloth. Edgar was ready. He swung the stool as hard as he could, smashing it against the man's skull.

"Quick!" he said, trying to keep his voice low. "Run!"

"You won't stop 'im!" said Kalen, grasping a bleeding nose as Kate threw herself out of the inn's front door. "You'll jus' make 'im angry!"

4

MURDER

Kate fled out into the market square and saw Artemis being pushed roughly into a cage. She forced herself to turn away and kept close to the inn's outer wall, hoping that no one would see her. There were too many wardens for her to risk helping him there. She had to find another way.

The sun shone straight into her eyes, leaving no shadows in which to hide, so she kept running. She leaped over bird bodies and piles of wood and tools, and squeezed past a row of traders' horses that were tied to a fence, eating hay from a rack. She considered stealing one of them, but she didn't know how to ride and, even if she could, a girl traveling on horseback would look far too conspicuous in the town.

She ducked between their warm bodies instead and headed for one of the gaps between the buildings, where a pair of open gates led her into a barrow alley: a road just wide enough for two horses and carts to squeeze past each other on their way to and from the market. There was a high wall on one side and a few tiny shops on the other, but everything looked abandoned now. Kate checked behind her. Edgar was pushing his way past the horses, making one of them stamp and snort, but there was no sign of Kalen. She knocked hard on the first door she could find and the wood swung back limply against the weight of her hand. The lock had been smashed and there was no answer from inside.

"Come on," she said quietly, stepping forward as the door creaked open and Edgar followed her through into the dark.

The air smelled of sage and rosemary and the floor crunched with scattered dry leaves. Edgar lit a match from a box in his pocket. Tall jars sparkled from shelves lining the walls and a pair of weighing scales had been knocked off the curved wooden counter, and left dented and broken where they fell.

Kate stepped over the scales and crept to the window. The curtains were closed, but she could see the front pane had shattered, covering the floor beneath them in fragments of green glass. She pulled the fabric carefully aside and peered out into the alley.

"What if the wardens are still in here?" whispered Edgar, shivering as the match went out and he began to light another.

"There's no one here," said Kate. "It looks like Eva and Parr put up a good fight."

"Do you think they're all right?"

"The wardens have them. What do you think?"

"I think this is all crazy," said Edgar, crunching his way over to her. "First those birds, then Artemis gets taken. There are mad guys underground and wardens everywhere else." He looked at Kate and then lowered his eyes. "That old guy. Kalen? What he said back there. It was all crazy talk. You do know that, right? On a scale of sanity that guy is completely out of his tree."

"I know that," said Kate. She tried to sound confident, but the truth was she did not know what to think. Even if Kalen had been lying about knowing Edgar, Edgar's behavior toward the old man had made her realize just how little she really knew about her friend. "*Does* he know you?" she asked tentatively.

Edgar looked away, refusing to meet her eyes. "He's probably just seen me around somewhere," he said with an awkward smile. "Like I said, crazy."

Kate wanted to believe him. "That's what I thought," she said.

Kate had known Edgar for three years, since the very first day he had arrived in Morvane. He had moved to the town from somewhere in the south and spent all his time lurking in the bookshop talking to customers, until Artemis had finally agreed to give him a job. He had never really talked about his life before he had come to the town. All Kate knew was that he lived alone in a basement room two streets from the market square and that his family were all gone, just like hers. It had never crossed her mind that he might have something to hide. He was just Edgar. Anything else . . . she was not sure she wanted to know any more.

The shouts of the people gathered in the market square carried down the barrow alley while Kate looked around their new hiding place. She knew the people who had owned that shop. They had been regular customers at the bookshop and were two of the few people her uncle counted among his friends. Now they were out there with the wardens—with him—and everything was falling apart.

"We should hide here," she said, trying to sound confident. "If we stay out of sight no one will find us."

Edgar pushed the front door back into its frame and pressed his hands against it when the broken lock would not catch. "This door's useless," he said. "We need something to push against it."

"No," said Kate. "Leave it. The wardens won't expect anyone to hide in an open building. They'll think it's empty and won't search it again."

"What about Kalen?"

"I don't think he'll follow us. Not with everything that's going on. We should be safe in here."

The next hour in that shop was the slowest of Kate's life. They hid behind the counter, side by side, and Kate sat in silence while Edgar concocted plans for their escape. He was whispering something about heading back into the warrens, dodging Kalen, and finding their way into one of the other quarters, but Kate was only half listening. Her own mind was filled with thoughts, confusion, and half-made plans to free Artemis from the wardens, which all seemed to end with their getting captured. Edgar must have known she was not listening, but he kept talking anyway, peering over the counter now and again to check for any movement outside.

"Maybe you were right," he said, ducking down as the shop's clock rang out the hour, making them both jump. "Maybe they won't find us in here."

"Maybe," said Kate. "Just wait."

Then the noises came.

First there was a shuffling sound and a sharp tapping noise from somewhere close by, though neither she nor Edgar were moving an inch. Then it came again. *Shuffle-shuffle-tap. Shuffle-shuffle-tap.* Kate tensed. Someone was outside, in the alley. Someone was walking along the cobbles.

"Did you hear that?" she whispered.

"What was it?"

"Wait here." Kate crept around the side of the counter and crouched low, making her way over to the curtained window. Edgar was not about to stand back and do nothing again and he followed close behind, peering out silently into the alley beside her. Neither of them spoke as a limping figure shuffled into sight, but both held their breath.

Kalen was back.

The old man's shoulders were hunched and his muddy face was stained with trails of blood. Kate crouched quickly beneath the window and peered over the window frame. Kalen's tight lips were drawn back in anger, his sharp eyes searching every shadow for movement, his ears scrutinizing every sound. Seeing him there, it was hard to imagine how they could have gotten so close to him in the tunnels and survived. Out in the open, he looked more vicious than ever.

Edgar stood up quickly against the shop wall, hiding himself in one of the curtains, and Kalen raised his head, sniffing the air like a dog. It was hard to tell exactly where he was looking. He was just standing there, waiting, his fingers playing upon the handle of a dagger at his side.

"Filthy rats," Kalen grumbled to himself, scraping his tongue under his nose to taste the dried clots of his own blood. "I'll find ya. Don't you worry. Kalen's comin'."

Something moved at the end of the alley, and Kalen stood up straight and alert, his dagger raised ready to strike.

"No!" he snarled. "Not you. Get back!"

"Lower your blade, Kalen, before I drive it through your throat." Kate heard the order before she could see who had given it.

Silas strode into sight, his gray eyes fixed upon the old man. Edgar tensed behind the curtain, and Kalen shuffled from foot to foot, looking back over his shoulder, planning his escape.

"You won't be able to run from me this time." Silas walked

right up to Kalen until he was close enough for Kalen to stab him if he tried. Kate waited for the older man to make his move, but he just stood there, hands quivering, looking down at the ground.

Silas's dark shadow swallowed Kalen as he stood over him like a predator. Kalen swiped his dagger in front of him, trying to force Silas away, but the weapon might as well have been made of wood for all the attention Silas gave it. He kept walking, making Kalen retreat instead. Then his hand shot out, clutching the old man's throat, raising him off the ground and slamming him against the alley wall.

"Ssssilasss!" Kalen's voice came out as a hiss.

"Where is she?"

Kalen grinned beneath a mustache of clotting blood. "Why would I tell you? It's 'cos of you I'm stuck in this rotten place. Argh!"

"Where?"

"She's a strong one," said Kalen. "Oh yes. Maybe I'll just claim 'er for myself, eh?"

Silas held Kalen firmly with one hand and drew a long sword from his belt with the other. The blade was so blue it was almost black, shining like a forged night sky. Kalen squirmed, trying to slash out again with his own blade, but he did not have the strength to land a good strike.

"What exactly is your plan?" said Silas. "Do you plan to kill me, Kalen? Many have tried, one of them even succeeded.

But as you can see, it was not as permanent a predicament as some would have liked. You told me the girl would be in the bookshop. Tell me where she really is."

Silas loosened his grip enough for Kalen to wheeze in a thin breath. "You'll . . . kill me anyway," he said, chuckling horribly with each word.

Silas rested his blade upon Kalen's shoulder. "And with good reason," he said. "Who was it who stood by while the High Council allowed one of the Skilled into their midst? Who was it who knew what that woman planned to do and yet said nothing—*nothing*—about it to me? If you had warned me about her, I never would have allowed her to get close. So do not *dare* to blame me for what has happened in your life when you had a hand in destroying mine."

"What can I say? The gold was good." Kalen grinned, showing off rows of loose cracked teeth. "'Course, that's all spent and gone now. Worth it, though. Ah, yes. It's not my fault ya walked right into 'er trap."

Silas's eyes flashed with anger. "You are the same traitor you have always been," he said. "The council stopped looking for you years ago because they thought you were dead. I should have told them where to find you, but instead you went free. You owe me far more than your worthless life. So, for the last time, what have you done with the girl?"

Kalen's face twisted into a look as smug as any man could get with a blade so close to his neck. "Losin' yer touch, eh, friend?" he said. "Time was you'd have had that little banshee locked up and halfway to Fume by now, an' I'd've been left dead and cold. Food for the rats, just for slowin' you down. Better get a move on. The council won't thank ya for keepin' 'em waitin'.'"

"This one's not for the council," said Silas, sheathing his sword, but keeping a firm grip on Kalen's throat.

"Then I'd finish 'er off quick. Dangerous, she is. Better off dead than breathin'. Wouldn't take much, I reckon."

"This blood," said Silas, noticing the stains across Kalen's robes. "Is it hers?"

"Maybe. Maybe not. My nose took a good bashin' along the way. She's got company with 'er, see. Da'ru's boy. He did this to me."

"Da'ru's boy?" Silas looked surprised. "Edgar Rill is here? In this town?"

"Ha! Didn't know that, did ya?"

Kate looked back at the curtain where Edgar was wrapped up with only his shabby boots poking out into the room. If he could hear the two men's conversation he wasn't showing any sign of it. Maybe Kalen *had* seen him in town somewhere, but how could a collector know his name?

"I'll be sure to thank him for what he's done to you when I find him," said Silas. "It's just a shame he did not finish what he started."

Kalen's face hardened. "Hey, now. You and me. We're

friends, Silas. Soldiers. Let's not forget that."

"I owe you nothing," said Silas. "You know what is at stake. That girl could be the key to everything and you have let her go. Do you at least have the book?"

"Have it? I've been 'ere all this time lookin' for the cursed thing. I've been listenin' from the cellars, sneakin' into houses at night. If anyone was hidin' it, I would know. It's gone, Silas. Gone to who knows where."

Silas tightened his grip, and the old man whimpered. "If you had not lost it in the first place, all of this would already be over," Silas said. "I would be free of this useless life and you might still have full use of your pathetic little mind."

"I tried!" squeaked Kalen. "It's not here, I tell ya."

"Then you have not tried hard enough," said Silas. "How do I know you have not just been hiding here, doing nothing, cowering away like the filth that you are?"

"You don't." Kalen grinned dangerously. "But at least *I'm* not some errand boy, trapped under a woman's heel!"

Kalen's laugh turned into a hacking cough, and Silas glared at him in fury. "The Skilled are our only link to *Wintercraft*," he said. "That girl is the only one they have not yet hidden from us, and you are wasting my time. You should have stayed in your tunnels, *friend*, where rodents like you belong."

The glass-covered floor crackled beneath Kate's boots as she listened from her hiding place. She tried to remain still, but her heel pressed gently against a large shard that she had not seen, and the sharp pop of crushed glass carried into the alley. Kalen's eyes flashed to the broken window. Silas saw him look and turned toward the shop, giving the old man the chance he needed. Kalen swiped his dagger up toward Silas's throat, but Silas's hand moved lightning fast, grabbing the blade so hard that his palm dripped blood. "Too slow," he said, turning the blade inward toward the old man's chest. "Haven't you learned anything, Kalen? The dead cannot die. You, on the other hand . . ."

"Wait!" Kalen cried, but it was too late. In one powerful move Silas thrust the blade up into his robes, driving the metal deep into his heart.

"One death for another," he said, letting Kalen bleed freely until his lifeless body slumped down onto the cobbles.

The alleyway fell silent. Kate dared to peer carefully out over the window ledge and saw Silas crouching down, pressing his hand to Kalen's forehead. The air rippled strangely around him, like heat rising from a roof on a wet summer's day, and everything seemed to slow down. Kate did not know what she was seeing. Silas was impossibly still, his eyes closed, concentrating on something she could not see. Kate had forgotten to breathe and only when the air settled back to normal again did the full horror of witnessing a man's death hit her. Her knees felt weak and she stumbled back.

"Kate!" whispered Edgar, abandoning his hiding place to help her.

That was all Silas needed.

He saw Edgar move, drew his sword, and strode toward the broken window. Edgar did not see him approach. Silas's boots made no sound upon the cobbles and no shadow crept across the shop floor. Only Kate saw him standing there just two steps from Edgar's back, his sword raised ready to strike.

"Move!" she yelled, pushing Edgar hard into the curtains as the blade fell. The sword missed, the point dug into the wooden floor, and the metal rang out.

Edgar stood frozen against the wall. Silas was inside the shop, standing right in front of Kate. Both of his hands were on the sword, but he made no attempt to free it from the floor. He just stood there, looking at her.

"Do you know who I am?" he asked.

Kate nodded firmly, trying not to give away her fear.

"Then you should know that no one escapes me once I have set my mind upon their capture. No bargains are granted, no freedoms or mercy are offered or given. You have something I want, and I believe you can help me find something I need."

Kate didn't know what he was talking about, and she didn't care. "Where is my uncle?" she asked, sounding far braver than she actually felt. "He's not one of the Skilled. He's not what you're looking for."

"I know that." Silas tugged his sword from the floor and raised it a little, enough to make Kate flinch. "I knew it as soon as I saw his face. The eyes do not lie, Miss Winters."

"How do you know my name?"

"I have been ordered to find you," said Silas. "And I believe you may be of use to me. But first . . ." He turned to Edgar, whose face was a picture of terror. "First I must put down the boy."

"No!" Kate shouted. The blue blade whipped up to Edgar's throat and stopped only a hair's breadth from his trembling skin.

"No?" said Silas. "Why not?"

Kate glanced at the dead body out in the barrow alley. "Because I . . . I'll go with you," she said. "You don't have to hurt him. He's not in your way. He won't stop you from taking me. Will you, Edgar?"

Edgar shrugged his shoulders as much as the blade would allow. "I was going to give it a bloody good try, actually."

"I'm not going anywhere if you hurt him," said Kate. "And I certainly won't help you."

"You will do as I say, or you will die right here next to your useless friend."

Kate thought fast, not knowing what to do, but Edgar had a plan.

With Silas distracted he took his chance, heaving on the green curtain with all his strength, making the rusted curtain pole break from the wall and spilling the wooden rings from its end. He had hoped to catch Silas beneath the fabric, but it was too heavy, and the curtain flopped straight down on top of his own head instead. Edgar scrambled blindly across the floor, dragging the curtain along, with Silas right behind him. Kate grabbed the weighing scales from the floor and threw them at Silas's knees, cracking the metal hard into his kneecap. The collector did not stop. He did not even limp; he just strode on, calmly chasing Edgar down until the boy finally managed to squirm from the curtain and bolt straight out of the shop door.

Silas stopped at the threshold, and Kate watched Edgar skid upon the bloodstained cobbles as he ran past Kalen's dead body. Her heart sank, and fear gathered like a lump in her throat as she realized he was not coming back.

The door at the back of the shop was blocked by a rack of fallen shelves, and a killer now stood between her and her only chance of escape. She was alone, unarmed, and there was no way out.

Silas sheathed his sword and turned on her. "The weak always run," he said. "There is no honor in killing a coward. Do not disappoint me by trying to do the same."

"You didn't give him any choice," said Kate, trying to convince herself that it was true, that somehow Edgar had to leave her behind. "What do you want?"

"You are a rare girl, Miss Winters. A diamond in the festering filth that makes up the rest of this worthless town. I have questions for you and you will answer them. Answer them to my satisfaction and your life will be made easy. Defy me and you will find me much less friendly than I have been thus far."

"You *killed* a man," said Kate. "You burned my home, took my family, and you just tried to kill my friend."

"Yet here you stand, untouched. Why do you think that is?" Silas walked toward her, and with every step the air felt colder. Fear trickled up Kate's spine, but there was nowhere for her to go.

"You were the one who brought the bird back to life," he said. "You are the only one I am interested in. You will help me find what I need."

"I didn't do anything," said Kate. "I don't know who you think I am. But you're wrong."

Silas's hand snapped forward and grabbed Kate's face, clutching her cheekbones as he stared into her eyes. His grip was river cold and would not let her wriggle away. The dead gray of his eyes moved like fog trapped behind circles of glass, and Kate found herself staring at them, unable to look away.

"I am not wrong," he said. "Your uncle has no more Skill in him than a splinter of rock. But you . . . I can see the power inside you. Young power from ancient blood, raw and untrained. Do you know how many people carry the Winters name here in Albion? Worthless people with no true link to the family by blood?"

Kate shook her head.

"Hundreds," said Silas. "One or two of them showed

some small promise, but they were nothing like you. You are the one I have been looking for, and you will come with me, or I will start slicing off those delicate fingers of yours. One . . . by . . . one."

Kate felt the chill of metal against her hand and she tried to snatch it away. There was a sharp snap of a lock and Silas cuffed one end of a long fine chain to her wrist, wrapping the remaining length of it around his hand. "A precaution," he said. "I do not intend to lose you again. Now, walk."

Silas dragged Kate to her feet and pushed her ahead of him to the shop door. She did not want to go out there, not after what had happened, and she deliberately tried not to look at Kalen's body lying on the ground. Silas led her toward it and made her stand beside him as he toed the fallen man with his boot. He knelt on one knee, wrenched the dagger from Kalen's body, and wiped it clean on the dead man's robes. An engraved letter K glinted along the blade. He pocketed it at once. "Unfortunate," he said. "But necessary."

Silas looked up to the roof of the shop, where his crow was perched patiently upon the gutter, fluffing its feathers against the wind. "Follow the boy," he said. "Do not leave his side."

"Edgar?" Kate tried to pull free of her wrist chain, but the metal gripped tight. "What do you want him for? Leave him alone!"

The crow clicked its beak and leaped into the air.

"As long as my crow is with him, I will be able to find

him," said Silas. "The Skilled may be able to do many things, but I possess a few tricks of my own. No one can escape me, Miss Winters. Not him. Not you." Silas held Kate still, and she watched the bird fly away until its wingbeats were lost across the rooftops of the town. "Kalen earned his death many times over," he said. "Your friend will have his own judgment to face. For now, you are my primary concern."

Silas pushed Kate farther down the barrow alley in the opposite direction to the market square, heading out into the maze that was the Southern Quarter's back streets. Kate looked around, searching for someone who could help her, but the few people she could see were already running from the collector, too terrified to challenge him for the sake of one girl. Her town belonged to him now.

Groups of robed wardens moved through the streets, herding frightened stragglers in the direction of the square, and Silas forced Kate to a stop as a black horse pulled a closed carriage along the road toward them. The carriage's sides and roof had been red once, but the paint had long since peeled away, leaving scars of worn red and black. Kate could not see the driver's face under the hood of his robes.

The carriage stopped right beside them, and Silas unlatched the door. "Get in," he said.

5

WINTERCRAFT

Edgar ran through the Southern Quarter, keeping to the shadows, trying not to be seen. His hands were sweaty and his heart was racing. He hadn't run this fast since . . . No. He wasn't going to think about that. He felt like a coward. A collector had Kate and he was running in the opposite direction. Any ordinary person would have tried facing Silas, tried to fight him and force him to give her back. But this was not the first time Edgar had run from Silas Dane. Fighting him would get Edgar nowhere. He knew what he had to do.

He kept running, ignoring the shouts of a few townspeople who were standing on doorsteps or leaning out of windows pointing at plumes of smoke rising from nearby fires. They must not have seen the wardens yet, but they were making enough noise to attract every one of them for a mile around.

Dark clouds brought heavy flurries of snow from the north, darkening the sky and filling the air with falling flakes of white.

Edgar dodged between the houses, looking for somewhere to hide, somewhere to plan, while above him, soaring high in the air, Silas's crow followed silently behind.

No one noticed the bird's wide wings outstretched above the rooftops as it kept pace, following Edgar until he was forced to take shelter from the heavy snow in a decrepit old house. It watched him force his way in through a boarded window, then it settled on the cornerstone of a bakery roof like a perfect gargoyle, waiting for him to make his next move. And as it sat there, the town of Morvane changed.

The snow lay like a blanket across the run-down streets of the Southern Quarter. Ruined roofs became beautiful again, dirty roads were given a fresh new mask of white, and everything sparkled in the rare patches of morning sun. The crow sat patiently, watching the door of the house until a comfortable carriage pulled by two gray horses rolled into sight, drawing the crow's attention away. It stood, suddenly alert, cocked its head, and shook its feathers dry. The crow knew who was inside that carriage. It could sense the unwelcome presence of an enemy. Someone it had learned to fear.

Instinct told it to fly, but duty to its master kept it locked to its post until the carriage rolled by, oblivious of both the bird and the boy hiding in the house. Only when it had passed safely out of sight could the crow settle again and return obediently to its silent watch.

~~<~ ❊ ~>~~

Across town, the carriage Kate was in was traveling fast. The windows were blacked out with thick cloth, so she could catch only tiny glimpses of the streets that raced by, but she saw enough to know that they were heading toward the Western Quarter—Morvane's oldest and most dangerous district. She tugged secretly at her wrist cuff, trying to force it up over her thumb joint, but it would not budge.

A broken hatch at the front of the carriage looked out on the driver's back, and biting wind surged through it, blasting snow into Kate's face and forcing her to huddle deeper into her coat. Silas did not move. He had not spoken since they had boarded the carriage. The snow churned around him, sending flakes drifting across his face, but while the flakes melted instantly against the warmth of Kate's skin, they clung to Silas's face far longer before melting away. When they landed upon his eyeballs they clustered together in tiny drifts along his eyelids. He did not even blink.

By the time the high archway marking the change of quarter came into sight, Kate's cheeks were so cold she could not feel them anymore. The carriage's wheels bounced and jolted so hard along uneven roads that she had to hold her seat to stop herself from falling off, and without even glancing at his window, Silas gave an order to the driver. "Here."

The carriage came to a gentle stop in front of a rough-looking boardinghouse. Silas unlatched his door and pulled

Kate out into the open, where the chill of the snow made her ears burn. The boardinghouse was easily the tallest building in the quarter, with three floors of square windows reaching up to a cracked circular window tucked beneath the distant eaves. Silas did not bother to knock. He wrenched at the door handle and pushed Kate inside.

The door led into a long corridor that was dark except for a single candle glowing at the end. A shadow moved in front of the light and a small man hurried up to meet them. He was old and plainly dressed, but Kate could not miss the gleam of a gold and ruby ring on his right hand. A ring like that could only belong to a man with powerful friends, so it did not surprise her when he greeted Silas by name.

"Mr. Dane," he said, bowing deeply. "A pleasure, sir, as always."

"Has she arrived?" asked Silas.

"No, sir."

"Then I will come down the moment she does. As far as you are concerned, this girl is not here. She does not exist. Do you understand?"

"Yes, sir."

The boardinghouse owner smiled creepily at Kate as Silas took her up the worn stairs to the upper floors. They climbed two doglegged flights and then a third that led right up to the attic floor. A door, to which Silas already had the key, stood upon a landing at the very top, and the room beyond was small and neat, with a narrow bed, an unlit fire, and a wooden desk inside. Silas locked the door behind them and went at once to the circular window, swinging it open so he could lean out over the street.

"What's going on?" asked Kate. "Who are you meeting here?"

"Someone who has been looking for your family for a long time," said Silas, crossing the room and locking one end of Kate's silver chain to the desk. "As far as she knows, there is only one Winters rumored to live in this town. I will tell her that your uncle is useless, just like the rest. If you stay quiet, there is a chance this day may not end badly for you."

"What does that mean?" asked Kate.

"Your parents never mentioned they had a child when the wardens took them," said Silas. "They were wise enough to know when to keep quiet and when to speak. A lesson you would do well to learn."

"What do you know about them?" demanded Kate, but a look from Silas was enough to silence her.

"What I know is irrelevant," he said. "All that matters now is what you know, and what you can do."

A long silence followed.

Silas stood beside the open window, not caring that Kate was left shivering in the dark. She sat down at the desk, trying to prize her wrist cuff open on the corner of the wood, and was just about to ask Silas for the woman's name, when a sudden pain burst between her eyes, like needles piercing the skin. A bright light flashed in front of her: pure white light, there and gone again in an instant. She blinked it away and had gone back to the wrist cuff when it happened again. The light shone more intensely this time, lasting for a few seconds and never weakening, even when she closed her eyes.

Silas glared at her with suspicion. "What is it?" he asked.

"Nothing. It's nothing. I—"

"The Skilled have far greater senses than ordinary people," he said. "Those senses can create visions of things the eyes cannot normally see. Tell me what you saw."

The pain stabbed again and the light flashed once more, sharpening into a vision of something that Kate knew should have been impossible.

She was looking out of a carriage window toward the arch that divided the Western Quarter from the Southern. It was the same route that Silas's carriage had taken, but she was not looking at a memory of her own journey. The carriage window was arched, not square, and the curtains were pulled wide open.

"What do you see?" Silas demanded.

Kate did not know what was happening. Icy cold surrounded her hands, chilling them until they were so frigid it felt as if her bones might snap. She tried to stand up, but she could not move. She tried to speak, but her throat made no sound. She could only sit staring at the same point on the wall, eyes fixed in silent terror as her body refused to obey her.

Her first thought was that she had been poisoned, but Silas had not given her anything to eat or drink. She had not felt the prick of a needle or smelled gas in the air. The cold spread along her arms, numbing them completely as a thin layer of frost traced across her fingers. After that, all she saw was darkness. Deep blackness, more complete than any darkness she had ever known. She felt lost within it. Held tightly in one place. Unable to move or speak or scream. All she had was the pulse of her blood racing through her veins to let her know she was alive, but even that was slowing down. Becoming fainter. Weaker.

Silas's voice spoke close by. "All Skilled have the ability to see into the veil," he said. "The boundary between this world and the next is opening around you. Let it happen. It will become as easy as breathing, given time."

Kate could not have stopped it if she tried. The cold was so intense that she became numb to it. Then the vision returned and this time she was glad of it. Anything to force the terrifying darkness away.

She was back inside the carriage, traveling swiftly beneath the arch. She tried to look around, but her view was fixed upon the window as the dark stones that made up the archway blackened the glass, forming a mirrorlike reflection within it. Kate focused upon it and found herself looking at a face. A woman's face that was not her own.

Then everything stopped.

The vision froze around her and everything was still except for the face: the face of a woman who had sensed something other than herself inside that carriage. The cold eyes within the glass began to smile and the finely painted mouth whispered a word. "Kate."

The shock of hearing her own name made Kate heave in a sudden breath. The vision broke and she was back in the boardinghouse with Silas standing right beside her. The frost melted quickly on her warming skin and she stared as her hands slowly regained their color, still shivering with cold.

"Someone's coming," she said, as soon as she was able to say the words. "She said my name. What . . . What happened?"

"You used the veil to see through the spirit of another," said Silas. For a moment, he sounded surprised, but his cold eyes gave nothing away. "She is the hunter and you are her prey. Given the right conditions, the veil can link two Skilled minds if they are focused enough upon each other, but it normally takes a tremendous strength of will to make such a connection possible. What did you do?"

"Nothing!" said Kate, tugging on her wrist cuff in frustration.

"For her to know your name, she must have been aware

of the link between you," said Silas. "When two minds join within the veil, it is possible for them to share memories. You must not let it happen again. I am surprised the Skilled did not find you long before I did. Your potential is even greater than I expected. How long have you been one of them?"

"I'm not one of them."

"Who taught you the ways of *Wintercraft*?"

"Winter-what?"

"Where is the book being kept? Did you read from it yourself?"

"What book? I don't know anything about any of this!" Kate was tired, confused, and angry. Her head still hurt from whatever had just happened, but already logic was starting to take over. There was no way she could have actually seen that woman in the carriage. The woman couldn't have been real. Kate's imagination could have created her by piecing together what had already happened that day with what Silas had told her. And as for the frost on her hands . . . there wasn't even a trace of it left now. Perhaps it had never been there at all.

"Da'ru will arrive soon," said Silas. "She must not find out that you are up here. Do you understand?"

Da'ru? Kate remembered the name. Kalen had called Edgar "Da'ru's boy," but she was sure she had also heard it somewhere else before. "Why is she looking for me?" she asked.

"The Skilled are a dying breed," said Silas. "She has her

plans for you. I have mine. You are going to help me find the book—*Wintercraft*—and with it you will help me do something that most people believe to be impossible. That is all you need to know for now."

"This is wrong," said Kate. "I don't know anything about the Skilled."

"Few people are able to choose their own fates," Silas said coolly. "Even fewer learn to accept the path that they are given." He returned to the window and looked down to the street.

"She is here," he said, as the rattle of carriage wheels carried up from below. "Stay quiet and do nothing. If you are found here with me, there will be consequences for both of us. You will not leave this room."

Silas stepped out onto the landing and closed the door. Kate waited until his footsteps were far enough away before sneaking over to the door, letting her chain snake silently across the floor behind her. The metal handle clicked dully in her hand. Locked. She bent down to look through the keyhole and saw something dark sitting in the lock. The key was still there.

Kate crossed the room as quietly as she could and creaked open some of the desk drawers, hunting through them for something long and thin to push the key out. The few ink pens she found were too wide to fit in the lock. All that was left were a few loose sheets of paper. They would have to do.

Kate grabbed two pieces, tore one of them in half and

rolled it tightly into a narrow strip that was thin enough to reach the key but strong enough not to bend against it. She returned to the door, knelt down, and pushed the second piece of paper under it to catch the key when it fell. Then she slid the rolled strip carefully into the lock, pushing the key gently, hoping it would not make too much noise when it hit the floor.

Gradually, the key worked loose. Kate tensed when it dropped, and the metal rang out hard against the wooden boards. She froze, waiting for someone to come up to investigate the sound. No one came. Once she was sure it was safe, she pulled the slice of paper back into the room with her fingertips, with the weight of the door key balanced precariously on one of the corners. She snatched it up as soon as it was in sight and dug it into the lock. The handle clicked and the door creaked open.

The length of her chain gave Kate just enough room to allow her to step out onto the landing, where she could hear distant voices talking at the bottom of the stairs. There was a woman's voice and a louder one belonging to the boardinghouse owner, but she could only make out his half of the conversation.

"There has been no talk of the Skilled in this town for ten years or more," she heard him say as she edged closer to the top of the staircase. "If there was a Skilled girl, she has not come this way. The people here have been more careful than in the south. No. No meetings. If any of them had passed through this town, you can be sure I would know."

"Very well," came the woman's voice, clearer now as Kate leaned out over the steps.

"We will call you if we require you again," said Silas. "Leave us."

Kate heard shuffling steps as the boardinghouse owner walked away and a door closed somewhere down below.

"These people are hiding something," said Da'ru. "What news do you have about the girl? Do we have her yet?"

"It appears Kalen's information was incorrect," said Silas. "The only Winters we found here was a bookseller with no family. He is already in custody and shows no aptitude for the Skill. This could have been merely a futile effort in the hope of regaining your trust. Kalen is known to be a desperate man, but the harvest is proceeding well nonetheless. Our presence here may yet prove worthwhile."

"No. There is someone in this town," said Da'ru. "A girl. I have sensed her."

"If so, then you can be sure she will be found," said Silas. "My men are scouring every street, and the town gates are locked. No one will get out."

Da'ru's voice fell quiet, and Kate had to strain to hear her words. "This is the closest we have ever been, Silas," she said, her words dark and dangerous. "I am certain the book is hidden somewhere in Fume. We will find it soon, and with a Winters to use it . . . I do not have to tell you what that would mean. The book is *mine*. That girl's family stole it from me, and if it takes the rest of my life, I will discover its secrets. Do not leave this town until your men are certain there are no Skilled left. Check empty houses, cellars, everything. I want that girl, Silas. Find her for me."

Kate backed slowly into the attic room, lifting up the silver chain so it did not scrape across the floor. Even if she could remove it somehow, Silas was right, there was nowhere to go—and as much as she feared him, instinct told her that she should fear that woman even more.

Kate locked herself in the attic room and pushed the key back under the door where Silas would find it. There was nothing she could do to help herself, not with so many people in the house. She stood in the shadows at the side of the attic window, forcing herself to concentrate upon anything other than the woman downstairs. From her viewpoint just above the rooftops, Morvane looked large enough to hide anyone. Anyone except her. She had been careless. After everything Artemis had taught her, she had allowed herself to get caught.

Thin pillars of smoke rose from faraway buildings that had fallen prey to the wardens' flames, and in the distance a crow was circling in the gray, snow-filled sky.

"Edgar," she whispered. "Where are you?"

Two streets to the south of the boardinghouse, Edgar was lost. He had seen the carriage pass outside his hiding place and, just like the crow, he had recognized it at once. Da'ru was in town. And if she was there, so was someone else who might be able to help both him and Kate.

He trudged through the snow, checking every street sign and house name, wearing a pair of stolen gloves and a stolen hat to keep warm. Three years of living in Morvane had taught him enough to stay away from the Western Quarter. But with news of the wardens' arrival traveling fast, the streets were empty, and there was no one around to ask for directions.

The Black Fox boardinghouse. He knew the name well enough. The owner was known to be a whisperer—an information monger—willing to share any secret for a price. Most whisperers were loyal to their towns and refused to have dealings with wardens and their kind, but this one was known to be both accurate in his information and indiscriminate in his choice of contacts, some of whom came from as far away as Fume. If anything important was happening in Morvane, the owner of the Black Fox would know about it. Da'ru was sure to stop there for information, if she had not been and gone already. But where was it?

At last, he spotted something familiar.

A gap between the houses gave Edgar a glimpse of a tall building with a circular window on its top floor. He squeezed down a narrow path and ran straight out in front of two gray carriage horses standing in the middle of the street.

He ducked back so the driver did not see him and spotted a boy a few years younger sitting alone on the boardinghouse step. The boy was hugging himself against the wind, with a blanket full of holes pulled tight around his shoulders. Edgar crept up to him. "Tom!" he whispered.

The boy looked up, his face brightening at once. "Ed?"

Edgar dared to take a few steps closer.

"Ed! What are you doing here?" The boy scrabbled to his feet, still clutching his freezing hands beneath the blanket.

"Shh!" Edgar ran the short distance left between them and clutched the younger boy's shoulders tightly. He checked him over quickly, making sure he was in good health, then he scuffed his hair as both of their faces widened into matching grins.

"Where is Da'ru?" asked Edgar.

Tom pointed back at the boardinghouse. "If she sees you here, she'll put the knife in you," he said. "She hasn't forgotten what you did."

"I don't care about that. It's you I need, Tom. I need some information." Edgar quickly told him what had happened to Kate, but Tom just kept shivering and looking back at the boardinghouse door, cringing whenever his voice raised above a whisper.

"You shouldn't have come here, Ed," he said at last. "Da'ru's in there. She'll know."

"Just tell me, which way are they taking the prisoners out this time?"

"She'll know that I told you. She always does."

"I'll be long gone before then."

"*I* won't be."

Edgar's face fell. "You know I can't take you yet," he said. "There are wardens crawling all over this town. Da'ru would catch us both before we were two streets away. One day . . . soon, I promise, but not now. I can't risk you getting hurt. You do understand that, don't you?"

Someone moved inside the building. Tom threw off the blanket and tugged at his torn clothes to make himself look presentable. "Go on!" he whispered. "She'll kill you if she sees you, Ed. She swore she would."

Edgar took off his hat and planted it on Tom's cold head. "That is *not* going to happen," he said. "Now, are we brothers or not? Which way are they taking the prisoners?"

Tom looked nervous, pulled off the hat, and stuffed it into his pocket. "They're going to stop the Night Train," he said quickly. "It'll pass through at sunset on its way back to Fume. But don't go out there, Ed. You don't know what's happening. Silas is out there!"

"We've already met," said Edgar, pulling off his gloves and pressing them and some of his matches into his brother's hands. "Look after yourself. Stay warm. I'll come back for you. You know I will."

Tom clutched the gifts in his shivering hands. "Wait! Ed!"

Edgar looked back at the boy in the snow and then a door

latch clicked, forcing him to dive into the darkness between two houses.

The shadows swallowed him completely as a well-dressed woman stepped out into the street; she could not have looked more out of place if she had tried. There Edgar was, crouching in one of Morvane's poorest streets at one of its most desperate times, and there she was, pristine and perfect, her silvery dress snaking across the ground, her boots jet black and delicately heeled, her elegant shoulders poised and relaxed beneath a hooded shawl of gray and brown fur. Wolf fur. Only one woman in Albion chose to wear wolf fur, such was her low regard for any life other than her own. Her long black hair was tied back and pinned with a pointed bone, her cuffs were edged with tiny rubies and her lips were painted gray. The owner of the boardinghouse stood behind her, looking like a well-used penny next to a freshly minted coin.

Da'ru ignored him, raised the fur hood, and let her perfect face disappear beneath its shadow, while Tom tucked his blanket into the back of his trousers, trying not to look over to where Edgar was hiding. Da'ru stepped aboard the carriage and Tom clung onto the luggage rack at the back, squeezing himself in like a lumpy traveling bag and tugging on his gloves as soon as his mistress was out of sight.

Edgar did not want to let his brother go with her, but there was nothing he could do. The horses pulled forward, and silently he watched them leave.

Anyone who saw that carriage would probably not notice anything different about it. The horses were standard grays, the wheels were plain, and the doors were unmarked, giving no hint to the real identity of its passenger. But Edgar knew very well who she was. Da'ru Marr: the only female member of Albion's High Council, and the only one who counted herself as one of the Skilled. Wherever she went, she brought trouble.

Edgar dug his bare hands into his pockets and tried to get his bearings. If the wardens were putting the prisoners on the Night Train, Silas would be with them, and he would definitely be keeping Kate close by. The train station was on the opposite side of town, so he had some time. It would take the wardens a while to move everyone there, even in those cages, and the train would not arrive until after dark. If he kept moving, he should be able to make it.

It was risky. The last thing Edgar wanted to do was go up against a town full of wardens. It would have been a lot easier for him to just sneak out of Morvane and try to disappear again, or at least find somewhere safe to hide until it was all over. But Kate was far too important to him for that. He wasn't about to just leave her behind.

His mind was set.

He had outsmarted the wardens once before. Now it looked like he would have to do it again.

Edgar was concentrating so hard on what he had to do that he did not realize that he was not the only one who had watched

Da'ru leave. Silas stood at the circular window, watching him disappear into the falling snow. He had to admire the boy. He was even more daring than he had expected. He ran his thumb across a deep scar on the palm of his right hand. A curling brand made by searing hot iron into flesh, the same brand that had once brought him back to life from the furthest reaches of death. It had never healed. After twelve years it was still as raw as the moment it was made, and sometimes he thought he could still see a few sparks of fire smoldering inside the wound, burrowing down a little deeper year after year.

He lurked by the window like a wolf in the shadows, waiting for the boardinghouse owner to climb the stairs. The key to the room lay in easy reach upon the sill beside him. The girl had already attempted to escape once; he would not make it easy for her to do so again. When the old man finally made it up to the landing, Silas opened the door before his knuckles had even touched the wood to knock.

The man smiled nervously on the other side.

"Good work," said Silas, tossing a small coin pouch into his hands.

"Thank you, sir. And . . . will there be anything else today?"

"No," said Silas. Outside, the snow was easing and Kate was watching him warily from the desk chair. "It is time for us to leave," he said. "The girl and I have a train to catch."

Back inside the black carriage, Kate sat beside Silas as they rolled their way speedily across town. But this time, Silas opened one of the curtains to make sure he wasn't being followed, giving Kate the chance to see her town for one last time.

The snow made it all look eerie and unreal. Children wandered without parents, dogs snuffled through the streets, and the black robes of the wardens were never far away, breaking down doors or wrestling people into cages. She thought about Artemis and about all the years they had spent worrying about this day. It had made no difference in the end. Artemis was gone. Edgar was gone. Kate was alone.

It was almost dark by the time she spotted the Night Train's thick tracks slicing through the town like a scar, carving a hard iron curve through the Eastern Quarter as it threaded from the trading towns of the north to the capital city of Fume in the distant south. Those rails linked every town in Albion like an ominous metal vein, and the people who lived close enough to see the Night Train pass by always closed their curtains against its eerie light. It was easier to pretend that it didn't exist, that it didn't choke the air with foul smoke and leave the heavy rumble of metal on metal thrumming through the ground long after it had gone.

The road they were traveling upon ran alongside a stone wall that lined the track's route, but Kate did not recognize this part of town. The houses were larger and grander than any other part of Morvane, yet few people lived there. The station cast too dark a shadow over that part of the Eastern Quarter. It made people uncomfortable. Kate had seen pictures of the station in books at her uncle's shop, but he had never let her see it for herself. Now that she was so close to it, she found that her curiosity had gone. She didn't want to see it anymore. All she wanted was to be back at home, getting ready for the Night of Souls, living life just as she had lived it the day before. But all that was impossible now. Silas had made sure of it.

The driver shouted out to someone up ahead. A gate screeched open and the carriage wheels crunched onto gravel, rolling past row after row of wheeled cages with flaming torches punched into the ground to light the paths between them. There were many more there than Kate had expected. What she and Edgar had seen in the market square must have been only a small part of the wardens' plans for the town that day. There were at least five times as many cages outside that station as there had been in the square, all filled with so many people that it was hard to believe the wardens had left anyone behind.

Most of the prisoners were yelling angrily at the wardens, rattling their bars, trying to find a way out. Others were trying to bargain with them, offering up their businesses or savings for a second chance at freedom, while the rest just sat there, quietly accepting the grim truth that they were no longer in control of their lives.

"Every one of these people will do their duty to Albion," said Silas. "Just as thousands of others have done before them. You are fortunate you are not one of them."

"My uncle is one of them," Kate said quietly.

"That part of your life is over. There is nothing you can do for him now."

The blazing torches lit up the night and, as the carriage turned, Kate finally saw the station with her own eyes. It was an ancient place, centuries old, built for a single track and one special train. Kate knew from her books that, long ago, the gravel where the cages now stood had been a beautiful garden where the coffins of Morvane's dead were taken before being carried by train to Albion's graveyard city. Friends and family would have gathered for a funeral in that garden before passing the coffin over to the bonemen—the keepers of the dead—who took it on to the train, ready to make its final journey south.

The bonemen were a select group of the Skilled who had devoted their lives to helping the spirits of the dead pass safely out of the living world and into the next. They had once been the sole guardians of the graveyard city, performing complex rituals, maintaining the tombs and graves of the many families interred beneath its earth, and ensuring that their remains were treated with respect long after their funeral day had passed. But that was before the wardens had claimed the Night Train for themselves, before the bonemen had been driven into hiding and one of the old High Councils had walled up the country's burial ground, transforming it into the great fortress city of Fume.

Fume was now a place for the wealthy, not the dead, and since the war with the Continent had begun, it had been the only town spared the threat of the wardens' harvests. Living in the shadow of the High Council came at a high price, but for those willing to pay it, Fume was the only place in Albion to feel truly safe. The tall memorial towers looked down over stone streets, built to house the High Council's most trusted followers and their families, while the extensive underground maze of caverns and tombs were left to lawless groups of smugglers and scavengers who managed to scrape out a living down in the dark. The needs of the rich were served by hundreds of servants and slaves, and none of them ever gave a thought to the thousands of dead still buried beneath their feet.

In its prime, Morvane's station had been a simple building built from black stone. The main structure straddled the tracks like a long tunnel and a large arched entryway jutted out into the garden, with a wooden door that was always open, ready to welcome the dead. That was how Kate had seen it in drawings copied from that time, but now it looked very different.

Without the garden to soften its dark façade, the station was a bleak, miserable place. It looked angry and broken. Rain and wind had worn away most of the entryway, leaving only the right-hand wall and a few crumbling pieces of the rest. The wooden door lay rotting on the ground; metal beams that had once held a curved slate roof were gradually being devoured by rust; and, alongside what was left of the main building, a decrepit clock tower stood like a sentry overlooking the tracks. Normally that tower would have been in darkness, but on that night its roof was alive with a crown of dancing fire. The wardens were signaling the Night Train, ordering it to stop.

Silas's carriage headed straight for the station, and as it rolled in through the entryway every warden stood to attention, acknowledging his arrival. Then a deep sound rumbled like the bowels of the earth, and somewhere to the north—still too far away to see—the oncoming train's great wheels began to slow down.

Inside the station, the first cages were already being moved across the platform in preparation for the train's arrival. But all work stopped and every prisoner fell silent when the ground began to tremble and a cold blue light seeped out of the darkness, tracing along the edge of the track's boundary wall and focusing into a single blinding beam that cut through the night like a knife. The deep noise sounded again. Closer this time and unmistakable. Silas's driver stopped the carriage right on the edge of the platform, where he climbed down, unhitched the horses, and led them quickly away.

Kate could feel the train approaching, but she still could not see anything but the light. The ground shook hard. Silas swung open the carriage door and the horn wailed again, deafeningly close. He pulled her out onto the slippery platform. Light flooded the walls, the rumble of wheels echoed through Kate's bones, and the Night Train thundered into the station, groaning and grunting like a vast, malodorous beast.

It was a moving stink of dripping oil, hot grinding metal, and burning fumes; a patchwork of heavy repairs, newly forged metal, and old hammered panels all riveted together into one scarred machine. Its massive wheels growled against the pressure of the brakes and its metal carriages rolled behind, each one windowless and terrifying, accompanied by the creaking sound of hanging chains.

The train was a monster. Its engine car was taller than a house, with a twisted steam chimney on top and a pointed grille mounted on the front, designed to push anything it encountered out of the way. Kate's head swam as a wave of putrid steam gushed from the wheels and tumbled onto the platform, carrying with it the hot smell of burning oil and churned-up dirt. The nearest carriage groaned as it settled to a stop, letting the train fall into silence, or as close to it as such a huge machine could.

The Night Train stretched back endlessly down the track, no longer the grand funerary train of Albion's last age, created to carry the dead to their place of rest, but a twisted ruin of what it had once been: a symbol of terror instead of hope. Its carriage doors opened one by one, filling the air with the shriek of sliding metal, then the first cages were rolled forward and the throbbing sound of machinery echoed inside, sending many of the prisoners into a panic.

The station was in an uproar. No one wanted to be put on that train, and their shouts were deafening. People fought at their locks, tried to squeeze through the bars, and two cages crashed onto their sides as their occupants tried desperately to escape. The wardens ignored them and stood in silence along the platform, their daggers glinting in the lantern light. They did not care if people shouted or fought or begged or screamed. To them, Morvane was just another town and they had already won.

"You will not be traveling with them," said Silas, turning Kate away from the shouting people and leading her toward the front of the train. "I want you where I can see you."

A set of three metal steps folded down from a door close to the front of the train and Silas motioned for her to step aboard.

Kate looked back across the station, wondering where Artemis was, among all of those people. Maybe if she did what Silas wanted, for now, he might make a mistake, or at least leave her alone long enough for her to free herself. Something told her Silas was not the kind of man who made mistakes, but that small hope was enough to make her climb those steps with a little less fear. She was going to get out of this, and she was going to help Artemis. She just didn't have any idea how she was going to do it yet.

Kate stepped up into the monstrous carriage and was met by the dull flicker of tiny lanterns swinging in groups from metal beams overhead, but other than those beams the roof was completely open to the sky. Dark clouds moved sluggishly through the night and the jagged remains of the station's roof crisscrossed above her. The Night Train was a bare skeleton of what it had once been. It had walls but no roof and no real floor but the girders needed to hold it together. One step to either side would have sent Kate falling through onto the tracks, and if the train was moving, she had no doubt someone could easily be dragged underneath.

"Keep moving," ordered Silas.

Kate continued slowly along the girder toward the center of the carriage. To her right three rows of cages hung from chains hooked onto the beams and three more matched them on the left-hand side, swinging precariously over wide open gaps in the floor. All of them were empty.

Silas unlocked one of the cages on the right and held it still while she climbed inside. "This is the quietest part of the train," he said, unclipping her wrist chain and locking the door behind her. "The wardens do not patrol this carriage, and I have sole possession of the prisoners carried here." He pulled a red blanket from a cage on the other side and forced it through the bars into Kate's hands. "Get some sleep. We will not reach Fume until morning and there will be plenty of work for you to do once we arrive. You will be no good to me without rest."

Kate shivered in the icy cold. Snow began to fall again, and she waited stubbornly for Silas to walk back out onto the platform before wrapping the blanket around herself for warmth. The great train's door slid shut and the finality of the sound reverberated through the walls. She rattled the cage door. The lock was bent a little from a previous occupant's attempts at escape and it would not budge, so she stood in the corner of the cage with the blanket around her, clutching her mother's necklace, not wanting to accept the truth.

She was trapped on the Night Train, helpless, just as her parents had been. Was this how they had felt the day the wardens had taken them away? How long had they survived? Kate knew that they had made it to Fume, but Artemis had never told her what had happened to them after that. She buried herself deeper in the blanket. She was about to take the same journey her parents had taken ten years before, and there was nothing she could do about it.

There was no way out, nowhere to go. All she could do was wait.

Crouching behind a wall just outside the graveled garden, Edgar would have done almost anything for a blanket. His toes were numb, his fingers ached with cold, and his skin prickled in the icy air.

Getting across town had been difficult enough. With time against him, he had ridden a stolen bicycle the entire way, pumping the pedals as fast as he could, taking shortcuts no warden would ever know about, dodging patrols and trying to stay out of sight while the Night Train drew closer to the town every second. He had made it. The train was still there. All he had to do was sneak on board. That part had sounded easy when he had first thought of it. Now, seeing so many wardens in one place, it was starting to look impossible.

Edgar was peering over the wall, watching for a break in the warden patrols, when a flutter of wings settled on the wall beside him, and he turned to look straight down the beak of Silas's crow. The bird strode proudly in front of him, not caring that it had been seen.

"Shoo!" said Edgar, slapping it away. "Get lost!"

The bird jumped deftly out of reach, lowered its head, and let out a loud, sharp call. *"Krrarrk!"*

"Stop that!" Edgar tried to grab hold of it, but it moved

too fast, marching stubbornly up and down the wall. "Fine." Edgar grabbed a chunk of stone and threw it at the crow's feet. The bird clicked its beak and flapped its wings, glaring at him.

"Didn't like that, eh? Next time it'll be your head," said Edgar. "Go on!"

The crow tilted its head to one side, as if listening to something far away. Then it snapped its beak viciously toward Edgar's nose and took flight, circling up to the nearest rooftop to keep watch from a place Edgar's stones could not reach.

"Great," whispered Edgar. If the crow knew where he was, it wouldn't be long before Silas sent the wardens out looking for him. It was time to do something.

"It isn't that hard," he told himself, looking out at the cages and shuffling his feet to keep warm. "Just stick to the plan."

For his idea to work, Edgar had to choose his moment carefully. With most of the wardens loading cages onto the train, there were fewer of them left to guard the ones farthest away from it. All he had to do was climb one of the cages, hide on top of its roof, and let himself be taken aboard.

He stood up as straight as he dared, watching the commotion that had started inside the station spreading quickly to the prisoners still waiting outside. Edgar knew that sound well. The sound of fear. He knew what was in store for the prisoners. The Night Train was the stuff of nightmares to most people, but to him it was far more than that. He had been ten years old the day the wardens had come to claim the people of his own home town. He remembered being pushed into one of those cages, holding his brother's hand and promising him that everything was going to be all right, even though he knew it wasn't. He could never have imagined that, seven years later, he would be waiting for it again, trying to find his way on board.

"This is it," he whispered, spotting a break in the patrols. He clenched his hands into fists, not at all convinced that he was going to come out of the next few minutes alive, and then ran into the moonlight, darting between the cages, searching for an empty one he could climb.

Some of the prisoners shouted at him as he sped past, but their voices were lost among the rest. Edgar ignored them. He couldn't afford to slow down and there was nothing he could do for them anyway without a warden's key. Then he saw them: a pair of wardens patrolling away from the rest, close enough for him to see the whites of their eyes. He ducked quickly behind the nearest cage and scrabbled beneath the wheels, waiting for them to pass by.

"Hey! You!"

He had been too slow.

For a moment, Edgar just stared at the two men as they ran his way. Then he rolled out across the dirt, sprang to his feet and was off at a sprint, barreling along like a wily mouse fleeing from two fast cats. He raced past five burning torches and made a sharp turn before colliding with a horse that reared up in fright.

"Argh!" He wriggled away from the horse's falling hooves, scrambled under a second cage, and changed direction. There was no time to climb on top of a cage now, so instead he did what no warden would expect him to do. He headed straight for the Night Train itself.

Groups of lanterns fanned out from the station as patrols began sweeping the rows one by one. The search was highly organized, making it predictable enough for Edgar to slip between two groups and sneak right into the station without being seen. Once inside, he crept along what was left of the main wall and ran across the northern end of the platform, jumping down onto the tracks between two of the train's enormous carriages. He ducked, pressed his back against the side of the platform, and stopped there to catch his breath and figure out his next move. Getting that far was amazing enough, but the train would be leaving soon and he still had to find a way on board.

Once all the front carriages were filled, the train's brakes steamed suddenly and the wheels began to move. Edgar heaved himself up on to the coupler that held the two carriages together and, as the train rolled forward to bring the rear carriages up to the platform, he struggled to keep his feet up off the tracks, dragging himself along on his belly and clinging to the coupler for safety. Every inch the train moved carried him an inch farther down the platform, past wardens and prisoners alike. He had to move. Fast.

Edgar had been carried right through the station by the time the train stopped again. His hands stung as he peeled them off the icy metal and began to climb hand to hand up a vertical bar fixed to the end of one of the carriages. Once up, the snow was falling so heavily it blinded him to everything farther away than two carriages in either direction. There was no way to tell where Kate would be, but if he stayed out in the open for too long he would be too cold to do anything other than curl up and hope the weather finished him off before the wardens did.

There was no sign of Silas's crow inside the station and, as the prisoners continued to be loaded, Edgar spotted some of the horse-drawn carriage drivers walking their horses down the platform ready to be taken aboard.

Horses?

Where there were animals, there was heat. If the train had a horse box . . .

Edgar set off, skulking along the edges of the carriage roofs, moving parallel to the horses as they made their way to the middle of the train. He moved quickly, concentrating on where he was putting his feet and daring to make the jump between carriages whenever one came to an end. His stomach turned with every leap. He felt exposed, the ground was too far away and he knew he would become nervous and fall if he looked down. Somewhere through the snow he heard Silas's voice, but the order he was shouting was nothing to do with him and so Edgar kept going, feeling like a fly on a dog's back, until the smell of hay and animals reached his nose, drawing him on with its promise of warmth.

He knelt on top of the only carriage he had found with a proper roof and looked down through a wooden grille at a collection of tired horses, each one penned in, giving off a welcome heat that drifted up through the bars and into his face. With two strong tugs, the old grille broke off in his hands and he dropped down into an empty stall. The neighboring horses stamped their hooves, sensing the presence of an intruder, but Edgar was too exhausted to care. He piled the hay up around him, letting his muscles relax for the first time in hours, and squeezed his freezing hands together, trying to warm up his blood.

He sat there like that for what felt like hours, watching the door and getting ready to bury himself in hay just in case a warden stepped inside. Then at last, the wardens' work was done. Edgar felt the train shudder and strain as its engine gathered power.

The horn sounded. Brakes hissed. Wheels turned.

There was no turning back now.

The Night Train hulked its way sluggishly out of Morvane's station, puffing heavily through the snow and grunting along a wide curve that took it through a gated arch in the town's eastern wall and out into the open country. Wandering animals fled before it as the great train gathered speed, dragging itself south with a fresh load of human cargo, slicing its way toward the distant city of Fume.

Kate was the only prisoner in her section of the train, but she was not on her own. Silas spent the entire journey watching her, his gray eyes gleaming almost white in the half-light. Just having him near her made Kate feel colder, and even when she shuffled around so she could not see him, she could still feel him looking at her. Snow blew in through the open roof, and she buried herself deeper in the blanket, trying to concentrate on keeping warm.

The train rumbled for hours through the overgrown fields

and hills of the wild counties, where wolves howled through black forests and stalked the riverbanks, out on their nightly hunt. Towns held their breath as the train smoked through them, and the glow of distant fires flickered around the base of the eastern hills where the residents of smaller villages kept watch, making sure the train passed them by.

The people of Albion had not always lived this way. The seas dividing the island country from its cousins had once been filled with huge-sailed trading ships carrying goods like wool, fruit, and wood to the Continent and bringing fine cheeses, oils, horses, and lotions back in return. Trade flourished. Towns grew. The wild counties were veined with roads and walking trails, and journeys between towns were commonplace. Wardens had not worn robes back then and they had not been feared. They had been trusted men—the towns' defenders—tasked with keeping wolves from the town gates and guarding the people who traveled across the wild counties in between.

The country had been great once. Its vast towns and grand architecture were the envy of every country on the Continent, but while the fighting of a war had not made life any easier, the rot had begun to sink in long before war had been declared.

For more than a thousand years, Albion had been ruled by the governing High Council. The council had thirteen members—usually men—who had shown distinction in many different areas of public service. Being chosen to wear one of the High Council's robes of office was the ultimate honor, giving the members a coveted place of responsibility at the very head of Albion's society, as lawmakers and defenders of the country's history and its people. The system ensured that only people who had proved their commitment to bettering Albion were put in charge of the decisions that would shape its history, and at first it worked, but it took time for ordinary people to recognize its one fatal flaw.

The power attached to members of the High Council lasted until death. Only then could a new councilman take an old one's place—and some people did not like to wait. Those who were hoping they were next in line soon began to take chances, often going so far as to employ assassins to speed up their ascension to the council's chambers, and those who were ruthless in their acquisition of power proved no less ruthless in their wielding of it. Under their influence the focus of the High Council gradually began to shift, and corruption spread like poison through the halls of the old ruling city.

Council members who resisted the greed of the others had a tendency to disappear, leaving their seats open for new blood more willing to accept changes in how things were done. Soon personal wealth meant more than anything else in the selection of new council members. The welfare of Albion became secondary to the greed and personal gain of those in charge of its laws, and council seats began to be handed down through bloodlines, offered to people who could pay their way into power, or presented only to those whom the existing councilmen knew they could trust. Shaped by such grasping and devious hands, Albion soon began to suffer.

No one really knew when the first change had come. There was no single moment, no sudden day when everything was different. Darkness crept slowly over Albion. The High Council became more secretive, the wardens gradually drew back from the wild counties, and without their protection to rely upon, travel between the towns became dangerous. People began to go missing on the roads and many chose to stay within their own walls, letting nature creep in around them rather than setting out to brave the world alone.

Within fifty years of the wardens' retreat the councilmen had become suspicious of their neighbors and wary of their own people. They were rarely seen outside their chambers. They recruited the wardens as their protectors and enforcers, called back the trading ships and put them to work patrolling Albion's borders instead. Within a hundred years, the towns had become completely isolated, their people linked by only two things: the High Council's laws and the Night Train's tracks.

At that time, the High Council's ruling city was a small town that lived within tempting sight of Fume's impressive towered skyline. The councilmen could no longer stand to see the greatest buildings of past ages being wasted on the dead, so with the help of their wardens, they took Fume for themselves, driving out the bonemen and killing any who dared to challenge the council's claim. The Night Train was left to rust in its station. Towns were forced to bury their dead in open spaces that had once been parks or greens or gardens. Life gave way to death all across Albion and nothing was ever the same again.

Within the protective walls of Fume, the councilmen led privileged lives, demanding more obedience from their people while offering them less and less in return, and when war came, the people accepted it without question, knowing they could do nothing else. No official reason for the conflict was given. Many speculated that Albion's broken trade agreements were to blame, but no one really knew for sure and the High Council saw no reason to tell them. People were simply expected to do their duty: to live quiet lives and to fight when they were ordered.

Albion had become a place of suspicion, doubt, and lies. The war dragged on, communities were torn apart by the wardens' harvests, and living beneath the shadow of an unknown war eventually became an accepted way of life. Years passed, and soon there was no one left alive to remember that life had been any different.

The people of Albion did not often like to talk about the way things had once been, and Kate was used to that way of thinking. Artemis had raised her to concentrate only upon what was there, right in front of her eyes. There was nothing to be gained from looking back, he always said; nothing except regret. But sitting in that train, listening to the creaking of her cage chains, Kate could not prevent her thoughts from turning to her own past and her memories of the place she was leaving behind.

She remembered the smell of her mother's oil paints and her father's laugh as he worked alongside Artemis in the bookshop and she knew that, despite everything that had been going on around them, her family had been happy once. Now they were gone, Artemis was missing, and their precious bookshop was nothing but a burning shell. Kate hugged her knees up to her chest. There was no doubt that Albion was dying, but it seemed that her little part of it was dying more quickly than the rest.

The clouds changed slowly from nighttime gray to patchy indigo, then pale violet and pink as the sun began to rise over the eastern hills. Kate's body ached with cold. The blanket was too thin to keep the deep chill of winter at bay and her mind kept drifting into short snatches of restless sleep. Silas Dane's face crept into her dreams, and the shivers of the huge train kept jolting her awake until eventually she heard the swooshing sound of stone arches passing overhead. The Night Train's brakes engaged, sending a loud squeal screeching from the hot wheels, and Kate sat up, knowing that the sound could only mean one thing.

They had arrived.

Fume was Albion's most fortified city, separated from the rest of the world by high outer walls and a wide river that had been diverted to circle it like a moat. Rows of empty stables stood along those walls, where travelers' horses had been kept before war with the Continent had been declared. Dozens of wardens stood guard along the city's perimeter and at the great black gates, ready to question anyone who wanted to pass through. But Kate could not see any of that herself. All she saw were more arches passing above her as the train slowed down, sweeping around a wide curve of track.

"Hold on to something," said Silas, still standing beside her. "Now."

Kate grabbed hold of the bars just before the cage swung hard and the entire carriage tilted forward, descending into a sloping tunnel that carried the train underground. They were gaining speed, darkness swamped the carriage, and the horn sounded again, echoing deafeningly from the walls as they swallowed the train. After that there was only the smell of smoke and choking heat as the lanterns flickered out.

The walls hugged dangerously close to the carriages and the ceiling was just high enough to allow the engine's chimney to pass through. Kate's eyes stung in the hot smoke as the train rolled deeper underground, beneath the river, beneath the city walls, and down toward the oldest foundations of the city. The screams of the prisoners sounded distant and unearthly. The train shivered so violently it felt as if it could fall apart at any moment, and still the tunnel continued curling down. Metal ground against metal, the brakes squealed, and the train slowed. Then the tunnel widened, soft firelight spread from a redbricked ceiling hung with lanterns and the mighty engine rumbled along the last few feet before coming to a final bone-juddering stop.

The wardens wasted no time. The sound of sliding doors shook through the train, and raised voices carried through the air. But they were not prisoners' voices Kate could hear. They were loud, confident, and they were all shouting at once. Silas threw open the carriage door and what Kate saw beyond it was as unexpected as it was terrifying.

The train had stopped at a station built into a cavern of earth that looked as though it was being held up by buildings from the past. The damp walls were a mass of stone pillars, half-ruined walls, statues, doorways, and arches positioned in places no one would ever be able to use them. Some jutted out at odd angles halfway up the sides of the cavern, half buried in the mud, and others were squashed on top of one another like layers in a cake. It looked as though someone had taken chunks of broken buildings and pushed them into the cavern walls, letting them sink in before the earth had hardened permanently around them.

Outside the train was a wide stone platform divided in two by a high wooden fence. The right-hand side was for the wardens and prisoners being taken off the train, and the left side was filled with people shouting at them, waving pouches of coins, and craning their necks to get a good look inside the carriages before anyone was brought out.

"Tailors!" shouted a woman, her shrill voice carrying above the rest. "I'll pay five gold for a seasoned stitcher, two for an apprentice."

"Housekeepers!" barked a man beside her. "Four gold apiece for a strong woman and boy!"

"Dancers!"

"Builders!"

"Bakers!"

"Servants!"

And so it went on. A rage of voices, all desperate to buy the prisoners as they would buy animals at a market. Offers were made, bids were argued and increased, and all the while cages were wheeled out of the carriages and the people of Morvane were fed into the belly of Fume one by one.

No daylight poured in to brighten the station. Braziers spat and hissed along the ceiling, arranged in line like a fiery spine, and there were two torch-lit exits to the left of the platform: one for the crowd and one with a fenced path leading to it from the prisoners' side.

Kate pressed her back against her bars, trying to stay out of the crowd's sight, but not before she had spotted something else waiting on the opposite side of the platform. A second train, sitting on a parallel track. Kate had never heard of a second train existing in Albion. Its engine was barely half the size of the Night Train's. It looked newer and more carefully pieced together, with carriages built like huge metal crates, its doors barred and its engine's metal skin shining a deep dark red.

Most of the male prisoners were not for sale, and they were pulled straight on to the red train, to the groans and disappointed shouts of the onlooking crowd. Kate watched as a small group of pickpockets were allowed to squeeze in through a gate and snatch whatever they wanted from the prisoners being taken on board. Cloaks, shoes, coins, anything that could be grabbed through the cage bars was taken, but the thieves paid a price for what they took. Not one of them skulked back into the crowd without a bruise, a broken finger, or at least a dazed look in their eyes once Morvane's men were through with them.

Kate looked for Artemis among the steady stream of people being wheeled across the platform, but there was no sign of him.

"Wait here," said Silas, walking to the doorway and kicking the three steps down on to the platform. "I will come back for you."

Silas stepped off the train into full view of the crowd, and the effect his presence had upon the people was incredible. All shouting stopped at once. The station fell silent as he swept his eyes around it, scrutinizing every face, every movement, and every breath taken around him.

Kate could almost feel his concentration. She could sense dominance emanating from him without his even saying a word. He was completely in control of every person in that station. Not one of them would dare to defy him. Fume was his city. His territory. In that place he was not just another face among many enemies. He was known and feared for reasons far beyond the reach of any ordinary warden. No one looked at him directly, careful not to attract his attention, and the air hung with the anticipation of his words. When at last he did speak, it was to give one simple instruction. "Carry on."

With Silas's blessing, the crowd burst into life again. The frenzied bidding continued, the station was a mass of ordered chaos, and then one bidder's shout stood out above the rest.

"Scholars. Historians. Booksellers! Paying a high price!"

"If you're not interested in this batch then keep your mouth shut," growled a warden, glaring at a small man who was waving a hat in the middle of the crowd. "Wait your turn."

Three more cages rolled by before the man called out again. "I represent a member of the High Council! I must be heard. Scholars! Historians! Booksellers! Name your price."

That got the wardens' attention.

Orders were passed along the platform. There was a burst of activity farther down the train, and a cage was lifted out before its turn.

"All right then. One bookseller. The only one we have."

Kate moved around her cage, trying to get a better look. There was only one bookshop in Morvane and, as far as she knew, Edgar had not been captured by the wardens. The only bookseller on that train had to be Artemis.

"Does he know his trade?" asked the buyer. "I require someone skilled in history and literature. Nothing less."

"He's all we've got. Either take him, or clear off."

The buyer pushed his way to the front of the crowd, money changed hands, and the warden gave another signal to his men. A cage was pulled forward by two brown horses and there, sitting inside it on his own, was Artemis, looking pale and sickly in the firelight. The man inspected him briefly— "He'll do"—then Artemis was rolled off toward the prisoners' exit tunnel and Kate could only watch helplessly as he was taken out of sight.

"Next!" bellowed the warden, pocketing the fat coin pouch.

She had to do something. She had to get out!

Kate was struggling to break her lock when a shout carried along the platform, a sound like a screaming cat ripped through the air, and green fire streaked past the train before exploding not far away. Silas turned, his face veiled in anger as a second streak chased the first—red this time—with a silver sparkle right on its tail. The crowd ducked as one, and a blaze of white sparks blossomed above their heads, accompanied by an ear-splitting bang.

Someone was setting off fireworks in the station.

Wardens converged on the source of the commotion and their frightened dogs struggled against their leashes as they barked and clawed the ground. Kate was too far back to see anything clearly. More explosions burst above the platform, a green flash erupted right above her carriage and when she looked up she saw someone slither down through the roof, grab on to one of the cages, and drop into the dark. The hot smell of hay and horse manure wafted Kate's way and a very disheveled-looking Edgar crept over to her with hay sticking out of his wild hair and soot from the cellar fire still clinging to his clothes.

"That should keep them busy," he said, grinning as another rocket whizzed overhead.

"Edgar! What are you doing here?"

"Helping you. What does it look like?"

"How did you—?"

"We don't have long. Silas'll find the fuses in a minute. They've got crates full of those things out there." Edgar pulled a long black key out of his boot and unlocked Kate's cage. "I got this off a wall hook three carriages back. I was starting to think you weren't on board. Most of the other prisoners are off now." The door swung open and he held out his hand. "Let's go, then."

"Artemis is here," said Kate, as soon as she was free. "I saw him."

"I know. I saw him too, but there isn't time to . . . Hang on. Trouble."

Kate followed Edgar's eyes. Silas was crossing the platform, heading right for their carriage.

"Quick! Climb up!" said Edgar, holding her cage as still as he could.

Kate jumped on to the bars and climbed them right up to the roof beams. She looked down once she had reached the top, but Edgar was gone.

Silas's shadow spread across the carriage, and Kate leaned back, trying to stay quiet. It took only a moment for Silas to realize she was gone, and the cages crashed together as he began searching for her.

She had to move. She had to get away from him.

The place Kate was sitting was only two carriages away from the Night Train's engine. She skirted the roof quickly and found the top rung of a ladder taking her right down to the tracks.

"You!" Kate heard Silas's shout in between two more screeching bangs.

He had found Edgar.

There was nothing she could do. If she went back, she would be caught—and what good would she be to anyone then? She forced herself to walk away from the shout, down a narrow worker's path squashed between the train and the station wall. Soon she was right beside the hot black engine and there were only two choices from that position: down into the tunnel, or back onto the platform. There was no way to know where that tunnel came out. Edgar was in trouble, and every second she wasted carried Artemis farther away. She had to risk the platform.

With fireworks still lighting up the air, no one noticed Kate climbing from the tracks and squeezing through a broken panel in the side of the wooden fence. Water dripped from the muddy ceiling like indoor rain and tickled her head as she slipped unnoticed into the crowd, most of whom had their arms over their heads for protection, pushing their way toward the arched exit behind them. She was just about to follow them, hoping to find Artemis somewhere on the other side, when Silas dragged one final prisoner onto the platform.

Edgar limped awkwardly into the light, squinting through a bruised eye. As soon as some of the braver bidders saw him they started counting what was left in their coin pouches, weighing up Edgar's value with eager eyes, but one look at Silas's face showed that he was not for sale. His eyes scoured the crowd. Kate ducked behind a tall woman beside her, and when she looked out again Silas was marching Edgar off to the prisoners' exit on foot. That must have meant something serious, because the crowd suddenly became angry, squeezing forward to glare and shout.

"Traitor!" spat the woman closest to Kate. "You've earned what you'll get, boy."

"Traitor."

"Traitor!"

Edgar turned to look at the heckling crowd. He was trying to put on a brave face, but Kate could see right through it. She knew he was scared and she pushed her way forward, determined to do something, *anything* to let him know she was still there and that he was not alone. She dodged around the heaving bodies and found herself squashed against the wooden fence as Edgar walked by. There was only one safe way to get his attention, so she shouted out loudly with everyone else.

"Traitor!"

Edgar looked up, recognizing her voice, and she raised her eyebrows in a small way that no one else could see, trying to send everything she wanted to say to him in one desperate smile. His face brightened a little when he spotted her and sank again as Silas grabbed the back of his neck, forcing him away.

Kate pushed back through the crowd and forced her way through to the exit leading to the city above. She climbed up a long twist of spiral steps, hoping that the two tunnels came out at the same place, but the narrow staircase was full of people. She tried to run, but the steep steps and heaving bodies made it difficult to move quickly.

A burst of sunlight met her at the very top, and she found herself standing in the middle of a busy path framed by high stone walls. There was no sign of Edgar or Silas anywhere, so she followed a handful of people in front of her and tried to look like she knew where she was going.

The thin path turned and split like a maze, with rusted hand-painted signs directing people to Narrow Way North, Traitor's Gate, Sunken Lake, and more. Kate lost sight of her guides while reading one of those signs and decided to take a chance and follow the path marked Traitor's Gate, hoping it would lead her to Edgar.

The way became dirtier and quieter the farther she went, until she had the feeling that the only people who took that particular path were those who were forced to. Then the path turned sharply and Kate froze, face to face with a pair of wardens. They were just guards, standing on either side of a small door. There was no way they could have known of her escape, but her terrified face must have betrayed her guilt, because both of them drew their daggers as one. Fear overrode everything else, and Kate ran.

The wardens gave chase, their bootsteps closing in upon her as she raced off down the pathway. She ran as fast as she could go, rejoining the main flow of people and pushing her way through them, and when the path turned sharply, she collided solidly with a small man in a tall hat.

"You there!" the man said, grabbing hold of her wrist. "What is your business here?"

"Let me go!" Kate struggled to free herself but the man held her tight, taking every kick and tug as he tried to get a good look at her face. Finally their eyes met and his face registered shock.

"You!" he said. "You're one of them."

Two wardens ran up the pathway in answer to the man's call, their bootsteps closing in on Kate, gaining every moment.

"Let me *go!*"

Kate tore her hands from the man's grip and raced off down the pathway with the wardens close behind. She ignored the signs, knowing they couldn't help her, and chose turnings at random, until suddenly she found herself at a dead end, with a wooden door sunk into the wall, bolted tight shut.

There was nowhere else to go. The wardens were almost upon her. She slammed the bolt to one side, heaved open the door, and ran through, not caring where her panic was taking her. And there, topped by a wide patch of perfect blue sky, Kate got her first true look at the grand graveyard city of Fume.

8

FEATHERS
& BONES

Fume was a city of darkness. The buildings were tall and angular, built from black stone and dark wood, each one reaching up to six stories high, casting shadows across the winding streets. Kate was standing upon a wide balcony at the top of the northern wall, alongside a spiral staircase leading down into the city itself. From that vantage point she could see the rest of the city's outer walls circling round like encompassing arms, reaching far beyond the horizon, and the pointed roofs of the towerlike buildings scratching at a layer of fog that balanced across them like a sickly blanket.

Every building was an exaggeration of other buildings she had known. Where Morvane had ordinary houses, Fume had clusters of tall towers huddled together like whispering old men and streets of grand homes with black slate roofs all shimmering with frost. It was powerful, aggressive, and magnificent all at once, built upon the bones of Albion's

SHADOWCRY

ancestors. Kate had expected to see riches, but nothing like this.

She looked behind her. The wardens had to be close, so she grabbed the handrail of the curling staircase that wound in upon itself impossibly tightly and headed down.

The metal steps creaked and wobbled beneath her, but she kept going, clinging on to the central post for balance and hitting the ground at a run, not daring to catch her breath as the staircase swayed with the weight of someone following behind her. The towers looked even taller now that she was underneath them: immovable monuments to the dead that not even the High Council had dared to strip away. She ran to the nearest street, past railings that circled the towers like iron skirts, and squeezed through the first gate she could find, ducking down behind a neatly trimmed hedge and trusting it to keep her hidden as she spied on the road.

Carriages trundled past her hiding place, but no wardens came. She was just about to creep out and risk checking the staircase when she heard a familiar voice close by.

"One more sound out of you, and I will slice you ear to ear."

Kate peered through the hedge. Standing in the street, as ominous as the city around him, was Silas, with Edgar by his side, bound to him by a wrist chain.

"I should have killed you when I had the chance," said Silas, raising a hand to the sky and letting his crow flutter down to land proudly upon it. "You always were trouble."

"She won't follow us, you know," said Edgar, his nervous voice a little higher than usual. The crow glared at him, watching his every move. "Kate doesn't know her way around the city. She won't know where we are."

"She'll know." Silas stopped for a moment, making Kate retreat farther into her hiding place. "I would have stripped that station bare in search of her if it would not have attracted unwanted questions," he said. "Perhaps this way is for the best. I have *you* now, Mr. Rill. The Winters family have always looked after each other, and you are as good as family to that girl from what I have seen. Wherever I take you, your friend will not be far behind."

"Don't count on it," said Edgar. "Kate's a lot smarter than you think."

"We shall see." Silas reached his hand into the street and a horse-drawn carriage with a blue crest on its door pulled up to the pathside. "The Museum of History," he said to the driver. "And don't spare the whip." Silas carried his crow inside and tugged Edgar in behind him like a disobedient dog. The carriage reins snapped hard and the gray horse trotted forward.

Kate didn't have to think about what to do next. If she lost Edgar now, she could lose him for good. She darted out from her hiding place, ran straight for the carriage, and grabbed hold of the luggage rack hooked on the back. She managed to jump up and push her left foot into a twisted loop of ornamental metal that caged the carriage's rear axle. The whip cracked, the horse gathered speed, and the carriage wheels spun at a racing pace until it was cutting through the streets faster than a wolf could run.

Kate's right leg hung down as she clung to the rack's cold metal, and she forced most of her weight into her left leg, trying to keep her balance. No one paid her any attention. There were dozens of carriages on the streets, many of them with people tucked into the luggage racks or riding on the roof—servants, she guessed from their bedraggled states—but none of them were traveling as fast as the one under Silas's command.

The carriage raced along streets decorated with stone statues, past low buildings topped with staring gargoyles that spat meltwater down on to the paths below. The driver was definitely taking Silas at his word. The whip cracked hard every few seconds, and the horse sped on, forcing well-dressed men and women to move aside to let it speed through. Most of the streets were built to match perfectly the architecture in the oldest parts of Fume. Kate was starting to think they were going around in circles when one of the wheels hit a stone on a tight turn and the carriage lurched sharply, almost sending her catapulting out on to the road. She clung on as it bounced along into a wide street lined with huge gray buildings, where, with a snort of relief, the horse finally slowed to a stop.

They were at the bottom of a high curve of shallow steps,

looking up at the once-grand face of what had to be the Museum of History. Its windows were tall and thin, tinted with green glass, and every one of them was still intact. A strange deserted feeling hung around that building. The same quiet stillness that settled over cemeteries, as if the dead were standing on those steps, still watching the living.

The carriage door swung open before Kate had a chance to move. Silas stepped out and pushed Edgar up the steps, heading for a door at the top while Kate unhooked her foot and dropped down from the luggage rack. Her left leg stung as the carriage rolled away, and she carefully ducked into the museum through an unlocked side door once Silas and Edgar had walked in through the front.

The door led to a short corridor and through to a narrow room lined with glass cases. There was no one around. From the look of the cobwebs hanging thickly from the ceiling, the museum had been abandoned for a very long time. Every case was empty, each one lined with faded fabric that bore the dark shadows of necklaces, rings, and gemstones that had once been held inside.

There were six doors leading out of the room, not including the one she had come in through, and all of them were shut tight. The first one she tried opened to an odd chemical smell. It was dark and there was no sign of Edgar, so she tried the second, which opened to a staircase leading down to a lower floor. Kate thought she heard noises echoing below: sharp footsteps heading the opposite way, but her experiences with cellars were bad enough to make her hesitate on the top step.

"*Silas.*" A woman's voice carried from behind a door to Kate's right, taking her by surprise.

The voice was strong and commanding, and Kate matched a face to it at once. It was the woman she had seen in her vision at the boardinghouse. The one Silas had gone to meet there. The woman called Da'ru.

Kate risked opening the third door as silently as she could. She peered through the gap, hearing Silas's voice on the other side. "Be careful, my lady. Remember where you are. Your voice is loud enough to call the dead."

Da'ru was standing beneath enormous skeletons of long-dead creatures that were hanging down from the ceiling. Silas walked toward her, his expression caught somewhere between obedience and hate. Kate could see most of the hall from where she stood, but Edgar was not there. The chain was no longer in Silas's hand. There was no sign of him anywhere.

"You have had long enough," said Da'ru. "Where is the girl? My officers informed me that you kept one prisoner separate from the rest on the Night Train, and yet she has not been delivered to the High Council. Why?"

"There was a commotion at the station," said Silas. "A boy was causing trouble and I had to deal with him."

"And the prisoner?" said Da'ru. "Where is she now?"

Silas hesitated, his eyes narrowing as he chose whether

to lie to her or not. "Secure," he said at last.

"Then you do have her?"

Silas nodded firmly, but his jaw twitched with anger.

"I should not have to come looking for you," she said. "Your first duty is to me. The only reason you are not locked away beneath the council chambers is because you have proved yourself useful. My name is feared for good reason, Silas. And you above all others should fear me the most."

Silas took another step toward her. "I fear nothing," he said.

"Then I suggest you pay closer attention to your work, or that will soon change." Da'ru locked eyes with Silas without a hint of fear, and Kate did not doubt the seriousness of her threat.

"*Boy!*" Da'ru's voice echoed around the hall.

Footsteps rattled along the upper level of the building and a young boy's face appeared on a gallery encircling the main hall. "I haven't found anyone yet, my lady," he said, bowing as he spoke. "I'll keep looking."

Da'ru turned back to Silas. "Where is she?"

Silas glared and said nothing.

"You would not be here if the girl was not close by," said Da'ru. "You will hand her over immediately, or I will have you thrown into a cell and charged with treachery."

"Your presence here threatens everything I have set in place," said Silas. "Leave. Now."

Da'ru smiled, raising her chin to expose her bare neck, and Kate saw something cruel and terrifying behind the beauty of her face. "Do not test me," she said. "You are nothing but a dog on a leash to me, Silas. The rest of the council may still trust you, but I know how much you would like to kill me if you could. You could take your revenge against me, right here and now, but you know what will happen if you do. Without me, the blood within your veins will slow and die. Your body will wither and what is left of your soul will be sealed inside your rotting bones, unable to live and forbidden to die. Your world will be silent. Your name forgotten. My wardens will bury your worthless body where it will never be found, and the only battle left for you to fight will be against the worms as they slither upon your skull and feast upon your eyes."

Silas stood unflinchingly before her, neither of them willing to give the other an inch.

"You already know that there are far worse punishments than a simple death," said Da'ru. "The half-life of the veil is a torturous place, and immortality lasts a long, long time."

Silas glanced in Kate's direction, just once, so quickly that she might not have noticed it. He relaxed his shoulders a little, and the tension in the room lifted as it looked like he was about to back down.

"Return to the chambers," he said to Da'ru. "I will deliver the girl. Assemble the council and tell them we shall perform the first procedure tonight."

"The council does not waste its time upon empty promises. She should be ours already."

"Leave her to me," said Silas, bowing his head a little and taking a small step back. "Trust me, my lady. Everything is going according to plan."

Kate backed away from the door. Silas knew she was there! But she couldn't leave. Not with Edgar still somewhere in the building. She ran as softly as she could back between the display cases. The boy was searching upstairs; he mustn't have found Edgar up there. Then she remembered the footsteps in the cellar. The second door was still hanging open, waiting for her.

The steps beyond were tight and cramped, leading down into a huge dark space broken only by pillars that held the main floors up. Sunlight crept in through flat windows squashed against the ceiling, but it was still too dark to see anything near the middle of the room. Kate followed the wall, staying close to the light, and walked past high tables stacked with specimen jars; some empty, but most sickeningly full. There were birds, frogs, fish, spiders, beetles, and flies, all dried and pinned to stands inside the green glass, or drowned in thick choking liquid that kept them preserved against time.

Something rattled on the other side of the enormous room.

Kate froze.

"Edgar?"

Her whisper was lost in the darkness.

Stuffed birds hung down from the ceiling and old feathers covered the floor, their spines crunching beneath her feet as she followed the edge of the table toward the noise. Then the sound came again.

A line of doors was set into one of the longest walls. They looked like storage cupboards, each one hooked shut upon a rusted latch, but one of them rattled hard as she made her way toward it. A length of wire jutted out of the space between the door and its frame, and Kate could hear someone talking to himself on the other side.

"Edgar?" she whispered. "Is that you?"

"Kate?"

Kate unhooked the latch, the door swung open, and Edgar—who had leaned against it to listen to her voice— flopped straight out onto the floor.

"Ow! You could've warned me!" he moaned, trying to stand up. His wrists were tied behind his back, and Kate knelt down to free them. "How did you know where I was?"

"Shhh! They'll hear you."

"Silas . . . left me in there!" said Edgar. "I was almost out, though. That latch would've given in eventually."

"We have to get out of here," said Kate, helping him up. "It's not just him anymore. There's a woman here. I think it's the councilwoman. She's right upstairs."

"Da'ru is here?"

Kate clamped a hand over his mouth. "Yes. Not so loud. I

know the way out. So just follow me and keep quiet."

Edgar nodded and she let him go. "Lead the way," he whispered.

Kate followed the tables back toward the cellar steps, trying to ignore the eerie faces of the dead creatures glaring out at her from the jars. The silence was frightening, and she was just about to say something to break it when Edgar grabbed her arm.

"Kate," he breathed. "Stay still." But it was too late. Kate looked over to where the steps began and saw a tall figure standing there. Silas. His gray eyes shone with an eerie light. His voice echoed powerfully around the cellar.

"There is no way out, Miss Winters," he said, stepping into the weak sunlight. "The rules have changed. You are in my world now."

9
THE COLLECTOR'S ROOM

There was a loud click, a buzzing sound in the wall, and a thin fuse burned along a glass tube in the ceiling, lighting a row of lanterns that illuminated the room with a faint orange glow. Kate looked for another way out. There were at least a dozen doors scattered around the room, but no way of telling which of them led out of the cellar or which were unlocked.

"I should have anticipated what happened at the station," said Silas. "Edgar Rill is well known for his inventiveness, though not for his success. The fireworks were an interesting choice of distraction, but failure is a habit your friend cannot seem to break. As it stands, your 'escape' was both temporary and convenient."

"I'm not going anywhere with you," said Kate.

"Then you clearly do not understand your position. I am not giving you a choice."

"You stay away from her!" said Edgar.

"There are only a few hours before I must deliver you to the High Council," said Silas, walking toward them. "We have work to do. We shall begin now."

Edgar grabbed Kate's hand and pulled her toward the first door he could find, leading her on to a staircase that led even deeper into the old museum. The stairs were steep and uneven. There was no handrail, so they relied on each other to reach the bottom, fleeing through the dark with no way of knowing where they were or how far behind Silas was.

Edgar stumbled when they came across a small landing and he knocked against a handle in the dark. "Doors!" he said, grabbing it at once. There were two, one on either side of them. Both locked. The only way open to them was down.

"Can you hear him?" Edgar panted. "Where is he?"

Kate kept running, trying to keep her balance on the awkward steps. None of this felt right. Why were they going down? They should have been going up. Into the city, into the light. The air changed as they ran, becoming stuffy and dank, but they kept going, right to the bottom of the steps, bursting through into the only unlocked room they could find.

"Check the walls!" said Edgar, slapping his palms against the stone. "Maybe there's a way out."

Their bootsteps echoed from the stone walls, but the staircase remained silent. Either Silas was still at the top, waiting for them, or he was lurking somewhere close by in the dark.

Edgar lit a match and looked around. "Oh no," he said, his face glowing in the light of the flame.

They were standing in a square room with three doors squeezed together along one side, each with a collection of switches and levers beside it. Edgar used the match to light a lantern hooked to the wall and he held it up.

"These must be Silas's holding cells," he said, testing the first door. "Every collector has a couple of places where he locks people for interrogation before handing them over to the High Council."

"So this is a prison?"

"Sort of."

"How do you know that?"

"I just do. This is not a good place to be."

Kate tried the other two doors. The first was locked, but the second swung open easily. Inside was a cell just a few feet wide. It smelled musty, as if it had not seen fresh air for a very long time.

"No wonder Silas wasn't following us," said Edgar, pushing past her and feeling along the cell walls. "He knew where we'd end up."

A strong hand reached across Kate's face, stifling her before she could scream, and the cell door thumped shut, sealing Edgar inside.

"What made you think I wasn't following you?" asked Silas, his voice faceless and terrifying in the dark. "Since you are so interested in disturbing my work, Mr. Rill, it is only right that you should take a closer look at it yourself."

Edgar's lantern light shone out through the window in the cell door.

"Let him go!" Kate tried to reach the handle, but Silas held her still.

"I warned you," he said. "This boy is not the escape artist he believes himself to be."

Edgar rattled the door, but it was stuck tight.

"He has served his purpose," said Silas. "It is time for you to serve yours."

Kate struggled against him as he dragged her back up the staircase to the first landing, where a door now stood open.

"After you," he said, forcing her inside.

Kate blinked in the bright light of a lantern that was already lit upon a low table, and Silas picked it up, leading her through a maze of rooms linked by archways. The museum may have been huge above ground, but those main floors were only the uppermost levels of a much deeper space. Most of the lower rooms held storage crates filled with forgotten pieces of bone, metal, coins, books, and everything else Kate could imagine, but the farther they went, the neater the rooms became, until they reached some that Silas had obviously claimed for himself. There were chairs to sit in and old paintings and weapons displayed on some of the walls, suggesting that this wasn't just an ordinary collector's hiding place. It was Silas's home.

Soon they reached a large room that looked much older than the rest. A fire crackled under an ancient stone mantelpiece set into the main wall and the air hung with the warm smell of old leather. Silas's crow was there, perched upon a bookshelf in the corner, watching Kate keenly as she stepped inside.

She tried her best to look calm when Silas pointed to a chair by the fire.

"Sit."

There was no hope of escaping this time. The museum's lower floors were like a maze. She would only get lost if she tried to run, so she did as she was told.

Silas took a plate of food from a table and passed it to her. "Eat," he said. "I have no interest in food anymore, but I find prisoners usually require it."

Kate's stomach growled at the sight of fresh bread, biscuits, and cheese, and the crow skittered closer, watching every mouthful that she ate.

Silas pulled over a second chair and sat down. "It is time for you to understand. Your life as it was is now over," he said. "Your home is gone, your uncle has been taken, and you are only just beginning to recognize the lies that have been told to you all these years."

"What lies?" asked Kate. "I don't understand."

"That is because you have been encouraged to be ignorant. There are those who have tried to protect you by hiding the truth about what you are, but I will not lie to you.

Being one of the Skilled brings nothing but persecution, fear, and death. You can accept it or try to hide from it, but you cannot escape it."

Kate put down her plate, unable to stomach the food anymore, and the crow fluttered over to it, stole what was left of the cheese, and scuttled under the table to finish it off.

"Why did you bring me here?" she asked.

Silas sat back in his chair, studying her face. "Do you know what began the war that has made Albion what it is today?" he asked.

Kate did not answer.

"For generations the leaders on the Continent have tried to cross our borders," said Silas. "And every battle that has been fought—every death, every kill—was caused by one single secret. That secret was the Skilled. The High Council are not the only ones who recognize the value of your kind. As a people, the Skilled are unique to Albion. There are no reports of anyone on the Continent having access to the veil. No one knows why, but while the Skilled have thrived here, other countries have long lived in the peaceful ignorance that this world is the only world there is."

"That's because it *is* the only one," said Kate.

"Really?" said Silas, looking genuinely surprised. "Are you sure about that?"

"Of course I am."

"Then you have far more to learn than I realized."

Silas stared at Kate, letting the silence grow between them until she was forced to look away. "Believing in a lie can be a comfort," he said. "But continuing to believe it when you have already seen the truth can be dangerous, if people decide to use that lie against you. You cannot deny what you have already seen. The High Council has always known about the Skilled, but it has been many centuries since they have shared the same goals. Almost four centuries ago, at the beginning of the last era, the High Council were tempted by science and turned against the old ways of the Skilled. They wanted to study them. Understand them. Pick apart their minds to find out exactly how they can do what they do. Their greed for knowledge drove the Skilled into secrecy and the council still hunt them to this day, believing that they are the weapon that will win this war once and for all, even though they were the ones who caused it."

"The Skilled didn't start the war," said Kate.

"No, the High Council did that by bragging to every Continental leader who would listen about how the Skilled can see into the world of the dead, heal the sick, and see the future. The Continent wanted a share of that knowledge. They wanted the Skilled, and the High Council refused to part with them. Curiously, to those who cannot enter the veil themselves, the secrets of death are a prize worth dying for. Tensions grew between Albion and the Continent over many years until eventually war began."

"Why would anyone go to war over something like that?" asked Kate. "Most people don't even believe in the veil."

"Believing is not the issue," said Silas. "The Skilled can prove the existence of life beyond this world. Knowledge like that is without price."

Kate did not know whether to believe Silas or not. No one in Albion really knew what the war was about. It had been a part of life for so long that no one even questioned it anymore.

"The existence of the Skilled caused the war that generations have lived with every day," said Silas. "The promise of their knowledge was enough to throw our world into chaos, but instead of standing up beside our soldiers to fight, the Skilled went underground, leaving the rest of Albion to fight its enemies alone. I have no love for the Skilled, Miss Winters. It is because of them that I have seen the veil for myself. I have seen the path of death and it has turned me away."

Silas drew the silver dagger he had stolen from Kalen's body, held out his hand, and drew the point of the blade across his palm, slicing it open so a trail of blood shone like a string of beads in the light. Kate watched in disbelief as his skin began knitting together before he had even finished the cut, and the blood upon it dried to a faint red dust.

"That's impossible!"

"That is what the High Council believed," said Silas. "Before they were proved wrong."

"How did you do that?"

"Twelve years ago a member of the High Council uncovered a rare book in an old grave not far from here. The grave belonged to a long-dead member of the Winters family. *Your* family. And within that book, she discovered a way for the Skilled to harness the power of the veil more deeply than just looking into it or using its energies to heal."

"Was that Da'ru?" asked Kate.

Silas nodded once. "Da'ru believed she could use the book's techniques to alter the link between a person's body and their spirit, and I was part of an experiment to prove that theory. Dozens of other subjects had already died from their exposure to the veil. I was the unfortunate one. I survived. Because of this, my blood does not flow like that of normal men. My injuries heal as quickly as they are made. My lungs breathe, but I have no need for air. Poison cannot kill me and fire does not burn."

Kate looked at Silas and saw the man in front of her clearly for the first time. There was something not quite right about him. Something beyond the fear that he instilled in people with his presence. Anyone could do that with practice. What Silas possessed was deeper than that. That cold feeling that Kate always felt around him; the way his gray eyes reflected nothing of the man behind them. He felt empty to her. It felt as if he was already dead.

"Imagine, then, a thousand more men like me," continued

Silas. "An army like that would be unstoppable, making Albion more feared than any other nation. That is the power the Continent wishes to claim for itself. The High Council are working toward the same goal, but the force of *Wintercraft* almost killed Da'ru the night she made me what I am. She would not survive a second attempt. For that, she needs someone who possesses a greater natural ability than herself, someone whose family possesses an instinctive connection to the veil. That is why she needs you."

Artemis had always taught Kate to trust only what she could see and feel. To him, the veil was a fantasy created by people who could not face the finality of death. But sitting there with Silas, the line between what was true and what was not blurred suddenly. Kate had never fully shared her uncle's skepticism toward the veil, and she could not help believing that at least part of what Silas was telling her was the truth.

"If that is true," she said, "why isn't Artemis one of the Skilled? He is a Winters."

"As I told you before, the Skilled are a dying breed," said Silas. "The ability is not always passed down through blood, and fewer are born with every generation. Your father had the ability to see the veil, your uncle does not. It is not unusual to see a difference within families."

Silas's crow shook its feathers and flapped up onto the fireplace, where it stood pecking at its claws.

"Are you one of the Skilled?" she asked.

"I was an ordinary man once," said Silas. "Now I am something else."

"But . . . when you send your crow after people . . . you can talk to it, can't you?"

"My relationship with the veil is very different from that of the Skilled," said Silas. "Animals use the veil far more than any of us. They understand it. All I have to do is listen."

"Then . . . you can hear what it says?"

"No. But there are ways to communicate that go far beyond the basic senses. You experienced that yourself when you saw through Da'ru's eyes at the boardinghouse. You were not using your own eyes at that time, you were using the veil. That is what I do. The crow's eyes become mine. We hunt together."

Kate tried to imagine how such a link could be possible, but after what she had already experienced of the veil, she realized that she was in no place to judge what was possible and what was not anymore. "If Da'ru almost died doing what she did to you, what makes her think that I won't?" she asked.

Silas leaned forward in his chair, his eyes meeting hers, as if this was the question he had been waiting to answer all along. "Because the book—*Wintercraft*—was never meant for someone like her," he said. "Each person has his own level of potential, and Da'ru reached hers long ago. However much she might deny it, her level of Skill is accomplished but not extraordinary. Her ambition far outweighs her talent, and it has taken her a long time to accept that. *Wintercraft* was written by your ancestors and was meant to be used by people with a far greater level of Skill than Da'ru. Your parents both came from families with strong Skilled abilities and you may well be the last of a pure Winters bloodline. Generations of potential exists within you. You are Da'ru's best chance of using *Wintercraft* to get what she wants. She does not care if it will kill you or not, but she intends to make you try."

"But . . . I don't know anything about any of this," said Kate. "The Skilled . . . the veil. And if you are one of Da'ru's men, why didn't you hand me over to her? What do you want me to do?"

Silas stared at her as if the answer should be obvious. "I had to judge your abilities for myself," he said. "You may be the most vital part of my preparations; the key to something I have looked forward to for twelve long years. You, Miss Winters, are going to help me to die."

10

MEMORIES

Kate was sure she had misheard him. "You want me to . . . what?"

Silas's frown deepened. "It is not as simple as it sounds," he said. "This body can no longer die by any ordinary means. What I need is something extraordinary. Someone capable of reaching beyond this world to the place where the real damage was done. What I need is you."

"But if you can live like that, why would you want to die?" asked Kate. "Surely for you . . . for *anyone* . . . not being able to get hurt would be a good thing."

"My body may heal quickly from the cut of a blade, but I still feel it," said Silas. "The tearing of metal against flesh, the hot smell of blood . . . Life is pain, Miss Winters. I am simply forced to endure it longer than ordinary men, and that is not acceptable to me. There is no cure for being human. *Why* I am looking for death is not the question you should be asking. For now, all you should be concerned with is *how*."

"But . . . I can't. That's not—"

"Your ability is not in question," said Silas. "Once we have *Wintercraft*, everything will fall into place."

"I've already told you. I don't know anything about that book!"

"Just because you do not remember it does not mean you have not seen it. I think you know more about it than you realize. The answer is already there inside your mind. And together, we are going to find it."

Silas moved before Kate knew what was happening, pressing his fingers to the sides of her head and bringing his face up close to hers. His gray eyes locked on to her own bright blues, and then all of her energy was sapped away, drained so completely that it was an effort even to blink.

It felt as though a hood of ice had been pulled over her head. Her forehead prickled with cold and a deep chill spread through her bones, moving down through her spine and trickling into every muscle until she could not move. Her fingertips burned as frost spread across her skin, icing her eyelashes and making her lips turn blue. Her heartbeat slowed, unable to fight against the cold. Her lungs fought hard for every breath . . . tightening . . . slowing . . .

Silas slid Kalen's silver dagger from his belt, pushed up Kate's left sleeve, and traced a shallow cut across the inside of her arm. Kate felt nothing except the cold as Silas captured

SHADOWCRY

drops of her blood in a thin vial and held it up to the light.

"All blood holds power," he said. "Da'ru will use this to prove your identity to the High Council. Be glad that I have taken it from you. She would have taken a lot more."

Kate tried to fight against what was happening, but the veil overtook her even more strongly than before.

"Tell me," said Silas, corking the vial and pushing it into an inner pocket against his chest. "What do you see?"

Kate's whole body stopped. Time stretched endlessly around her and then, in the midst of that wide unbroken stillness, her mind burst spectacularly into life.

First there were colors, lights, and sounds. Kate felt as though she was moving, but Silas was still right in front of her. Then the colors merged into fractured images of places she knew and people she remembered: Edgar dropping down through the Night Train's roof . . . Morvane's market in full swing . . . the view from her bedroom window . . . and her father in the bookshop when she was young, teaching her how to spot a rare book among the ordinary ones.

"There. Go back to that memory," said Silas. "Let me see it again."

Kate was so lost in what was happening that Silas's voice took her by surprise.

"Concentrate!"

Her thoughts obeyed him, even though she did not want them to, and she was wrenched back into her memory of the bookshop, where her father was inspecting a book with a magnifying glass.

"Your parents let you see many rare books that passed through that shop," said Silas. "Your mind can remember them all. Show me more. Show me this one."

The view shifted to a place Kate had never seen before. She was standing in the middle of a room high up in a circular tower with windows all around her, looking out over the vast cityscape of Fume. A book lay open on a desk in front of her: an old book with curled pages and words written in faded ink, and Da'ru sat behind it—looking younger than Kate remembered. She wrote something on a piece of parchment, rolled it up, and pressed it into Kate's hand. But the hand that took it was not hers. It was a man's hand, worn and strong.

"Let the council know that I am ready to present my findings," she said. "Silas has been kept in isolation for two years and the results of every test continue to exceed all of my expectations. The council may not approve of my methods, but they cannot deny the results. It is time for them to see Silas for themselves. I am trusting you, Kalen. Convince them to speak with me again. Tell them what you have seen. Take the book with you as a token of trust, but do not let it out of your sight. Perhaps now they will finally recognize the value of my work."

"Yes, my lady." Kalen's gravelly voice spoke from the place Kate's throat should have been. His hand reached for the book and closed it, revealing a dark purple cover with silver studs around the edges and the shimmer of polished oyster shell running in bands across the leather. A title glistened in the sunlight. One word written in faded silver leaf:

WINTERCRAFT

"Inform me the moment they send for me," said Da'ru. "And if any of them try to harm the book in any way . . . kill them."

"Yes, my lady." Kate's mind swiftly left Kalen and Da'ru behind, already searching out the book within her memory. She returned to the bookshop—to Artemis this time—and found herself looking through the eyes of her younger self into one of her earliest memories, one she did not even know that she had.

"I told you, it is too dangerous!" said Artemis, arguing with her father over the bookshop counter.

"This is not your decision, Artemis! Anna and I have already decided. It is the right thing to do."

"They can't ask you to do this!"

"They can. You, me, and Kate are the only ones left that carry the Winters blood. The book belongs with our family. Why don't you understand that?"

"Because it's not right. What about Kate? Are you going to risk putting her in danger for the sake of a stolen book?"

"Nothing is going to happen to Kate. And this is far more than just a book, Artemis. It is history, and who knows what else it might be one day. We are going to do this. It doesn't matter if you agree with us or not. That book will be safe here with us, where it is meant to be."

Artemis thumped his fist upon the counter, the only time Kate had ever seen him lose his temper in that way. "This is wrong, Jonathan. How do you know they are telling the truth? How do you know they're not just trying to protect themselves by getting this thing out of Fume?"

"Because they stole it from a warden—from Da'ru Marr's best man himself! They have already taken enough risks to get Wintercraft back. The rest is up to us now."

"So," said Silas, his voice breaking into Kate's thoughts. "The book was stolen from Kalen and handed to your family. Da'ru always believed he had sold it to the Skilled to line his own pockets. She thought he was a traitor. It appears she was wrong."

Kate was not listening to him. The veil was already taking her to the next memory she had of Wintercraft, and before she could stop it, her mind replayed the first night she ever spent in the bookshop cellar's hiding place. A night that happened just a few days after that argument: the night the wardens took her parents away.

She remembered looking out through the eyeholes in the cellar wall, watching her parents taking Wintercraft out of a secret space beside the chimney breast. They were talking too quietly for her to understand them, but they were both afraid. Her mother hid the book in her dress pocket, wrapping it in a torn strip of cloth. Then there was a loud crack above them and the cellar door smashed from its hinges, clattering down the steps as four robed men broke their way in.

Kate remembered watching her father fighting them off and her mother drawing them as far away from Kate's hiding place as she could, so her daughter would not be found. She saw the flash of silver as a blade was thrown through the air, stabbing deep into her father's shoulder. She saw the warden who came to retrieve it and heard her father's scream as the warden wrenched the dagger out.

That warden gave the order for her parents to be taken up to the cages, and as he carried the dagger held ready at his side, Kate saw the letter K shining upon the blade, stained red with her father's blood. Kate knew that man at once. Kalen. But he was younger and healthier, before the madness had taken over his mind. Kalen had come to Morvane to find the book and clear his name. He was the enemy she had seen in the cellar that night. He was the one who had taken her family away.

The image faded. Silas was back in front of her and Kate could feel the prickle of cold on her skin once again. Her lungs burst into life, her heart raced up to speed, and she was back in the museum, back in the firelight.

"What . . . was that?" she asked, her throat stiff and sore as Silas lowered his hands from her face.

"That was a glimpse of the half-life," he said. "The first level of the veil that a Skilled mind learns to enter, where memory becomes reality. You cannot stop now. You must return."

"But I saw the book . . . and Da'ru . . . inside a tower. I've never been there."

"That was one of Kalen's memories," said Silas. "I took it from him in the moments before he died. The soul remembers every aspect of a person's life at the moment that it ends: every sight, every sound, every thought. Kalen's search for *Wintercraft* consumed the final years of his life. When he died in that alleyway, his spirit was exposed to me. The memories I needed were easy to find. I shared that memory with you because it was important for you to see. Now go back. The veil must become familiar to you. You must travel even further along the path into death if you are going to be of use to me."

"No," said Kate, flinching away from him. "Leave me alone!" She knocked her chair over and stumbled to the door, throwing back the bolts with shivering hands as Silas sat and watched.

"It took Kalen just a few weeks to find your parents, but he did not find the book," he said. "The Skilled were not there to help your family when it mattered most, just as none of them are here to help you now. It seems Artemis kept you away from them for good reason. Clearly he did not want to put you in any more danger. Your parents had already done enough of that."

"You don't know what you're talking about!" snapped Kate, fighting with the door as tears sprang into her eyes.

"The Skilled convinced your parents to risk their lives and yours to protect *Wintercraft*, and Kalen took the wardens to Morvane that day because of them. From what I have heard, your uncle fled from the bookshop the moment the wardens arrived. That cowardice saved his life. If he had stayed, he would be dead."

"Artemis is not a coward!" said Kate.

"He ran like a rabbit, leaving you and your parents to your fate. I have seen him lie for you. He protects you and treats you like his own child, but he does it out of guilt. He gave in to his fears that night, saving himself and leaving your parents to face their enemies alone. Then again, perhaps he was happy to see them being taken away. Your uncle was powerless within your household before the wardens came. Perhaps he wanted your parents to die."

"That's not true!"

"Your family was the reason Kalen harvested your town ten years ago," said Silas, "and you are the reason I chose to harvest it this time. The Winters family has a talent for attracting danger, and that danger has always been connected to the same thing. Tell me where *Wintercraft* is. Tell me what happened to it and you will have no reason to hide anymore. It will all be over."

Kate rattled the door. The bolts would not open. They were stuck tight.

Silas stood up and began walking toward her. "Since the night Da'ru unearthed the book she has been plagued by visions of the dead," he said. "They disturb her dreams and torment her days. She believes that ancient spirits of your family cursed her for taking *Wintercraft* from them, yet she still wants it back. She will do anything to find it and, if she does, you can be sure that you and your uncle will be the first to suffer. You saw what was left of Kalen. He was Da'ru's closest ally, yet she poisoned him into madness just for losing *Wintercraft*. The man I killed in the barrow alley was barely a shadow of the warden he had once been. His mind was lost. If you insist upon making things difficult, I could easily do the same to you."

Kate's head swam with dizziness. The effects of the veil were still upon her and an old memory blossomed in the confusion. Silas's link to her thoughts was already broken. This memory was for her alone. A memory Silas could not see.

She remembered being very young again, hiding between the shelves in the bookshop and pulling books out of place, leaving rough piles of them behind her on the floor. Artemis was there, but he had not seen her. He was too busy talking to a woman standing in the shop doorway. A small woman in a black hooded coat.

"It is unfortunate that it has come to this," she said. "There was nothing anyone could do."

The woman would have easily passed unnoticed in any crowd, but Kate remembered her eyes clearly enough. They were dark and strange, like black puddles of oil with rims of bright blue tracing around their edges.

"Then . . . it's true?" Artemis looked at the woman, willing her not to give him the news he was dreading.

"I am sorry, Artemis. They are dead."

"No."

"You have my word. We did everything we could."

"No! How? How could this happen?"

"Anna was carrying Wintercraft. She passed it to one of our people when the wardens moved her from the train, but she was seen. Da'ru Marr heard about what she had done and had her executed as a traitor. Jonathan tried to stop them. He stole a key and freed himself from his cell, but it was too late. Anna was already dead. He attacked the first two wardens that he saw, unarmed, and was killed that same night."

Artemis walked blindly over to a chair by the bookshop fire and dropped down into it with his head in his hands.

"What do I tell Kate?" he said quietly. "How do I tell a five-year-old girl that her parents are gone?"

"Tell her that they did what they set out to do," said the woman. "The book is safe. We will make a place for it in the ancient library, somewhere it will never be found." She walked to Artemis and placed a broken silver chain with a gemstone pendant gently in his hand. "We found this afterward," she said. "It belongs to Kate now."

Artemis's fingers closed around the chain, but he did not raise his head.

"It is not too late. You can still join us. We can protect you. Both of you."

Artemis looked up, his eyes damp with tears. "Just like you protected Jonathan and Anna?" he said bitterly. "We do not need your kind of protection."

"Artemis . . ."

"Get out," he whispered.

"Perhaps, one day, you will change your mind," said the woman. "You will see that it is for the best."

Artemis laughed coldly, and the woman turned to leave.

"Tell Kate her parents carried the name of Winters well," she said. "Da'ru only learned who they were after their deaths. If she had known whom she had captured, I believe their lives would have been a lot worse. Death may well be a blessing for both of them."

"Get out!"

The woman nodded once, then swept out of the door as smoothly as the breeze, leaving Artemis hunched in front of the fire, weeping in the dark.

Kate was sure now of one thing. Her parents had died trying to protect *Wintercraft*. Artemis had warned them the book was dangerous, but they had protected it just the same.

"It's gone," said Kate. "The book is gone."

"You are lying."

"We kept a box . . . inside the cellar fireplace. Artemis hid the book in there when he heard the wardens coming. You destroyed the book. When you burned the bookshop, it burned too."

The lie came easily to Kate, but Silas was not fooled. "There are two vital facts you should know before you lie to me again," he said calmly. "First, I am a man of my word. I keep my promises and do not make them without fully intending to carry them out. And second, there is no secret you can keep from me, now that I know how to enter your mind."

Kate felt the veil creeping around the very edges of her consciousness and she stepped back from Silas, trying to blink the feeling away.

"If the book could be destroyed so easily, do you not think someone would have rid the world of it long before now? And do you really believe I would have burned your shop if I had not been absolutely certain *Wintercraft* was not inside? If it was there, I would have known. I would have seized it, found you, and we would not be having this pleasant conversation. Your work would already be done."

Silas's growing anger smothered the room. Kate's back reached the wall. There was nowhere else to go.

"We have no more time," said Silas. He grabbed her arm, pulled her along the wall, and snatched something down from a high shelf. "Remember, it is your fault that we have come to this."

The point of a needle shone in the firelight and a vial attached to it glowed a deep, dangerous blue as Silas stabbed it down into Kate's arm, releasing a trickle of poison into her blood. She tried to pull away, but the liquid spread like fire through her veins. Sounds became distant, her limbs felt heavy and her knees weakened under her, sending her crumpling to the floor.

Silas's crow fluttered up onto his shoulder, and Silas stood over her as unconsciousness carried her senses away.

"This could have all been much easier," he said.

Kate woke to a dull thumping sound. She was underwater, but she was breathing somehow. Her hands went quickly to her face, where a mask covered her mouth and nose, feeding air into her lungs. She panicked, dragged the mask off, and thrashed her arms, fighting her way to the safety of the surface, only there was no surface to reach, just a hard barrier closed tightly over her head, sealing her in. Kate slammed her hands uselessly against the glass as a face appeared behind it: a face that was not Silas.

She choked in a mouthful of water and snatched at the bubbling mask again, terrified she was going to drown. Then the face stepped back, a deep grating sound rumbled around her and the water level plunged, draining away quickly through a metal grille beneath her feet. Kate dropped to the floor, choking and gasping for breath as Da'ru peered in through the glass.

"That was your first failure," she said, her voice echoing

around the tank. "As a Skilled, you should have been able to see me and speak with me inside the veil without returning to full consciousness. I am disappointed in you, Kate."

The room outside the tank was lit by dozens of candles and Kate saw a group of people gathered in the light. She was not in the museum's cellars anymore. She was in the center of a grand room, surrounded by twelve men in formal clothes seated behind a curved table draped in green cloth. The vial of blood Silas had drawn from her lay half empty at the very end of the table, and the man closest to it was hunched over a pile of papers, writing notes. Silas had taken her to the High Council. The experiments had already begun.

"She did not even enter the first level of the veil," said Da'ru, turning away. Kate watched her through the glass, glaring at her with pure hatred. "I should have let her drown."

"That would have been a mistake."

A dark shape moved in one of the corners, and Silas stepped into the light of the room. He blended into the shadows so perfectly, Kate had not even seen him.

"Immersing the girl was pointless," he said. "The elements do not react to her the way they did to the others."

Da'ru ignored him as if he had not spoken at all. "We shall attempt a more direct approach," she said. "The bloodbane dispersed extremely quickly in her blood. That is a small sign of potential, at the very least. She may yet prove interesting. Release her."

The boy from the museum scuttled out of an alcove in the wall at his mistress's word and unclipped four heavy clamps that kept the tank fixed to the floor. The glass shuddered, and with a sudden creak of wheels and rope the tank's walls rose up into the air, leaving Kate standing clothed and dripping wet on the round grate. She could not remember anything that had happened between the museum and where she was now, but whatever danger she had been in with Silas, her situation had clearly become much worse.

"You promised us results," said one of the councilmen. "This girl looks like yet another pointless waste of our time."

"Excellence takes time," said Da'ru. "Manipulating the subjects' connections to the veil is a delicate procedure. It cannot be rushed without forcing them too far into death. If my studies are correct, this girl may be able to manipulate the veil in ways we have not yet seen, even without the tools and careful conditions usually employed by the Skilled. If she is useful to us, you can be sure I will discover it."

Da'ru gave the boy a signal and he darted forward again, clipping one end of a short chain to Kate's ankle and the other to the grate in the floor.

"Bring in the body," Da'ru commanded the moment he was done. "And be quick!"

The boy scrambled to obey and disappeared into the next room, emerging moments later pulling a low table behind him. A dark red cloth covered whatever was on top of it, and

Kate stared at the body-shaped bulge, expecting the worst. What if it was Artemis under there? What if he was dead? She tried to prepare herself for the worst, determined not to react too strongly if it was true. Then Da'ru nodded, the boy pulled back the cloth, and the dead person's identity was revealed.

Kalen's body looked almost exactly the same as the last time Kate had seen it, gray and cold and still, except that his sunken chest was bare and the wound Silas's sword had made had been stitched together with crosses of thick black thread. The sight of him laid there made bile rise up in Kate's throat, but a deeper part of her was glad to see him again. There was the man who had stolen her parents, laid out, dead and cold. The manner of his death no longer mattered to her. Silas was right, Kalen *had* earned his death. All that mattered was that he was gone.

"This body is all I want you to concentrate upon now," Da'ru said, as the boy wheeled the table right up in front of Kate. "One of your townspeople stole this man's life and now you will return it to him."

"The townspeople?" Kate's eyes flashed toward Silas.

"Quiet!" Silas said firmly. "The councilwoman did not order you to speak." He glared at Kate with such fury that she did not dare say any more.

"You are here to work, girl. Not to talk," said Da'ru. "You will show the High Council exactly what a Skilled mind can do. Now, return this man's soul."

"I can't," said Kate. "I don't know how to do that. And even if I could, I wouldn't."

Da'ru's back straightened, her eyes bristling at Kate's brazen challenge to her authority. "You will."

"Not for you."

Da'ru moved toward her like a snake ready to strike. Kate thought she was going to hit her, but instead Da'ru smiled calmly, snatched hold of Kate's hand, and pressed it hard onto Kalen's chest. Kate immediately felt dizzy, as if she had been spun around too fast, her head pounding as the coldness of the veil closed in around her again. But this time was different. She felt like she was falling forward, falling *into* the dead man himself. The veil descended quickly, swamping her senses before she had a chance to fight against it, and the twelve councilmen all watched with anticipation.

Whatever Da'ru had done, it felt as if something had broken within Kate. She tried to fight back, but she didn't know how. Then her mind lifted and, instead of a flood of memories, she saw something she had never seen before.

She was standing within a vast hanging mist of silvery light, as if time had stopped in the middle of a moonlit rainstorm. The air shimmered with tiny lights, but when she held out her hand, she could feel nothing except the cold. At first, she was sure she was alone, but if she concentrated she could hear faint voices all around her, gentle sounds that whispered and moved.

"Who's there?" Her voice was swallowed by the mist, carrying much farther than she would have thought possible, until it reflected off something in the distance and returned to her as a tiny echo. Then something answered, whispering her name as the mist closed in.

"She has passed into the second level of the veil!" said Da'ru. "Silas. Do you see her?"

Kate did not hear Silas answer, but Da'ru's voice reassured her that—wherever she was—she was not completely lost. She started walking through the mist, concentrating on Da'ru's voice as the only connection she had back to her life. But the farther she walked, the less anything seemed to matter. She felt so peaceful in that place, so content and relaxed, that she was tempted to give in: to let go of the testing room, the High Council, and Silas, and to let the veil claim her completely. But then she thought of Artemis and Edgar, of Morvane and home, and she knew that somehow, she had to get back.

Kate stopped walking and focused on picturing Kalen's body on the table in front of her, ignoring the overwhelming feeling that was desperately trying to pull her on, so close and so beautiful . . . and then something changed. The tiny lights faded to a distant glow and Kate no longer felt as if she was being drawn along. Something like water lapped gently over her feet, the whispers died away, and Kate had the feeling she had done something very wrong.

The silver mist cleared a little around her feet and she looked down at a reflection of herself cast upon shallow water. Her boots were submerged—and she then looked out across the perfect waters of a wide blue lake. She listened for Da'ru's voice again but heard nothing. Even the water was silent.

All she could do was stand there, stunned by the complete beauty of what she could see, until she sensed something moving beside her. In any other place, perhaps she would have been afraid, but instead she reached out, calmly brushing her fingertips through a surging current of invisible energy that felt ready to snatch her up if she got too close. She knew at once she was looking at the way into death, the only safe path leading directly through the veil to whatever lay on the other side. All she had to do was let it take her.

Kate did not know how long she stood there mesmerized by the gentle call of death, and she only stepped away from it when she sensed the air around her shift and become heavier, distracting her from its presence long enough to break its hold upon her. Something had moved beside the energy current: a pocket of dark energy that disrupted everything around it like a stone in a fast-flowing river. The water shrank back away from it, and even death moved aside as something stepped out of the rippling void.

Kate's first thought was of Kalen—she did not want to see him, dead or not—and then the shape took on a more solid form, moving toward her until it was real enough to reach out and touch.

"*Impressive,*" *said Silas, stepping out of the mist as casually as someone walking across a room. "To come this far yourself . . . even Da'ru did not expect that.*"

"*I didn't do anything,*" *said Kate. "What's going on? How did I get here?*"

"*You resisted death. By connecting you with Kalen's body, Da'ru exploited a weakness in the veil, allowing your spirit to be drawn through to this place. But there is more to do if you are going to save yourself. My plans do not involve your death, so you must do as you were instructed. Return Kalen's soul to his body, before Da'ru decides you cannot control your skill enough to be of use to her.*"

Kate's consciousness switched briefly back to the testing room, where she saw her hand still pressed to Kalen's stitched wound.

"*Find him,*" *said Silas.*

"*No,*" *Kate said firmly. "He deserves to be dead.*"

"*And do you want to join him? Da'ru will do it without hesitation. She will sever your spirit from this life at the first sign of failure. Her ruthlessness has led many of the Skilled to their deaths. Do not let your stubbornness lead you to yours. There is a time for everything, and this is not the time to fight her.*"

Kate did not see Silas step behind her. He moved as if he was a part of the veil, not caught within it, and he reached around and held his hand against her forehead, forcing her to focus upon what she had to do. She did not feel the touch of his skin, only a brush of cold air. There was energy within it: a force that intensified slowly, radiating out from his palm.

"Do not fight against the veil," he said. "Embrace it."

The silvery mist flooded all of Kate's senses at once. Suddenly she could smell the water, feel the touch of the wind, and hear whispered voices drifting close to her again; only now she could also see the whisperers themselves, shadowed forms caught within beautiful flashes of dancing color, filling the surface of the lake like patches of floating moonlight.

"These are the lucky ones," said Silas. "Each one of these souls has a chance to enter death when they are ready for it. Kalen's death was a clean one. He should be here."

"I can see him," said Kate, her eyes drawn to an energy drifting alone near the center of the lake. A bubble of hate rose up inside her, but she forced it back down.

"Good," said Silas. "Allow him to see you."

Silas helped Kate bring Kalen's spirit closer. The soft shape gathered form as it moved toward her, becoming more solid, more human, its face twisted into a dark, mocking smile. Silas sensed her anger growing as Kalen drew near enough for her to touch, and in the moment when Kalen's cold soul connected with hers that anger flared up against him, fierce and uncontrollable.

Silas let go of her and shouted, "Now!"

Kate's consciousness plunged back into the testing room as energy burst through her hand and struck Kalen's chest like a lightning bolt. Kalen's body heaved in an impossible breath, and his eyes glared wide and furious as his spirit settled back into life.

Kate's hand sprang away from him. Silas was standing right beside Da'ru, looking as though he had not moved an inch, and the twelve councilmen were completely transfixed by the man on the table: the man Kate had managed to bring back from the dead.

"It is not possible!" said one of them, daring to stand up, before Kalen's arm snapped out and clutched Kate's throat in a deadly grip.

"Gotcha now, girly," he grinned, poisoning the air with a glut of rotten breath. "Thought you'd got away from me, did ya?"

Silas rounded the table and Kalen's mouth drew back into a snarl. *"You!"*

Silas struck instantly, plunging Kalen's silver blade straight down through his neck, ending his life before he could say another word.

"Silas!" Da'ru's face contorted with rage. "How dare you interfere!"

Silas left the dagger where it stood, the silver *K* still shining in the candlelight. "My duty, as always, is to the High Council," he said. "This man's mind was gone. He would have killed the girl and without intervention he could have easily turned upon you or any number of the councilmen in this room. I could not take that chance. The girl has proven her worth, but the subject's actions made him a threat. I was forced to eliminate him."

Da'ru glanced around at the councilmen, who were all still staring at Kalen in disbelief. "You have gone too far, Silas," she said quietly.

"I did only what had to be done."

Da'ru walked toward him and Silas met her gaze, revealing nothing.

"Perhaps you are right," she said, her words dripping with threat as she glanced back at the listening councilmen. "This will not be the last time the girl is put to work, after all." She turned to address the twelve men, hiding her anger with Silas beneath a dark mask of authority. "I am sure we can all agree that this experiment has been a fine success."

Kate's body was shivering. She sat down on the floor as the councilmen all spoke at once, each demanding an explanation for what they had just seen. She was too weak to move. Too tired to think. This was more than bringing a bird back to life. To be able to reverse death . . . to make a long dead body breathe again. It should have been impossible—yet she had seen it with her own eyes! She did not know what to believe anymore, but if this was what being a Skilled meant, then she wanted nothing to do with it.

Finally the talking was over, and when the last of the councilmen had left the room, Da'ru ordered her boy to wheel

Kalen's body away as she turned her attention back to Kate.

"Up," she said, signaling a warden to pull her to her feet. "We have a cell waiting for you. You will rest there tonight and recover your strength. I have more tests to prepare. We shall continue our work in the morning."

Kate looked up at the councilwoman's face and saw something moving around her. The air shifted as the veil drew closer. Images swept across her eyes, and her thoughts were lifted suddenly out of the tower and into a vision of a place she had never seen before.

She was standing in a crowd of people, somewhere out in the open. The crowd were wearing feathered masks—the kind usually worn upon the Night of Souls—and Da'ru was there, with a bonfire blazing beside her, her eyes dangerous and wild. Silas was behind her, his blue blade drawn ready for battle. Kate could not see what he was looking at, but fear rippled through the crowd as many of them tried to run. She did not understand what the veil was trying to show her until everything faded except for Da'ru, and in the distance Kate saw the silver current of death slowly closing in.

"What is it?" demanded Da'ru, breaking Kate's concentration and making the vision fall away. "Silas? Explain this. Did you see the girl's eyes? What just happened here?"

"The experiment has exhausted her," Silas said quickly. "I will take her to her cell myself."

"Speak, girl! Tell me what you saw."

"It was the Night of Souls," said Kate. "Everyone was afraid."

"Delusions," said Silas, pulling her away. "Your fantasies are of no interest to the councilwoman. Save them for your cell. You will have plenty of time to indulge them there."

"Wait," said Da'ru, forcing Silas to stop. "The Night of Souls is still two days from now. What else did you see?"

Silas shot Kate a warning look as she tried to remember.

"There was a ceremony," she said. "You were wearing a locket. A glass one, I think. It looked like it had blood on it."

"The locket?" Da'ru glared at her suspiciously. "What do you know about that?"

Kate looked straight into the councilwoman's green eyes and saw uncertainty in them for the first time. She knew then what the vision had been showing her, and the thought of it made her smile. She slid her arm out of Silas's grasp and faced Da'ru without fear.

"At that ceremony," she said. "You are going to die."

12

TRAPPED

"In." Silas held a door open for Kate, ordering her into a room lit by glowing firelight. For a cell, it was not what she was expecting. It was bright and warm, and the sight of a soft bed was enough to make her realize how tired she was.

For Kate, entering that cozy room was like walking out into the summer sun. The cold that had sunk so deeply into her bones began to retreat against the woody air of a welcome fire, and she felt the numbness fade from her skin as the water that clung to it evaporated. She knelt in front of the fire at once, letting its flames warm her face until her cheeks turned red.

"This room will be your cell tonight," said Silas. "Da'ru has ordered that you be treated well, despite your defiance toward her. Appreciate these comforts while you can. They are not offered to everyone."

There was only one window in the room: a wide arch of clear glass looking out over the buildings that made up what

Kate supposed were the High Council's chambers. Silas walked over to it, signaling for the two wardens to go outside, and waited until they had closed the door.

"Da'ru is keen to gain your trust, especially after your interesting revelation back there," he said. "The next time you see something that you cannot explain, I expect you to keep it to yourself. The more you give Da'ru, the more she will take from you. That would be costly for both of us."

"I gave her what she wanted," said Kate. "Whatever happens, it will be no more than she deserves."

"You saw something that was not meant for you," said Silas. "Da'ru will not let this 'foresight' of yours pass easily. She has devoted her life to manipulating the veil and yet you have just shown more of a connection to it in one night than she has been able to develop across many years. She must decide if you are an asset or a threat. If she cannot control you, she will kill you, so you must stay here and you *will* be quiet. You have already drawn too much attention to yourself. As far as those guards out there are concerned, you will be as silent as the dead. Do you understand?" He waited for her to answer.

Kate nodded that she did.

"You are fortunate I was the one to escort you here," said Silas. "Anyone else might have seen talk of the councilwoman's death as treason and have taken action against you. People have been executed for far less in this place."

Silas stood there for a moment, then he walked out of the

cell and locked the door behind him without another word. Kate heard him giving orders to the wardens outside and she ran to the door, peering out through an eyehole set into the wood. Silas glanced at the eyehole from the other side, as if he knew she was standing there, then he turned and walked silently down a long empty corridor, leaving the two wardens to stand guard.

Kate could hear people moving on the floors above and below, but despite all of the distant sounds of life around her, she had never felt more alone.

She turned her back to the door. Thoughts like that would get her nowhere. There had to be some way out of this room. All she had to do was find it.

Driven by new purpose, Kate stuffed the eyehole with a rag she found on the floor and decided to explore her prison. It did not take long. The walls were bare stone, enclosing a bed, a tiny fireplace, and a washstand with soap, towels, and a jug of hot water. Next to the bed was a table with a lit candle upon it and a tray covered with a white cloth. She lifted the cloth carefully to find a glass of water, an apple, and a plate of sandwiches underneath. Food could wait. She had to get out of her freezing clothes, and that water was not going to stay hot forever.

She undressed quickly and put her boots and clothes to dry in front of the fire, before rinsing her hair and scrubbing her skin clean. When she was finished, she wrapped herself up in a towel and found a pile of dry clothes folded in a box at the end of the bed. She pulled out a long skirt and a red sweater and tugged them on, before throwing a blanket around her shoulders and running her fingers through her clean hair.

Dawn was still a few hours away. It was time for a plan.

She tested the window. Locked. Even if she could break the glass, she was at least three floors up, overlooking a guarded courtyard, and she could see no way down. The walls all looked solid enough, but she inspected them anyway, feeling around for secret doors or loose stones. She found none. Even the chimney was too narrow for her to squeeze through, and a grille had been fitted over it just in case anyone was desperate enough to try.

It was not long before Kate was forced to accept her situation. There was no way out and nothing she could do to help herself escape that place. She ate some of the food to keep her stomach quiet and curled up on the bed, determined to check the entire room again in the morning, before finally giving in to the comfort of the fire and letting its warmth carry her into a restless sleep.

Kate woke some time later to the sound of a key turning in the door. She grabbed one of the bed blankets, flung it around herself, and pretended to be asleep. Then the door opened and someone stepped into the dark room.

The candle on the bedside table had burned out, and her hand tightened around its wooden candlestick as the door clicked shut. Footsteps crept across the floor. The intruder skirted the bed, fingered the blankets, leaned over, and— "Kate?"—the candlestick struck the intruder's head with a sharp crack and Kate squirmed away. He flopped onto the bed, groaning in pain.

"Ow! What was that for?"

Kate stopped halfway to the door. "Edgar?"

"Of course it's me. Did you have to hit so hard?"

"What are you doing here?"

Edgar sat on the bed, rubbing his sore head, and Kate threw open the curtains to see him more clearly.

"No! Wait!" he said, as the moonlight streamed in. "I have to explain something first."

It was too late. He smiled nervously, and Kate stared at him in disbelief.

Edgar was wearing the long black robes of a warden.

He was trying to act relaxed, but he was sweating. Kate gave him what was left of her water and he gulped it down at once, the glass shaking in his hand.

"I told the wardens I'd been sent to check on you," he said. "To be honest, I thought I'd be rat food by now. This is going a lot better than I hoped."

"But how did you get out of the holding cell?" asked Kate. "I saw Silas lock you in!"

"Not so hard really, when you know how. All the collectors put a dead-switch inside their cells, just in case a prisoner turns the tables and locks them in instead. Not all of them are as tough as Silas, you know. He'd probably never need something like that, so it's a good job he's just as paranoid as the rest. Took me ages to find it, but it was there."

"How could you possibly know that?" demanded Kate, stopping in the middle of pulling on her boots.

Edgar looked at her uneasily. "You don't want to know."

"Yes, I do. What happened to you before you came to Morvane? You told me Kalen was lying when he said he knew you, but you were the one telling lies. He did know you from somewhere, didn't he?"

"I promise, I'll tell you everything as soon as we get out of here."

"That's not good enough."

"It has to be. We don't have time to talk right now."

"Then what are you doing here? We can't get out!"

"Ah, but I have some inside information." Edgar pointed at the window.

"It's locked," said Kate.

"Not for long." Edgar walked to the window. Kate heard the lock click and a tiny key sparkled in his hand. "All thanks to my brother," he said. "Tom was with Da'ru in the testing room. He works for her and he told me where to find you. He risked a lot to get me this key."

"Your brother works for a councilwoman?" said Kate. "What else don't I know about you?"

Edgar threw open the window and looked out across a sheer drop. "The wardens are going to change guards down in that courtyard soon." He dragged off his robe and pushed it into Kate's hands. "Here's the plan. You wear this. Go straight out of that door, turn right at the end of the corridor, and head down the first staircase you see, all the way to the bottom. I'll be waiting for you there."

"I can't do that! They'll spot me in a second!"

"They won't. They'll just think you're me."

"And how is that good?"

"Wardens don't ask many questions if they think you're one of them. Trust me, you won't get caught."

"What are you going to do?"

"Me? I'm going to climb down there."

The last thing Kate could ever imagine Edgar doing was climbing out of a window into a place full of wardens and, from the look on his face, he wasn't too sure about it either. He looked like he was going to be sick.

"All right," she said, throwing the robes back into his arms. "But you're using the corridor. I'm climbing down." She pulled on her coat.

"You don't know where to go!"

"I'll manage." Kate tied her hair back, twisted the skirt into a knot at her hip, and tucked the fabric into the waistband. Once it was secure she clambered out onto the ledge.

"Tom said there are hand- and footholds carved into the

wall," said Edgar. "It's a secret way down, left over from when this used to be a warden's room. Look to the right. You'll see them."

"I can see one," said Kate, trying not to look down.

"Kate, please be careful."

"I'm all right," she said. "Go."

Kate clung to the window frame, focusing upon the wall. The wind howled around her ears, swirling up from the square below, and the sun was starting to break upon the horizon, casting long rays of gold across the rooftops. She slid her foot into the first foothold she could find, let go of the window just long enough to grab the lower lip of a tiny stone arch, and then edged her way along, step by step, heading diagonally down the wall.

Darkness was Kate's friend, for now, but at every moment she expected to hear a shout or a warning, or see arrows come spearing up past her ears. Nothing came and the secret path took her right to the ground, where an archway hid her from a pair of wardens who were just starting their patrol. She dropped down from the last foothold, freed her skirt, and ducked behind the stones, not daring to move until she saw movement off to her left. Edgar was there, hiding on the opposite side of the square, waving cautiously across the courtyard, which now looked much wider and dangerously exposed. There was no way either of them could cross it without being seen.

Something flapped above Kate's head, and she looked up to see a crow perched inside one of the footholds. Silas's bird. And if it was there, Silas had to be close.

Whatever Edgar's plan had been, there was no time for it to work now. She could not risk leading Silas to him again. They had to separate. She had to find her own way out.

Kate did not see Edgar's look of fear as she left without him, or see him crawl around a low hedge to avoid a warden who was heading his way. But Silas saw it all. He was on his way down from the testing room tower, carrying a stolen vial of what was left of Kate's blood. He had no intention of allowing Da'ru to use that blood in her work. The councilwoman may have lost *Wintercraft*, but she had learned enough from the book to make that blood a very dangerous tool. He could not risk her using it against Kate, not until his work was done.

Silas did not know how Kate had escaped from the holding room, and he did not care. He took the steps two at a time, his coat trailing through the stone dust as he slid the vial into the pocket at his chest and swept out into the open air.

She was out and she was his.

Kate ran into a quiet wing of the immense council chambers and raced along corridors and through empty rooms, checking every window to find some way out. All she saw were more buildings, more courtyards, and endless grassy squares. The place was a maze and the wardens were everywhere.

Most of the doors she found were locked, so she was forced to cut through a dining room where two long tables were already laid out for breakfast. A door hung open at its farthest end: a servants' door, meant to blend in with the rest of the wall. She ran straight for it and found herself inside a network of passageways built right into the walls.

The cramped pathways were dusty and tight, with passing places sunk into them at regular points wherever the thicker walls allowed. Kate often had to duck inside to let busy people pass, but no one questioned her. Many of the servants she saw there looked as bedraggled as she did, heading off to build fires, serve breakfasts, lay tables, polish floors, and do a hundred other tasks that kept the council chambers running smoothly.

Suddenly the passageway came to an end and Kate squeezed out into a busy kitchen filled with steam and smells and shouts. Most of the workers were younger than she was, boys and girls stolen from their own hometowns, stirring, baking, boiling, and frying under the keen eyes of three older cooks. Kate was not sure where to go next, until a young girl carrying a bowl of potatoes looked her way, glanced at the nearest cook, and then changed direction, heading straight for her.

"You're one of them, aren't you?" she whispered. "Your eyes are different. I can tell. Edgar told me you might come this way."

"Edgar was here?"

"He was looking for you a while ago. He said if you came here without him, I had to show you the door." The girl pointed to an iron hoop halfway along the wall. The door behind it was so well disguised that Kate never would have spotted it on her own.

"Is Edgar coming back?" asked the girl.

"I hope so," said Kate, trying to smile. "Thank you so much."

"Good luck."

Kate left the girl behind and stepped through the door into a short hallway that led straight outside. The fresh air chilled her skin, and she ran out onto a path edged by an iron fence that was far too tall to climb. Beyond that fence, the city rose like a black forest, and a carriage path led from the council chambers right down into the city itself.

Kate followed the fence until she found a missing railing that left a wide space between the bars. She squeezed through and set off running down the edge of the path toward the safety of the nearest street. She was so busy worrying about what might be behind her that she did not spot the man waiting up ahead until it was too late.

He stepped out in front of her, snatched her up in his arms and pulled her into the hallway of a narrow old house. Whoever he was, Kate was not ready to be taken without a fight. She bit and scratched and punched and squirmed until the man cried out in pain and two more hands grabbed her in the dark.

Lanterns gathered around her, and five dirty faces glowed in their light.

"Is she the one?" asked a man behind her, holding a light close to her face before she managed to free her arm and knock it away.

"She fits the description."

"And she's right where Edgar said she would be."

"What's your name, girl?"

"Do you really expect her to tell us that?"

"If it is her, then where's Edgar?" asked the first man. "Isn't he meant to be here?"

A woman's voice rose above the rest. "I think Edgar may be lost to us," she said, moving around to stand in the light. Something about her was familiar to Kate. Her hair was short and flecked with gray, and her eyes were pitch black, edged with blue, like shining drops of oil.

"It's you," said Kate, remembering her at once. "I saw you. At the bookshop."

The woman smiled kindly. "If you are who we think you are, then it has been many years since we last met," she said. "Perhaps if we introduce ourselves, you will understand why we are here."

The woman reached out for Kate's hand and this time Kate did not resist. A gentle warmth spread across her fingers and, for the first time since Artemis had been taken, for no reason she could explain, Kate felt safe.

"She is the right one," said the woman. "She is scared, understandably, but she is no threat to us."

"Tell that to my nose," grunted one of the men, whose face was swelling quickly after taking a full punch.

The woman ignored him, never taking her eyes off Kate. "We are going to let you go now," she said. "We have a lot to talk about, so please do not try to run."

The men released their grip, letting Kate stand by herself.

"Who are you?" she demanded, glaring at them in the light of the lantern.

"You have no reason to fear us," said the woman. "We are just like you, Kate. We are the Skilled."

13
THE CITY BELOW

Ever since Kate had first learned about the Skilled, she had expected them to look different from most people in some way. Not one of the people standing around her was extraordinary, but the one feature they shared was unnaturally dark eyes. Kate had heard that the more time the Skilled spent looking into the veil, the darker their eyes became, and even in the brightness of the lantern light their eyes looked as though their pupils had leaked out to overtake everything else, leaving just a faint line of true colors circling the edges.

Kate realized she was staring and looked away.

"My name is Mina," said the woman. "Edgar asked us to wait for you both here. Do you know where he is?"

"No," said Kate. "We got separated."

"He was worried that might happen. We have no choice but to go on without him. Here, he left this for you." Mina handed her a tiny roll of paper tied with string.

Kate recognized Edgar's handwriting on the outside of the roll. "But . . . how do you know Edgar?" she asked.

"We have known him since he was a boy," said Mina.

The men all nodded. "He's a good lad," said one of them. "He's had no kind of life. No kind of life at all."

Kate was confused. Was there anyone in Albion who *didn't* know Edgar?

"There is no time to read the letter now," said Mina. "But soon. When we are safe. The council will not find you where we are going. This way."

Kate held the little letter tightly as the Skilled led her down into the house's cellar. One by one they stepped through a door disguised as a stack of shelves and came out upon an underground path that was very different from the tunnels Kate had seen beneath Morvane. This path was not just an ordinary tunnel; it looked as though it had once been above the ground. Its walls were the fronts of two rows of houses facing one another, light came from candles propped on outside windowsills, and the path was wide and cobbled, with worn wheelmarks where carriages had once run.

The few windows that had survived the years reflected the group's lanterns as they walked past, but the houses had only bricked-up arches marking where doors had once been, and the rooms inside had long since been buried under fallen earth.

"Will Edgar be able to find us down here?" asked Kate.

"He knows the way," said Mina. "But I do not hold much

hope for his safe return. It will not take long for the wardens to see through his lie. We all told him it was foolish to go back."

"Back? Back where?"

"I will explain everything soon. For now, we must walk."

The understreets seemed to wind on forever, linked together by staircases and bridges that spanned deep chasms sliced into the earth. Looking over the sides of those bridges was like looking down into the underworld. Some of the chasms had people working in them, hanging from long rope harnesses and chipping away at the rock, while others were abandoned and so deep that it was impossible to see all the way to the bottom.

"Grave robbers," said Mina. "In the bonemen's time, the Night Train carried coffins here, and they laid the bodies to rest in long tombs that run deep beneath our feet. Fume's towers were built as memorials to the families laid to rest beneath them, but since the High Council took it as their capital they have made it a place to be feared, not respected. The bonemen are gone and the Night Train carries the living into slavery, war, and death. That is not the way things are meant to be."

Kate dared to lean out a little farther over the side.

"Do not let them see you!" whispered Mina. "The wardens are the grave robbers' enemies as well as ours, but the grave robbers would not hesitate to report us if they decided it was worth something to them."

Mina's group did its best to stay out of sight and headed down a narrow tunnel that had been cut into an old rock fall. Mina unlocked a green door hidden behind a flap of cloth and Kate followed her into a beautiful street lit by tiny lanterns hanging down from its ceiling. It was an arched cavern lined with red bricks and metal frames that protected the houses underneath from collapse. Every one of them was as perfect as the day they were built. There was even a working fountain in the very center and lanterns edging the paths, giving the street a warm, friendly glow.

"This is where some of the bonemen used to live," said Mina. "If your uncle had listened to me years ago, you would already call this place home. I am only sorry we could not bring you here sooner. You will be safe here. My home is close by. We will talk inside."

Mina took Kate into a small well-kept house and sent the others away, but some refused to leave.

"She could be dangerous!" said one. "The High Council kept her alive. What do you think she gave them to deserve that?"

"I think she gave them hope," said Mina. "Something none of us have had in a long time."

"Look at her eyes! They are already half dark, and she is too young for them to have colored so quickly. Da'ru has forced her too deeply into the veil. If she was not guided there properly, shades may have followed her spirit back out. She may be corrupted."

"This girl is too strong for that," said Mina. "As you can see, she is one of us and she needs our help."

Kate tried to listen to what else was being said, but they lowered their voices too much for her to hear. Whatever Mina said to them, it worked. The group left her and Kate alone. Mina locked the front door and, noticing Kate's uneasiness at being locked in, immediately pressed the key into her hand.

"You are not a prisoner here," she said. "This street is the safest in the City Below. Edgar hid here with us when he first escaped the High Council. Did he tell you about that?"

"He didn't tell me anything," said Kate. "Edgar escaped from the council?"

Mina regarded her carefully.

"He says we can trust you, and he is not a boy who trusts easily. He must think a great deal of you to go back to the chambers after all this time."

"I didn't even know he'd been to Fume before," admitted Kate.

Mina took her into a small room where two comfortable chairs sat on either side of a table spread with a deck of picture cards. "Edgar left this place three years ago," she said, gesturing for Kate to sit down. "He always was a good boy. Cunning and quick. Never frightened of danger."

"That doesn't sound much like Edgar," said Kate.

Mina gathered up the picture cards and shuffled them as she talked. "We all change in order to survive," she said.

"Edgar was taken from his family at a very young age. The councilwoman Da'ru Marr bought him and his brother Tom from the Night Train. Edgar was one of her servants for more than four years. As far as most of the wardens in the chambers know, he still is."

"He *worked* for Da'ru?"

"Not by choice, you understand. When Edgar was thirteen he escaped from the chambers. He tried to take his brother with him, but Tom was not where he was meant to be that night and Edgar had to leave him behind. Da'ru knows he will come back for his brother one day, so she always keeps Tom close, hoping to draw Edgar out. There is nothing she dislikes more than a traitor."

"Edgar walked right past the wardens outside my room," said Kate. "If they knew who he was, why didn't they just arrest him then?"

"Da'ru would never admit that one of her servants had tricked his way into freedom," said Mina. "Most wardens would assume Edgar had been working in one of the other towns on her behalf and that now he had come back. The men stationed on the Night Train were mostly new, so they would not have recognized him, but the High Council rarely change their chamber guards. Edgar was counting on them to recognize his face. That was how he planned to get you out. The moment Da'ru learns he is back, she will hunt him down. No one enjoys being deceived, which is also why my people are so reluctant to have you here. They think you have been corrupted and that bringing you here will invite danger into our homes."

"I'm not dangerous," said Kate.

Mina did not look convinced. She laid three cards face-down on the table. "You may believe that now," she said, "but they do have good reason to be afraid. Last night there was a shift in the veil, and the minds of the Skilled were blinded to it for a short time. That only happens when a powerful soul connects with the veil, an event so rare that none of us here have experienced it in our lifetimes. Even the shades were agitated by it. Do you know what a shade is?"

"Spirits?" said Kate. "I've read about them. Spirits of the dead who have not been able to leave this world behind."

"But you do not believe in shades, do you?" Mina turned the first card faceup. It had a painted picture of a tree upon it—an enormous tree with wide branches spreading out across mountains, rivers, and groups of tiny people.

"I don't really know what to believe anymore," said Kate.

"That is often the first step on the path to knowledge. You do not have to understand what life shows you, you only need to be open to it."

"What are those?" asked Kate, pointing to the cards as Mina turned the second one faceup. Its design was much simpler than the first: its two halves painted in black and white, with a gray silhouette of a person standing half in one side, half in the other.

"They are windows," said Mina. "Sometimes the cards reveal truths that we cannot yet see within ourselves or others. I am using them to learn more about you."

Kate did not know if she liked the idea of that. "What do they say?"

Mina pushed the two cards toward her. "Sometimes the veil likes to keep its secrets," she said. "You are a mystery, it seems. Even to the cards. There is nothing definite here. Only possibilities. Your path is not yet clear."

Kate saw a look of worry cross Mina's face. "What about the third one?" she asked.

Mina slid the last card off the table and put it in her pocket. "This one is not for your eyes," she said. "I already know what it will say." She gathered up the rest of her picture cards and smiled. "The shades are very interested in you," she said brightly, trying to lighten the mood. "Do not be afraid of them. They can be troublemakers, but they cannot do any real harm. There is a lot for you to learn and the Skilled will help you if we can."

Mina looked at Kate sadly, and the room slipped into silence.

"Well then," Mina said, standing up. "First things first. There is a room you can use while you are staying here. I will show it to you now so you have time to read your letter. After that, when you are ready, there are important matters we need to discuss." She left her picture cards stacked on the table, and

Kate could not help looking back at them as Mina led her out into the corridor.

Mina's spare room was right at the back of her single-story house, set deep into the wall of the cavern. There were no windows, but it was still airy enough to be comfortable, and Kate was glad to have somewhere she could be alone.

"I'll cook us some food," Mina said on her way out. "You can't have eaten well since you left home. Take as long as you need here and come along to the front room whenever you're ready."

"Thank you," said Kate. "For bringing me here and telling me about Edgar. I don't know if he would ever have told me himself."

"You don't have to thank me, child. I am sure he would have told you everything, given time. The boy is quite taken with you. Though I am not certain even he knows it yet."

Mina smiled as she left and Kate made sure that the door was propped open before sitting down on a cushioned chair. Edgar's letter was still in her hand. She unthreaded the string, unrolled the page, and began to read.

Kate,

I know you'll have questions, but if you're reading this it means I can't answer them yet. There are things you don't know about me. Mina will explain if you still want to know, but believe me, you have more important things to think about right now.

Mina says she knows where Artemis is! One of Da'ru's men bought him from the wardens at the station. She's making him work for her now. The Skilled know how to get to him and Mina's promised to take you there whenever you want to go.

You can trust these people, Kate. They're my friends.

I hope you're okay. Stay safe, and don't worry about me. These wardens aren't as smart as they think. I'm sure I'll think of something.

See you soon.

Edgar

Kate read the letter twice.

She had left him behind. Edgar had risked so much to help her and she had left him behind.

Kate rolled up the letter and tucked it away. If Mina knew where Artemis was, she had to speak to her. If there was a chance she could find him, she had to know for herself.

She caught her reflection in a mirror as she left the room. She looked tired. Her blue eyes were washed out and there were black veins appearing within the blue that had never been there before. She looked away from the glass, refusing to think about what those veins might mean, and walked out into the corridor.

A muffled shout from the front room made her stop halfway.

Kate froze. The window next to the front door was hanging open. She was sure it had not been like that before. She looked down the corridor. The entire back of the house was built into the ground. If something bad happened, that door was her only way out.

She walked toward the front room, concentrating so hard on listening for Mina that she did not feel the floorboards flex beneath her as someone closed in from behind. She did not see a faint shadow pass across the wall, or smell the scent of blood upon the air.

Kate peered into the front room and saw Mina lying still upon the floor.

Too still.

She bolted for the door, only to be grabbed before she could even push her key into the lock.

"Very well done, Kate," said Silas, pressing his hand over her mouth before she could shout for help. "I see your friend had something to do with your escape. Perhaps I underestimated his skills after all."

Kate squirmed in his arms but he would not let go.

Silas pushed her into the front room, forcing her to step over the dead woman on the floor. Mina was lying on her side, her eyes wide and empty. In her hand was the third picture card, the one she would not let Kate see. On it was a picture of a skeleton laid out on a platform inside a tomb: a picture that could only represent one thing. Death.

Instinct made Kate reach out a hand to try to touch the dead woman, desperate to recall her spirit to life as she had done with Kalen, but Silas held her back, refusing to let her try.

"At least you are showing more confidence in your abilities," he said, smiling at her as she struggled against him. "The Skilled will believe you did this. They will not protect you, now that you have murdered one of their own. None of them know that I am here and you will keep it that way, unless you think your new friend needs some company on her journey into death?"

Silas tightened his grip so that it hurt, and Kate stopped struggling.

"Good. Now . . . you will return to the tunnels. You will look at no one. You will speak to no one. Each time you disobey me, I will take a life, and the blood of those people will be on your hands. Do you understand me?"

Silas bullied her to the front door and Kate looked out at a group of people talking by the fountain, each of them oblivious to what had just happened inside the house.

"Now," said Silas. "Walk."

Kate looked back to say something, but Silas was already out of sight.

She knew she looked suspicious as she walked along that street; it was impossible not to, with a madman tracking her from the shadows. She could not see where Silas had gone, but some of the cavern's buildings were set away from the walls and surrounded by fences, giving him plenty of opportunities to pass unseen. Soon the Skilled would go into the house to look for Mina, and any trust Edgar might have earned for her would be gone. She wanted to tell them what had happened. She wanted to warn them, but all she could do was walk.

"Kate?"

Kate's eyes flickered up, just for a moment, and the man whose nose she had punched on the surface waved to get her attention from the other side of the street. Kate looked away quickly, concentrating on walking to the green door.

"Kate!"

She heard footsteps close in on her as the man jogged to catch up, but she did not turn around. Her hand went to the door handle, hoping that it was unlocked.

"Hey! Where are you going?"

The man pressed his hand lightly on her shoulder. Then it slid away, his throat squeaked quietly, and she heard his body drop to the ground.

"I saw you look," Silas whispered in her ear. "Step through."

The door opened easily against Kate's shaking hand. The Skilled were right; she was dangerous. She had led a killer right into their sanctuary.

Kate felt Silas's presence move closer behind her. She was on her own now. No one was going to help her. She walked out into the tunnel, not daring to look back.

14

THE SPIRIT
WHEEL

Silas ducked through the low tunnels and strode across underground bridges. He moved so fast, Kate found it hard to keep up, and when she lagged behind he turned back and dragged her along until they were far enough away from Mina's red-bricked cavern for her to be impossibly lost.

"You look weak," he said, leading her through the dark. "Weaker than I expected."

"You didn't have to kill that man."

"I am an honorable man and honorable men do not lie. You were warned of what would happen if you drew attention to yourself. The consequences are yours to bear."

"What about Mina?"

"Her life was unimportant and her death was convenient. She knew her time had come."

Silas stopped at a crossroads with nothing but darkness on every side, and he stood there, listening for something, before pulling Kate up a steep staircase to a pair of arched metal doors. "Do you know where you are?" he asked.

Kate could barely see anything, but a thin strip of daylight filtered in through the gap between the doors and Silas let her step forward to take a look.

"We're on the surface," she said.

Kate recognized the smoky smell of the streets. The doors looked straight out onto an alleyway with a cluster of tall black towers gathered at its farthest end. They could have been anywhere in the city. She had only seen a small part of it and it had all looked the same to her. There was no way she could know where they were about to come out.

"And this?" said Silas. "What do you make of this?"

Kate turned, and when her eyes became used to the shadows again she saw a carving set into the wall. It was a stone circle, measuring about one foot across, with a row of circular tiles sunk into a channel around its outer edge. Each small tile carried a different symbol, and the large circle in the center was carved with the shape of a crescent moon. She had never seen anything like it before in her life.

"This is a spirit wheel," said Silas. "Part of an ancient system that the bonemen once used to help people find their way around Fume and the City Below. Place your hand on the moon and ask it where we are."

"It's a wall," said Kate. "It can't tell us that."

"This is far more than just a wall," said Silas. "There

are thirteen of these circles in the City Below, seven in the City Above and four that have yet to be uncovered, though they certainly exist. Each one of them can remember more than a single person could experience in ten lifetimes, and inside each of their hearts is a soul locked away for eternity to serve the needs of the living. Most of these circles have gone unused for centuries, the souls within them knowing nothing but silence. For that alone they deserve your respect. Now, do it."

Silas pushed Kate toward the wall. Her hands went out in front of her, her right palm touched the moon, and the symbols around the circle began to move. She tried to step back, but she could not pull away. Her hand was stuck fast.

"Stop struggling," said Silas. "It will only take longer."

Kate watched as the stone tiles ground steadily around the circle, sinking back into the wall one by one, switching places and rearranging themselves, all of them moving at once. Kate recognized many of the symbols easily: a book, a bird, a skull, a snake, a flame, an eye, an arrow, the sun. Then the air rippled gently in front of the stones and some of them flipped over to reveal secondary symbols on their undersides, mostly numbers and arrows, as well as more complicated carvings that she did not understand.

The tiles began to slow. Kate's hand still would not come away from the wall, and when the tiles stopped, one symbol glowed very gently at the top. It looked as if a tiny flame was flickering behind it, drawing her attention to a tile carved with a single flake of snow.

"It recognizes you," said Silas. "That same symbol was found on the coffin where Da'ru first found *Wintercraft*. It knows you are a Winters. And here," he pointed to a second symbol illuminated a quarter of the way around the wheel. "A crescent moon. The wheels use their central carvings as reference points. Simply put, it is telling you that a Winters is standing by the wheel marked by the crescent moon. It appears the spirit inside it is still reliable."

"How do you know about these wheels?" asked Kate.

"They are well known to anyone who has lived in Fume for any length of time," said Silas. "When people first moved into the city, they saw them as wonders and used them almost every day. The technique is very simple. You interpret the symbols in terms of your question. Each tile can have many meanings, but the simplest is usually correct."

"So, there is a spirit trapped somewhere inside there," said Kate. "How does it know my name?"

"Fume has many secrets, Miss Winters. It is no concern of mine that you are ignorant of most of them. Now, ask it if it knows where to find your uncle."

"Artemis? Why?"

"Da'ru has sent many servants and wardens into the City Below these last few days," said Silas. "Your uncle was bought at the station and sent down among them. I believe Da'ru has those people working on something and I intend to find out what. Ask."

The tiles moved immediately without Kate even thinking about it and one was illuminated near the bottom of the wheel: a single open eye.

"That means yes," said Silas. "If the answer had been no, the closed eye would have been chosen. Where is he?"

Kate hesitated, torn between the danger of leading Silas to Artemis and the need to find him herself. Some of the tiles around the wheel tapped together but did not move, as if sensing her indecision.

"I will not ask you again."

Kate had no choice. Her thoughts cleared and the wheel moved at once. The tiles rattled and scraped for a lot longer this time, and Kate and Silas watched as four bright symbols settled together in a group at the top. The snowflake, a book, a doorway, and a key.

"What does it mean when they're together like that?" asked Kate. "Where is Artemis?"

"Da'ru has opened it," Silas said quietly.

"Opened what?" said Kate. "Where is Artemis?"

Before Silas could answer, something sharp pierced Kate's palm from inside the wall, and the circle released its hold on her. She snatched her hand away and a bead of blood gathered on the surface of her skin as a tiny glass point sank back into the center of the moon, taking some of her blood with it.

"What was *that?*"

"A spirit wheel tests a person's blood when they ask about areas open only to the bonemen," said Silas. "A group of tiles is meant to be read together. The snowflake represents your uncle, the book and doorway indicate a place of books, and the key means a secret or a lock. If this is correct, Da'ru has somehow found her way into the bonemen's ancient library, one so well hidden that it has proved impossible to find for centuries. It was said that only the bonemen could ask the spirit wheels for its location. Da'ru makes every one of her new servants use one of the wheels, just in case they carry the right blood to be shown the way. I doubt it is a coincidence that she found the library the very day your uncle was sold into her service. And if he carries the blood of the bonemen"—the wheel sprang into action and Silas smiled—"that means you carry it, too."

This time it was not only the outer symbols that moved. The central moon sank back as well, turning on its axis to reveal a reverse side carved with a perfect spiral.

"The blood of the bonemen is the key to more knowledge than you can imagine," said Silas. "Da'ru has been searching for their library for years. It is no secret that the Skilled already know its location and she believes they have hidden *Wintercraft* inside. I need that book, Miss Winters. We must find it first. Ask the wheel to show you the way."

Kate pushed her hand warily against the stone and the

tiles settled into place at once. Silas studied them closely, but Kate already knew what they would say. If she was going to hide something important, there was only one place she would choose. In the deepest place, the darkest place. Four tiles were illuminated: a skull, an ornate number three, a horizontal line, and an arrow pointing down.

Silas translated them out loud. "Third tomb cavern. Lowest level. This way."

The city beneath Fume was even larger than the one above. Hidden beneath the foundations of the upper city's tall black towers were staircases that curled impossibly far down into the darkness and paths so narrow they were no more than cracks in the earth. As they went deeper, those narrow ways widened into vast chambers linked together by corridors, like beads on a string. More stone bridges hung over dizzying drops and from them Kate caught glimpses of eerie streets and buildings flecked with distant lantern light.

"The Skilled are not the only people who hide down here," said Silas. "Keep moving."

Silas did not seem to mind the darkness and dankness that closed in around them. He moved like a shadow, with a stolen lantern in one hand and his blue-black sword sheathed at his side; Kate wondered again why a man as strong and ruthless as he was would want to deliberately end his existence.

Kate's reflection followed her along the windows of a

sunken street and twice she flinched, thinking that the face she could see in the ancient windows was not her own. She began to sense movement everywhere, in every shadow, every window, and she could hear strange sounds whispering on the air. Each time she heard something, it became harder to dismiss it as pure imagination, and when she reached a corner filled with black windows she heard a shade's voice clearly for the first time.

"Winters."

Kate felt something break, as if a barrier had fallen, and a wave of cold wrapped around her, drowning out everything except the presence of hundreds of spirits that she could not see. She sensed them as they had been in life, their stories flashing through her thoughts.

". . . she is listening . . ."

". . . traveling with him . . ."

". . . Silas . . ."

Some of the voices seemed to shrink back in fear. Kate stood still, not knowing what to do.

". . . find the book . . ."

". . . keep it safe . . ."

". . . she can release us . . ."

". . . prisoners . . ."

". . . bound by blood . . ."

Up ahead, Silas stopped and looked back at her with suspicion. Kate forced herself to catch up, her heart racing as she ran. Ghostly forms gathered in every window she passed, whispering to her, watching her. She dared not look back.

"... *guard the book* ..."

"... *return for us* ..."

The voices faded as she left the windows behind, stepping at last into the glow of Silas's lantern light. "You look pale," he said.

"Just tired," Kate said, trying to disguise her feelings.

"The dead cannot be trusted," said Silas. "They will say anything to attract attention from those who can sense them. Ignore them, and stay in the light. This is no place to be lost on your own."

After the disembodied voices in the tunnel, Kate found herself wanting to stay close to Silas and became worried every time he walked too far ahead. There was no way to know how long they had been underground. Other than giving her directions on how to negotiate difficult steps and corners, Silas did not speak. The silence was so complete that she could hear her pulse rushing in her ears as she walked.

"There," Silas said at last, pointing toward a distant light. "We are close."

Kate's heart lifted. Artemis was somewhere nearby. She followed Silas to the very edge of the tunnel mouth, overlooking the wide gulf that was the third tomb cavern.

The tunnel emerged halfway down the side of the cavern,

and the cavern itself was so deep that Kate could not see the bottom or the top. A few graverobbers clung to ladders and harnesses on the opposite side, dodging swinging oil lamps and falling rocks as they grabbed on to tiny ledges and scraped their way into the sealed tombs that had been hollowed out of its walls. Each of them looked filthy and wild, and they crept like spiders through cracked openings in the rock, stripping the tombs of everything that had been buried with the dead and sending it up in wire baskets to the top.

"This is where we climb down," said Silas, rattling a long ladder that led deep into the bottomless gloom. "You will follow me or I will leave you here and you can try to find your way back alone. I'm sure those thieves will find your bones sooner or later."

Silas stepped confidently onto the ladder, hooking the lantern onto his belt as he descended quickly into the dark. Kate looked out over the edge. The ladder seemed old, but given the choice between trusting it and being left there alone, she would take the ladder. Artemis must have come this way. And if he could climb down that ladder, so could she.

She swung her first foot out onto a rung, then the next. The wood felt firm under her feet, and with both hands gripping white-knuckle tight, she trusted her weight to it and followed Silas down.

Each step felt like an eternity. Kate had never been afraid of heights, but this place was different. It felt as if the depth of the cavern was making her body twice as heavy, trying to pull her down faster than she wanted to go. If she could have seen the bottom it would not have been nearly so bad. Silas took the ladder two rungs at a time, taking the light farther and farther away until Kate was hunting for rungs in the dark. She tried to catch up, gaining confidence with every step. Then her foot slipped, a rung snapped, and her feet flailed. She screamed as her hands lost their grip, her fingers slid from the wood, and she fell back, plunging straight toward the distant chasm floor.

She fell down . . . down . . . trying to snatch hold of the ladder in the dark. Silas's lantern blinded her as she passed it, and something tugged hard on her arm. Silas looked down at her, a strong hand clasped around her wrist. Kate reached up to hold on to him with her other hand, and he held her firmly, bringing her back toward the ladder. The moment she was close enough, Kate reached for the ladder and cautiously regained her footing. She clung there for a few moments, not wanting to show any weakness, before gradually continuing her descent.

Kate took each step slowly, until at last her feet touched solid ground. She misjudged the final step and stumbled back to the floor, but she was too relieved to care. She tested her wrist where Silas had grabbed her. A bruise was blossoming around the bone, and it was difficult to move her hand.

"You were lucky," said Silas, stepping down beside her.

"An inch farther and you would have been out of my reach. There are wise ways to enter a tomb cavern. Falling is not one of them."

He held out his hand to help her up, and Kate saw that he too had not come away unscathed. His wrist joint looked misaligned, and the bones cracked loudly as they straightened themselves again, making him wince with pain.

"I wish mine would do that," she said.

"You are not badly hurt," said Silas, pulling her to her feet. "Your body will heal itself just as surely as mine, given time."

Kate looked around. The cavern was long and narrow at the bottom, shaped like a long wave carved into the earth, but there was no sign of a library, or anything else. It was hard to see past the chunks of stone on the chasm floor and the dust thrown up by their feet as they negotiated a path around the edge. It looked like the grave robbers had thrown anything of low value onto the cavern floor, littering it with broken pottery, pieces of wood, and loose dirt and bones excavated from the tombs.

Silas tested every raised stone in the wall in case it was a handle of some kind, and while the two of them hunted for hidden doors, Kate dared to ask him something.

"If we do find the library down here," she said, "will you help my uncle?"

"You will be safe for as long as I need you," said Silas. "The same applies to him."

"Could you help him escape?"

"Why would I want to do that?"

"You were the one who brought him to Fume. What if . . . what if I promise not to try and escape again. If I get you the book, whatever it takes, will you help him then? Will you protect him from the wardens? Help him stay alive?"

"You will find the book simply because I demand it of you," said Silas. "Your promises mean nothing to me."

"I'm just asking you to let him live. Please. You'll still have everything you want."

Silas lowered his scarred hand from the wall and turned to face Kate. "You are not responsible for his life," he said. "We all live and die alone. You will learn that in time."

"He is family," said Kate. "We look after each other."

Silas turned back to the wall. "That is something I know nothing about," he said. "Families lie. They leave and they forget. We do not have time for this. As long as you obey me, the bookseller will live. Now do as I say and find this door."

Kate did not know how Silas expected her to find a door down there. It was pitch black and the spirit wheel's directions had not been very specific. The fire-glow from the grave robbers' swinging oil lamps flickered like stars above them and Silas's lantern light reflected from tiny pieces of rough gemstone embedded in the walls, making them sparkle and move as he hunted for anything that looked out of place.

They had walked more than a thousand steps and

searched only a tiny fraction of the cavern when Kate stopped. Everyone who had ever searched that cavern would have done exactly what they were doing now. They were going about it the wrong way.

She stood still, letting Silas wander ahead, and as the light of the lantern moved farther away, she tried to put herself in the place of the people who had built the city below. Kate guessed that the library had to be easy to find if Artemis had found it so quickly. Maybe people with the blood of the bonemen just knew where it was. What if she had not been receptive to the clues?

Kate closed her eyes and concentrated on finding the door. Nothing happened. There was no sudden pull. No sign to point the way. She opened her eyes again and found Silas standing right in front of her.

"This cavern is old, isn't it?" asked Kate.

"One of the oldest."

"What did it look like before the grave robbers came?"

Silas touched the wall and a fragment of blue gemstone broke off under his hand. "Most of it was lined with lapis before they stripped it away," he said. "This lowest section is supposed to have been decorated with a mosaic of an ocean, with fish and other useless things set in precious stones across the floor and the walls. I never saw it for myself. It had all been chipped away long before the High Council got here."

Kate tried to picture it as Silas had described. "What about light?" she asked.

"It is a tomb cavern," said Silas. "The dead do not need light to see it."

"But we do. And so would anyone else who came down here."

"If this is your attempt to waste more time—"

"Why do the grave robbers hang their oil lamps down on ropes?"

"In case they need to escape quickly from a warden patrol," said Silas. "They can pull everything up and be gone in moments. What is your point?"

"Da'ru and Artemis would have carried their light down here, like us. So would the bonemen."

Silas looked at the lantern, then at the walls. "I fail to see the relevance of any of this," he said.

Kate grabbed the lantern and walked back to where the ladder met the floor. A small metal hook was sunk into the wall beside it. She ran her hand across the ruined wall, feeling the deep welts in the stone where the grave robbers stealing the lapis had cut too deep.

"Everyone assumes the bonemen wanted to hide the library," said Kate. "But what if they didn't? What if it was just an ordinary place in their time? And when they disappeared, people just assumed it was a secret place because no one knew how to get into it."

"Except for the Skilled," corrected Silas.

"Maybe. But Artemis is not one of the Skilled. He can't

do anything any ordinary person can't do. If he found it, anyone can."

"Why would the spirit wheels test for the blood of the bonemen if the library was not a secret place?" asked Silas.

"There are places in the council chambers where ordinary people can't go, aren't there? The council don't want people wandering around their private rooms; maybe the bonemen didn't either. People were able to visit Fume back then, to come and pay their respects to the dead. What if the bonemen wanted to keep some areas of the city to themselves? They didn't need wardens to stand guard over everything; all they had to do was restrict information to anyone who asked about it."

"You are making a lot of assumptions," said Silas.

"The grave robbers didn't find the library because they weren't looking for it," said Kate. "And I think the wardens did not find it because they were looking too hard. Here!"

Silas followed her to where another metal hook jutted out of the wall just above her head, exactly like the first. "And?" he said when she pointed to it, clearly unimpressed.

Kate lifted the lantern up onto the hook and let it swing there as she studied the wall more closely. "Why would that lantern hook be there if there wasn't something around here to see?" she said. "If that mosaic was still intact, I bet we'd be able to see the door easily, but with all the damage the grave robbers have done to the walls, no one has noticed it. The bonemen must have made the door blend in with the wall and they wouldn't ruin the look of a mosaic with a big door handle. So if there's no handle, there has to be another way to open it." Her hand went to a small black stone, too neat and square to have been part of the cavern rock, and she pushed.

Something rumbled gently within the wall, a small door swung slowly back and the smell of old ink and leather wafted from the depths of a shadowed corridor lined with books.

The two of them stood staring into the dark.

"See?" said Kate quietly. "It wasn't so well hidden after all."

Silas left the lantern on its hook and drew his sword. "Stay close," he said, walking forward as distant voices carried from within. "And say nothing. Leave everything to me."

Kate followed him in, hoping that Artemis was still somewhere inside. Then there was only the smell of the books, the sprung feeling of a wood floor beneath her feet and the sound of a lock dropping into place as the door closed quietly behind them.

15

THE ANCIENT LIBRARY

It was hard to see where they were going without the lantern, but Kate could sense that they were entering an immense space. The air was clear and cool, and the sound of voices carried from somewhere nearby. The path opened out a few steps ahead of them, and a silhouette of railings rose up in the dim light, blocking their way.

Silas stopped walking and held her still. "Officers," he said loudly. "Step forward."

Kate looked on in horror as two wardens stepped out of the dark. They bowed at once, refusing to raise their heads until he gave the order.

"Very good," he said firmly. "You have taken a fine ambush position. If I were an intruder I would not have detected your presence." Silas sheathed his sword and the two wardens bowed again, putting away their daggers.

"Da'ru has sent another girl to aid the search," he said,

pushing Kate toward the two men. "I hear there was a bookseller brought here from the town of Morvane."

"Yes, sir."

"Put the girl to work alongside him. I have my own business here. I will not be disturbed."

The wardens bowed together and one of them took hold of Kate's arm, making the cut Silas had made there burn and sting. "Come with me," he said.

Kate looked back at Silas, who was now holding on to the railings, looking out into the darkness like a captain on the deck of a ship. The railings made up part of a long balcony, and the warden took Kate over to a flight of stairs which curved down into an enormous room. She stopped at the very top and looked out at the view Silas had already seen.

The ancient library was not just a room, it was a vast chamber.

The staircase spiraled down to dozens of towering bookcases lined up in long rows beneath an arched red-brick roof, and there she could see people carrying lanterns and candles that created pools of orange light in the dark. Some were balancing on narrow platforms that ran around the uppermost shelves, and others were wheeling themselves on railed ladders that reached taller than a house, pulling handfuls of books out for inspection, leafing through them and forcing them back in again out of place. They were so far along the shelves that it was hard to believe they had only been searching the library for two days. There had to be thousands of old books down there. *Wintercraft* could be any one of them.

The warden followed Kate down the steps and when she reached the bottom she looked up and saw Silas watching her from the upper balcony. Loose pages littered the floor between the disordered bookshelves, and the warden took her to the row along the easternmost wall, the only place in the chamber that was still relatively neat and tidy.

"You will work here," he said, pointing along the row. "The others will tell you what to do."

The warden left her there without a light and Kate could feel the bookcases looming over her like sad sentries witnessing the destruction and disarray. The cavern was so huge that the voices of the other workers did not carry right to the edges, and a strange silence hung around her as she walked down the row, heading toward a candle propped at an angle upon the floor.

"No, no, no. I don't need help. Go back. I'll work faster alone."

A figure was kneeling just outside the glow of candlelight and he struggled to his feet, leaning on a stick for support as Kate drew closer.

"Row sixteen needs another pair of hands. This one's full of nothing but poetry and fairytales. No point wasting anyone else on it. I'm fine on my own. Go back." The man gathered up a handful of open books from the floor and quickly pushed them back onto the shelves.

Kate quickened her step. She knew that voice. "Artemis?"

"I'm not moving. I don't care what they say . . . What? How do you know my name?" Artemis picked up the candle and held it high, squinting to see who had spoken. His cheek was bruised and his right eye was swollen, but it was definitely him. He looked tired and nervous as he stood his ground, waiting for her to come into sight. "Oh!" He lowered his candle the moment he saw her face.

"It's all right," she said. "It's me."

"Kate? How . . . ? Kate!" Artemis abandoned his stick and limped toward her, reaching out his arms and pulling her into a hug.

"I hoped you would remember the way out . . . but when I saw the fire, I was worried that . . . Kate, I thought you were dead! What are you doing here? Is Edgar with you? Did the wardens get him, too?"

"I think he's all right. He's here in Fume, but we got separated."

"I'm so sorry," said Artemis, still clutching her tight. "The fire . . . I couldn't stop them. I couldn't—"

"It's not your fault."

"I just wanted to keep you safe."

"We don't have much time," said Kate, slowly pulling away. "The man who gave the order to burn the shop. He's here."

"The collector?" Artemis's face hardened at once. "Where is he?"

"He's here in the library, watching from the balcony," said Kate. "A lot's happened since we left Morvane, but I think I have a way to get you out of here. I just need you to do something for me."

"Anything," said Artemis.

Kate chose her words carefully. If Artemis had found the book, he would have hidden it well and there was no way she would be able to find it without him. She needed his cooperation. She had to get this right.

"I know what you're looking for," she said. "If you know where it is, if you have it, please give it to me."

Artemis looked along the shelves behind Kate and once he was sure no one else was nearby, he spoke very quietly. "We are looking for *Wintercraft*, a book of old Skilled techniques," he said. "What makes you think I have it?"

"Because you're the only one down here who knows exactly what you're looking for. You've seen the book before. You knew the Skilled were going to hide it here. I think you might even know where it is."

"Shhh!" said Artemis.

"The Skilled sent you those messages from the south, didn't they?" said Kate.

"That doesn't mean—"

"I know they put the book here to protect it, but we have to find it. It's the only way to get us out."

Artemis's face dropped. He limped back to the shelves

and picked up his stick. "Do you know how many people have died because of that book?" he said. "I can't believe anyone still wants it. The High Council think that they need it. They think it will give them answers. That it will somehow end the war and make their lives so much easier, but it won't. *Wintercraft* is dangerous, Kate. The book is a lie. It always was."

"I know what it is."

"But you have never actually *read* it. Believe me, I have. It is a collection of impossible theories, written by a group of people no one remembers, about something that could never happen."

"What makes you so sure?"

"Shades? Wandering souls? Spirits returning from beyond the veil? It's impossible! How could any of it be real? The dead stay dead! We know that better than anyone."

"You saw me bring that blackbird back to life," said Kate.

"The Skilled are healers, that's what they do. They preserve life by healing the body. They do not have any power over the soul. The veil and spirits and everything else, it's a nice idea but there's no real truth in it. You know that."

"My parents thought it was true."

"I loved Jonathan and Anna," said Artemis. "I tried to understand their lives. I did. For years I wanted to believe that it was all true. I wanted to see what they told me they could see, but there is nothing there. It is all a lie. The veil does not exist. And even if it did, *Wintercraft* is all about corrupting its natural balance, allowing people to abuse life and manipulate death. I would not want to live in a world where anyone had that kind of power. Just the idea of it has been enough to drive the whole of Albion into chaos at the hands of the High Council, and it was enough to turn the entire Continent against us. We can't let the council have it, Kate. They're all crazy. They don't have the slightest idea what they're doing."

"Why not let them have it?" asked Kate. "If it's as harmless as you think, it won't make a difference, will it?"

"Because it doesn't matter what *I* think the book means," said Artemis, struggling to keep his voice down. "All that matters is what *they* think it means, what *they* think it does. The council are taking it all far too seriously. They will follow its words, step by step, thinking they can command spirits, bind souls, and achieve the impossible. They will keep experimenting on the Skilled, taking the lives of innocent people. Innocent people like you, Kate. They will keep failing and they will try again, and everyone else will pay the price."

Kate felt frustration welling up inside her, but she fought against it, forcing it back down. "Don't you want to get out of here?" she asked.

"Of course I do!"

"Then help me find the book. We can't leave here without it. All we have to do is hand it over. Then we can go home."

Artemis shook his head firmly. "No," he said. "You don't know what happened last time. If you knew what I had done—"

"I know exactly what happened," said Kate, stepping closer. "I know what happened to my parents. You warned them not to take the book, but they didn't listen. The wardens found them and they died for it."

Artemis looked up at her in shock. "How could you— ?"

"I know why you ran. You were scared and there was no way you could have helped them. But if you hide the book this time, the same thing that happened to my parents will happen to us. I know you want to keep it safe, but I would trade anything to get you out of here alive. Nothing is more important than that."

Artemis looked down at her as if she was five years old again. "Listen to me, Kate," he said. "These people cannot be trusted. Whatever deal you have made with them, they will turn their backs on you the moment you hand over the book. They will promise you anything to get what they want. It was not worth risking your own life to save mine. You should not have come here."

Artemis turned away from Kate and anger blistered inside her. She grabbed his shoulder, forcing him to face her. "Which is more important?" she demanded. "Staying alive? Or protecting a book that you think is useless anyway?"

"Kate, you're hurting me."

"I came here because I wanted to help you. I know the veil is real. I know what the Skilled can do and I know how dangerous *Wintercraft* can be, but we have no other choice.

No matter where you hide it, they are going to find the book eventually. At least this way we have a chance to get out of here. Why won't you listen to me?"

Artemis said nothing, but when he looked straight into her eyes Kate was sure she saw a look of fear cross over his face. Realizing she had been holding him, she let go. "I'm sorry," she said.

"So am I," said Artemis, rubbing the pain from his shoulder. "I don't know what that collector did to you, Kate, but if you want the book so much, it's the least I can give you to help put things right." He limped a few steps along the shelves to a waiting rail ladder. "Up there," he said, rolling the ladder a few steps to the left and holding out the candle for her to take. "Twenty-third shelf up, fourth book to the right. There's a knot-latch. You'll see it."

"How did you find it all the way up there?" asked Kate. From the look of Artemis's ankle, he would not have been able to manage one rung, never mind however many it would have taken to climb up there.

"I didn't," he said. "But it's there. When the Skilled hid it here, one of them came to see me again at the shop. She told me that it was our family's right to know where the book was being kept at all times. She even offered to bring you and me here to see this library for ourselves, but I refused. 'Farthest row on the right. Two hundred paces. Twenty-third shelf up. Fourth book right.' Those directions have stayed in my memory for ten years. I would have needed a guide to find the library if I hadn't used one of those wheels, but once I was in here, I knew exactly where it would be. Half of our family died for that book. I never want to see it again, but if you need it, it is yours. I'll leave it to your conscience to decide what to do with it this time."

"Thank you," said Kate. She took the candle and climbed the ladder, taking extra care to test each rung as she went.

The knot latch was an old trick. Not many people knew the trick, but it was simple enough to spot when you knew what you were looking for. Kate found it exactly where Artemis said it would be—a secret spring-button disguised as a knot in the wood—and she pressed it.

Something clicked. Kate balanced the candle on the shelf, pulled a handful of books out, and found a thin flap of wood beneath them. She lifted the flap carefully and put her hand inside, adjusting her hold on the ladder to keep her balance as she wriggled a small leather pouch out of the hidden space. Kate tugged the cords from its drawstring neck and a small book slid out of it onto the shelf. She could smell its age, and she wondered how many other hands had touched it; how many people had died to keep its words a secret. Its cover was exactly as she had seen it within the veil, stretched in old purple leather with ancient silver lettering that still sparkled in the candlelight.

⤜ ✳ ⤚

WINTERCRAFT

The spine creaked and snapped gently as she opened it, sending brown fibers drifting into the air. The old paper was crinkled and cracked, the pages clinging to the spine by the thinnest of threads, but the ink was still dark enough to be readable.

Kate read the only words written on the first page.

Those Who Wish to See the Dark, Be Ready to Pay Your Price.

A shout of surprise echoed up from below, and it was only then that Kate sensed how high she was above the ground. She clung to the ladder for safety and looked down. "Artemis?"

It was too dark to see anything. She stuffed the book back into its pouch, grabbed it and the candle in the same hand, and clambered back down the ladder as fast as she could.

"Artemis?"

"Kate, no! Stay up there!" Artemis cried out in pain.

Kate stopped twenty rungs from the bottom, close enough to see Silas's gray eyes looking up at her.

"Your warnings are unnecessary, Mr. Winters," he said. "I have no interest in taking your life. All I want is the book."

Kate climbed down the last few steps and saw Artemis curled up on the floor with Silas standing over him, one boot pressing down on his injured ankle. "Stop! Don't hurt him!" she said.

Silas's sword shone deep blue as he stabbed it into the library floor beside Artemis's neck, splintering the ancient wood and sending shards of it across Artemis's face. "Give me the book," he said, lifting his foot from Artemis's leg and pressing it against his neck instead, forcing his quivering throat closer to the blade.

"It's yours," said Kate. "Take it!"

Silas held out his hand. Kate passed the pouch to him and he checked inside it before tightening the strings again and tucking the precious book into his coat.

"Now we leave." He wrenched his sword out of the ruined floor and grabbed Kate's hand.

"Leave her alone!" cried Artemis, struggling to his knees, trying to heave himself to his feet as Silas dragged Kate away. "You've got what you wanted! Leave her. Please!"

Silas kept moving, pulling Kate along past the bookshelves and moving quickly through pools of light cast by people working on a platform overhead. Kate looked back at Artemis's face until it was swallowed by the darkness. Her candle blew out and she let it fall to the floor, listening to the blood pounding in her ears as they raced between the shelves. Silas may have gotten what he had come for, but she was leaving something far more precious behind.

Silas stopped suddenly as they came up against a solid

wall. Kate could feel the coldness of the stone and Silas's hand upon hers as he forced her palm against it.

"Ask it to show us the secret way," he ordered, his voice vicious and cold. "Ask it how to get out."

A sharp point stabbed into Kate's skin and the sound of a moving spirit wheel rumbled through the wall. The tiles rattled into place around her hand and the floor shifted beneath her feet.

Silas pulled Kate back as part of the floor slid to one side and revealed a shaft thick with cobwebs, with rusted metal hooks marking where a ladder had once been. Kate could smell water. Deep water.

"There's no way down," she said.

Silas peered out over the edge of the hole. "Only my way."

Then, without warning, Silas pulled her to his chest, engulfed her in his arms, and jumped.

← 16 →

THE THIEVES' WAY

Kate and Silas plummeted down through the hole and plunged feet first into deep black water. Kate's blood pulsed deafeningly in her ears and she fought hard to swim up to the surface. Her heavy clothes pulled her down, but she kicked hard and burst, gasping, out into the air.

"Artemis!" she sputtered, as the secret door ground back into place above her head.

Kate struggled against Silas's grip as he dragged her up onto a wide point of stone that jutted out into the calm river, and then the shock of the cold water hit her, making her shiver. She cried for her uncle, her only chance to help him lost. "We left him behind," she said. "I can't believe we left him behind."

"Do not waste your time crying for a fool."

Kate glared at Silas, angrily wiping her tears away.

"You are out of Da'ru's reach," he said, looking across

the water. "We have the book. That is all that matters."

The stone they were sitting on was all that was left of an old jetty. Most of the wooden landing stage had rotted away, leaving behind only the mooring posts where boats had once been tied. The skeletal remains of a forgotten boat lay moldering beneath the water, a large oil lantern spluttering light from the ceiling was dangerously dim and two more lanterns farther along had already gone out. No one had been to fill them in a long time.

"I know this place," said Silas. "It is the Thieves' Way. A smugglers' tunnel."

The light splash of oars echoed along the walls and a puddle of light turned around a distant bend.

Someone was heading their way.

"Stay here." Silas slipped silently back into the water, as lithe as a fish, and disappeared beneath the surface. Kate clambered to her feet, soaked to the skin, and looked up. Artemis was so close, but the shaft she had fallen down hung over the water and the ladder that had once led up to it was long gone. There was no way to reach it.

She looked out over the river, trying not to think about how far underground she was and how far she was from home. There was no sign of Silas. He had not even come up for air and there was only a faint ripple in the water to mark where he had been.

The sound of oars splashed closer and the dark shape

of a rowboat paddled into sight. Kate could see two men on board, one holding a lantern out over the front, the other rowing steadily behind him. The boat traveled low in the water, weighed down by sacks overflowing with bones and old pottery that were slumped around the two men.

Kate did not like not knowing where Silas was and she definitely did not like the look on the lantern carrier's face when he spotted her standing there alone, soaked and shivering in the dark.

"Hey! What do you make o' this?" he said, patting the shoulder of the man behind him. "Where do you think this 'un came from?"

Kate stepped back until her spine was pressed against the wall.

"Looks like a runner," said the rower, twisting his neck to look around. "Serving girl maybe. Reckon there's a reward going? Rich folk'll pay good money to get their servants back."

"The whisperers haven't said anything about a missing girl."

"Maybe she's fresh out. The whisperers mightn't even know about her yet."

The lantern carrier grinned. "Turn the boat," he said. "They'll name her soon and we'll be ready when they do."

The side of the little boat scraped against the stones as the rower steered it in to the bank, and the lantern carrier stepped off onto land before it came to a full stop.

"Nice an' easy," he said, approaching her warily, as if she were a wild animal. "Don't want no trouble now, do we?"

Kate spotted a short knife tucked into his ragged belt.

"That's right. Nice and—" The man's sharp eyes locked with hers and he stared at her, fear claiming his face as his hand reached quickly for his knife.

"She's one o' them!" he cried. "Get out of here, Reg! Row! Row!"

The man turned on his heel, skidding on the wet ground in his hurry to get back to the boat. But his friend was already gone. The oar blades lay abandoned on the water and Silas stood in the center of the little vessel, dripping wet, looking wilder and more dangerous than Kate had ever seen him before. The lantern carrier gave a small cry of fear. Silas leaped for the bank and with one sharp snap the man's neck was broken. His body slumped onto the jetty and one lifeless arm stretched out and floated upon the water, bobbing gently beside the boat.

"Get in," Silas said to Kate. "And throw some of these sacks out. They'll only slow us down."

Kate stared at the dead man. It had been so quick, so sudden.

"Now!"

Kate climbed into the boat and pushed the bags out one by one while Silas balanced the lantern on the bow. He had killed the two boatmen just for being in his way and seemed to have forgotten about them the moment they had breathed their last breaths, but Kate could not take her eyes off the dead lantern carrier. If she leaned far enough, she could reach his hand: the same hand that had held his useless knife, which was now sinking to the bottom of the river.

Silas dipped the tip of his sword in the water, letting the ripples reveal the current's direction, and when he looked away, Kate got rid of one last sack and reached out to touch the dead man's hand, hoping it would be enough.

"I'm sorry," she whispered, feeling the energy of the veil rushing to her fingers and leaping out like lightning through her skin. The man had not been dead for very long and she did not feel the same pull into the veil as she had felt with Kalen. She was not even completely certain that anything would happen, and so she jumped when the man's neck cracked suddenly back into place and his hand moved slightly in the water. The lantern carrier's eyes snapped open, his pale face caught in sheer surprise as life flooded back into his body.

"Sit down," ordered Silas, taking his place at the oars.

Kate looked back as the little boat headed out into the middle of the river and there, in the very edges of the lantern light, she saw the man's chest heave in a sudden, living breath. He sat up, one hand going immediately to his neck, watching the stolen boat float away.

With a few powerful strokes the boat soon left the lantern carrier behind and Kate sat on her narrow seat, hugging her knees and resting her head upon them, wondering if he was going to be all right.

"That piece of filth would have sold you to the wardens for a pitiful price," said Silas, looking up at her from beneath his eyebrows, letting her know he knew exactly what she had done. "Your compassion was undeserved. Do not waste your time on his kind again."

The Thieves' Way was a sluggish river, its current too weak to carry the boat very far. Silas had to work for every foot they traveled, and the boat cut slowly through the tunnels, the silence broken only by the slap of the oars and the squeak of rats scuttling away from the light. Kate wrapped herself in a blanket to keep warm and, if she concentrated hard upon the sound of the water, it was almost possible to forget that Silas had just killed two men, that Artemis was still trapped, and that Edgar was missing. But when she closed her eyes all she saw was the fear on the lantern carrier's face—the same look that Artemis had given her in the library. The last thing she had done was betray him. She had left him behind and now she might never see him again.

"It will take some time to find our way out of here," said Silas. "I know some of these tunnels, but there are many paths in which to get lost. I will need to get my bearings, and there is no use in your just sitting there wasting time."

Silas took *Wintercraft* out of his coat. The leather pouch was damp, but it had protected the book inside from the worst of the river water.

"Read it," he said. "There is a lot in there for you to understand."

Kate did not want to read anything. She wanted to throw the book into the river, tear it, or burn it, but she knew Silas would stop her.

"Greater minds than yours have hunted for that book for centuries," said Silas, noticing the look of rebellion on her face. "Many would kill to possess it."

"Just like you," said Kate coldly.

"*Exactly* like me. And you are here to make sure those people did not die for nothing."

Kate heard the darkness in his voice. He was in no mood to be challenged and she was too cold to argue with him.

"You should appreciate this opportunity," said Silas, his oars splashing across the water as they passed beneath the dark shape of a ceiling lantern that had flickered out. "*Wintercraft* is unique, and as a book alone it should be of interest to you. The people who wrote it had their own ways of dealing with the veil. They did not see the point in being able to glimpse one of the greatest mysteries of the world and not do anything with it. They were Skilled, like you, but they pushed themselves farther and deeper into death, stretching the bond that linked their spirits to the living world. Many went too far and died for their work, but that, I believe, was the point. Very little worth knowing is discovered without risk."

"Have you read the book?" asked Kate.

"I know enough to be sure that it is no use to me without someone who understands the veil completely," said Silas. "You are that person. You cannot doubt that you have a natural ability. This book will help you to hone that ability even further."

"I don't see how," said Kate.

Silas scowled at her, impatience spreading across his face. "You will not find the writers of *Wintercraft* mentioned in your history books," he said. "Your ancestors, and people like them, called themselves Walkers. Some lived among the bonemen, but they had more of an affinity to the veil than most of the people who worked with the dead. Walkers embraced their higher level of natural abilities and trained their own spirits to walk fully into the veil, as you have already done. The Skilled did not agree with what the Walkers were doing. They preferred to watch the veil, not enter it, and they continued to study it from a distance, choosing not to push themselves into the unknown."

"So the Walkers knew how to go into the veil," said Kate. "That's what *Wintercraft* is about?"

"There is far more to it than just that," said Silas. "The Walkers had one thing in common that ordinary Skilled did not. Whenever they entered the veil, frost spread across their skin, just as it spreads across yours. It is a phenomenon so rare that no one has even tried to understand why so few people react that way. The Skilled chose to ignore it, seeing it as something to be prevented rather than explored, and at the time *Wintercraft* was written, they turned their backs on anyone who could enter the veil in that unusual way. The people they cast out grouped together, and so the Walkers were formed. They decided to examine their abnormality and explore it for themselves and, judging from that book, many of them succeeded. You should be looking to them for your answers, not to the Skilled."

The book felt warm in Kate's hands, so warm that the watery cold that had gripped her fingers slowly began to fade away. There was something very strange about that book. It felt as if she had owned it for a long time and the longer she held it, the more she felt as if it belonged to her.

"The Skilled would have driven you out eventually," said Silas. "They would have lied to you and stripped your abilities down until you were as limited and closed-minded as they have always been. No good can come of a Walker who lives her life in their hands."

A gentle whisper echoed around the river walls but Kate ignored it. She had to think. Anything else was just a distraction.

"I have no reason to lie to you," said Silas, and despite everything else Kate knew about the man, she believed him.

She opened the book reluctantly and, in the light of the boat's swinging lantern, began to read.

Wintercraft was divided into seven sections, each with a title that would make anyone but the most determined reader put down the book and never open it again. The title of one section—"The Tearing of a Captive Soul"—made Kate think the Skilled might have been right to turn the Walkers away, but as she read on, the book revealed its own strange story.

From the different colored inks and styles of handwriting, it seemed at least twenty people had contributed to the creation of *Wintercraft* over a long period of time. Most of them had been obsessed with stretching the essence of a person's spirit to the breaking point, but as far as Kate could see, they had only ever experimented upon themselves, leaving what was left of their notes to be finished off by someone else after their death.

The neat handwriting of one Walker detailed her early experiments into using the veil to heal the body. She included a list of complex equations that Kate did not understand and detailed instructions for a process she called "Focused Reunification," which could magnify the healing energy of the veil by focusing it on a specific spot instead of spreading it across the entire body at once. That one woman had suffered dozens of deliberate injuries in order to test her theories, from a cut hand to a broken leg, and had to instruct an apprentice to apply her healing techniques when she discovered that she could not channel the veil to heal herself.

Wintercraft was a complicated text, meant to be studied

slowly, not skipped through in a single night. Kate found herself leafing through many of the pages, turning past the more intimidating subjects, such as "Compelling the Dead to Speak" and "Wearing the Second Skin," which—in spite of its gruesome title—was something Kate had already managed to do when she had seen the world briefly through Da'ru's eyes. She turned instead to the section that looked most useful to her, one named simply "Life & Death."

The writing there was small and cramped, and extra pages had been pushed in to accommodate the extensive research that had been done into the subject, but the central concept was simple enough. According to that section, the Walkers saw the worlds of the living and the dead as exactly that: two separate worlds overlapping one another, between which a person's consciousness could eventually move at will. To help Silas pass into death, all someone had to do was open a tear in the veil and let his spirit wander through. That was the theory, but Kate read that section twice and was still none the wiser about how she should go about it. The book might as well have asked her to jump from a tower and trust that she could fly.

Silas was guiding the boat steadily through a junction of seven mazelike passages when Kate reached a section of the book where the ink was mostly green instead of black. She tried to concentrate on the words, but she had been reading for hours and the events of the day were starting to catch up with her. Her eyes became heavy, the oars broke the water like a heartbeat, and she fell asleep clutching *Wintercraft* tightly in her hand.

Kate woke suddenly, not realizing she had been asleep, and found herself huddled on the floor of the boat, leaning against the stern. Shadows hung around her, thick stifling blackness, and her heart sank. They were still underground.

She pulled herself up into her seat. Silas was working the oars at a steady speed, but the candle in the lantern had burned most of the way down. He must have been rowing for hours, though he did not look tired. He did, however, have a rag wrapped over his nose and mouth that hadn't been there before. Kate's nose twitched, instantly becoming aware of a foul smell in the air. "What *is* that?" she asked, trying not to breathe.

She glanced over the side of the boat. Somewhere along their journey the underground river had fed into the city's system of sewer tunnels. The water was filthy and thick. Kate choked on the stench and dragged her blanket up to her face, struggling to block it out. She couldn't be sure, but she thought Silas's eyes were smiling. Beneath his mask he was laughing at her.

Silas steered the boat down the central tunnel, where the river split into three. Ladders led upward at regular points along the walls, but he was in no hurry to use just any of them. Instead, he counted them carefully and turned the boat in toward the wall at the fourteenth. "This shaft leads into a quiet part of the city," he said, tying the boat to the lowest rung. "Climb up and do not draw attention to yourself."

Kate scrambled onto the bank, dropped her blanket, and pushed the book into her coat pocket, needing both hands to climb the ladder. By the time she reached the top her eyes were watering with the smell. She forced a circular door open through sheer strength of will, then heaved herself out between a cluster of short black towers, and slithered on to the cobbles. Silas stepped up smoothly behind her, threw off his rag mask and looked around. It was early morning, and his eyes reflected the light of the winter sun as he pulled Kate to her feet.

"It is the day before the Night of Souls," he said quietly. "This way."

The snow had melted, and most of the streets were empty except for the most dedicated of carriagemen trundling around looking for an early fare. Silas ignored them, preferring to stay on foot, and he kept to the lesser streets where the towers were built closest together and the paths were too narrow for the carriages to pass through. Kate followed and was just starting to think that the collections of towers looked somehow familiar when they stepped out onto a wide street, right opposite the abandoned museum.

Kate and Silas climbed the steps to the main door, and there Silas hesitated. The door hung limp on its lowest hinge, its lock smashed, the way beyond exposed and black. He drew his sword, wrenched the door the rest of the way off in one pull and stepped inside.

Intruders had been in there, and whoever they were, they had not entered quietly. The huge main hall was completely ruined. Display cases had been smashed, upturned, and gutted on the floor; an old wooden counter had been crushed in two; and the skeletons of creatures hanging from the ceiling had their wires cut, leaving their bones scattered and unrecognizable on the floor.

Silas stepped farther in, watching for movement and picking a path through the debris. He did not care about being quiet. Anyone inside that building would be dead soon enough. He descended the stairs to the lower levels like a shadow. The pillar room was a mess: specimen jars smashed, work tables demolished, and the floor covered in slick shards of wet glass.

Kate followed him down to the rooms he used as his home, but those rooms were even worse than the first. Someone had torn his way through them, leaving Silas's possessions strewn everywhere. He kept going, toward the room where he had taken Kate before. The door's hinges hung loose, the fire was out, but someone had lit a small lantern upon the wide stone hearth, and the remains of a meal were left on the table.

Silas crept in, sword at the ready, and a deep scratching noise scraped behind the fireplace, making Kate stop in the doorway. Silas heard it, too. Loose soot trickled down the chimney and he advanced upon it, pressing his ear to the wall. Lightning-fast, he ducked into the chimney, reached up and grabbed a foot that kicked out in the darkness, sending soot spilling into the room. He dragged the foot and twisted it, making the chimney climber lose his grip and fall down hard, flailing and fighting as Silas pulled him out.

"Let me go! Let me go!"

Silas pinned him down with a foot upon his chest and raised his sword with two hands, its point down ready to strike. The squirming prisoner fought for his life, trying to push him away. His face was filthy, and half covered by the black hood of a warden's robe, leaving just one frightened eye visible in the lantern light.

"*Stop!*" shouted Kate, but too late.

The blade flashed as Silas drove it down.

The sword stabbed hard into the ground beside the intruder's left ear, pinning his hood back and revealing Edgar's frightened face.

"So, the boy with nine lives returns," said Silas. "Where are the wardens? How many of them are here? What did Da'ru promise you in return for invading my home? Answer now . . . or I take the ear."

Edgar threw his hands up to protect himself. "Wait! Wait! I didn't do anything! I can explain!"

"Speak!"

Edgar looked over at Kate and slowly let his hands fall. "I was just hiding down here," he said. "When the wardens came . . . I thought they'd followed me, but th-they wanted something else."

"You've made yourself very comfortable for someone who is only hiding," said Silas. "Why did you come here?"

"Da'ru knows I'm back in the city. I didn't want to lead her to Kate or the Skilled, so I came here. I figured you'd had plenty of chances to kill me so far but you haven't. When you took me out of the station you could have handed me right over to Da'ru, but you didn't. If you really wanted me dead, I wouldn't be here right now. So when the wardens saw me . . . this was the safest place I could think of to hide." Edgar looked up the long blade beside his head. "I guess I was wrong."

"Yes, you were," said Silas, twisting the blade to graze Edgar's ear. "If the wardens did not come here looking for you, what *were* they looking for?"

"They say you're a traitor. They think you helped Kate escape. They've sent the dogs out to look for your trail."

Silas twisted the blade again.

"I'm not with them!" Edgar said.

"You were once," growled Silas.

"So were you." Edgar held up his sooty hands in peace. "I promise you, I have nothing to do with this. Why would I lie?"

Silas pulled his sword back, letting Edgar sit up. "What did the wardens want here?"

"I don't know. A book, I think, but I don't reckon they found it. When I heard them heading down here I hid up the chimney, but . . ." Edgar stopped himself, looking as if he wished he had kept quiet.

"What?"

"That bird of yours. The crow. I think it was in here,

following me. There were wardens in the corridor and I heard noises as if it was attacking someone. Two of the wardens were laughing about it. I think they took it with them."

Silas did not need to hear any more. Da'ru knew of his treachery and the wardens had captured his crow. It was only a matter of time before she used the veil to find him. He had to enter death. He had to break the bond binding him to the half-life and he had to do it now.

"Bring him with us," he said to Kate, sheathing his sword and heading for the door. "It is time."

"Time for what?" asked Edgar, as Silas swept out of the room. "Kate, what's going on? What are you doing with *him*?" His sooty nose wrinkled as she helped him up. "And what is that *smell*?"

"You're not too fresh yourself, you know," said Kate.

"I think I can guess why the dogs haven't sniffed you out yet," said Edgar. "I've been squashed up a chimney for who knows how long. I've got an excuse. What did you do? Go swimming in a sewer?"

"Close enough."

Kate glanced at the door and, deciding she had some time, pulled Edgar's letter out of her pocket. The paper had dried out since being soaked in the underground river but the ink had run, making what he had written barely readable.

"Ah . . . right," said Edgar, shifting uncomfortably as Kate handed it to him. "I can explain this. What did, er, Mina say about it?"

"She didn't have much of a chance to say about anything," said Kate. "Silas soon saw to that."

"What? He didn't . . . ?"

"Mina is dead," said Kate, her voice colder than she meant it to be. "The Skilled found me outside the council chambers, right where *you* apparently told them I would be. Silas followed me, and now Mina is dead. What's going on, Edgar?"

"I don't—"

"Mina told me about your time with the High Council. I know you have connections with the Skilled. I've just found out that Artemis has been getting letters from them for years, and for some reason three years ago you just happened to move to Morvane and start working in our bookshop. It doesn't make sense. You're linked to everything somehow and I want to know how."

"I don't know anything about any letters to your uncle," said Edgar.

"Were you spying on him?"

"No! I wasn't spying!"

"They sent you to Morvane, though, didn't they? They told you to come to our town, so you could watch us for some reason. Was that all part of some plan? Did they know I was one of them? Did they know then that Silas was going to come after me?"

Edgar held up his hands. "Now look," he said. "No one knew exactly what was going to happen. Mina saw things inside the veil and, as usual, everything went wrong."

"What kind of things?" demanded Kate. "What did she see?"

"You might not know it, but your family was well known in this city," said Edgar. "Your father was one of the best healers the Skilled knew and your mother was one of the Pinnetts. The Pinnett family came from a long line of true seers. Did Artemis ever tell you that?"

"No," said Kate. "He told me her family were bakers."

"Well, they weren't," said Edgar. "Your mother told Mina that she was going to marry your father right after the first time the two of them met. She said the veil had shown her that he had a responsibility to carry on his family's legacy and that she was supposed to help him do it. She knew she was going to die young and that her child was going to be in danger and would need Mina's help. This was after only one meeting, remember, long before you were even born, but she was certain it was true and Mina believed her."

"Why does any of this matter?" asked Kate.

"Your mother moved to Morvane to live in the bookshop with Artemis and your father. Mina didn't like that. She said they would be safer in the City Below. She tried to get them to move to Fume for years, but they always said no. Your father never wanted to leave the bookshop and after what happened to them in the end . . . I suppose Mina felt responsible. After they died, she tried to talk Artemis into bringing you to the city, but we both know he didn't want anything to do with the

Skilled; mixing with them was just too dangerous. When the wardens starting hunting the Skilled, Mina got worried and—it's true—she sent me up north to keep an eye on you."

"Why?" asked Kate. "Because of something my mother said years ago?"

"It was more than that," said Edgar. "The veil warned Mina that a powerful new member of the Skilled was about to be discovered and would need her help. The words in the warning were almost exactly the same as those your mother had once said to her, and she couldn't ignore it. Artemis was about as Skilled as my left boot. Mina knew it wasn't him the veil was pointing at. It was you. She wrote letters to him, asking him to send you to her for your own safety. He wouldn't listen. She warned Artemis that you were in danger, but he was sure Mina was just making it all up. He didn't believe that trouble was coming, but Mina was sure it was only a matter of time. When Artemis found out that the wardens were coming, it was already too late."

"So that's why you came after me on the Night Train?" said Kate. "You were just doing what you were told. Doing whatever Mina asked?"

"No! I came after you because you were in trouble. I've seen what Da'ru does to people and I didn't want that to happen to you. Do you think I was just going to let Silas take you off somewhere and not do anything to stop him?"

"I don't know!" said Kate. "Everyone else seems so sure

they know what's best for me. Why didn't anyone just tell me what was going on? Why didn't *you* tell me?"

"Would you have believed me?" said Edgar. "Would you even have listened to me?"

"I probably would have said you were crazy," admitted Kate.

"That's exactly why I *couldn't* say anything. I wanted to help you. I *liked* you. I hoped the 'being in danger' stuff was just Mina getting things wrong, but when you brought the bird back to life in that cellar . . ." Edgar's shoulders slumped and his eyes met Kate's. "I never wanted to hurt you, Kate. We're friends. I wouldn't want anything to change that."

Kate wanted to believe him. She wanted to believe that Edgar hadn't just become her friend because someone had told him to, but she still felt betrayed. No matter what Edgar's reasons were for traveling to Morvane, she couldn't believe that for three years he had kept them from her. Kate always thought Artemis worried too much, but he had trusted Edgar, never guessing that he was anything more than a young boy looking for work in a new town. If someone like Edgar could lie and get away with it for so long, she was starting to think Artemis had not worried enough.

"What I don't understand is why the Skilled trusted you," she said, softening a little. "It's obvious Silas has known you for a long time. You were only with the Skilled a few months, but Mina told me you'd worked for Da'ru for years."

"I never *worked* for Da'ru. She *bought* me and my brother. We were just expected to work hard and do as we were told. If Mina hadn't . . . If Mina had had a chance to tell you everything, then you would know that I already *knew* the Skilled. My parents were in contact with them all their lives, just like Artemis. When the wardens came to my town, they were among the ones taken away to be used in Da'ru's experiments. Two days later I heard that both of them had died."

"I'm sorry," said Kate.

Edgar looked down at his feet. "They knew it might happen. Mina and the others tried to get me and my brother out of the council chambers a few times, but they never really had a chance. After that, I started passing them information: who the High Council had captured, which towns they were going to harvest next, and whenever I could help one of the Skilled, I did. Me and Tom managed to help some of them escape. Most were captured again, but a few got away. When Da'ru finally got suspicious about my part in it, I knew it was time for me and Tom to get out, but as you can see that didn't really go to plan. The Skilled sent me up north so I wouldn't be found. They told me about a bookseller they thought had potential and so I went to Morvane, where I met you. After that . . . I just did my best. I was trying to help. I never wanted to lie to you, Kate."

Kate took the letter back, rolled it up neatly, and tucked it away. "I don't think anything ever goes to plan," she said, picking up the lantern and pushing the handle into Edgar's hands. "What happened wasn't your fault, I suppose. And none of it really makes a difference now, does it?"

"So . . . we're okay?" Edgar asked hopefully.

"Being in this city gives people a strange view of things. All the hiding and the secrecy . . . and I've only been here a few days," said Kate. "I suppose I can understand why you did what you did. I'm just sorry you didn't trust me enough to tell me about it sooner."

"Then we're still friends?"

Kate held out her hand. "Friends," she said.

They shook hands awkwardly and Edgar grinned. "Silas was right, though," he said. "I do have more of a knack of getting people into trouble than getting them out of it. Just look at where we're standing!"

Kate realized they were still holding hands and gently pulled hers away. "Silas hasn't done anything to either of us yet," she said. "Right now, we just have to do what he says."

"Wait!" Edgar stopped her on her way to the door. "You're not really going after him, are you?"

"I have to."

"Why?"

"Because there's nowhere else to go. Do you really think he would just let us leave?"

"I think if we run fast enough he might not have any choice."

"And we'd be on the wrong end of that sword of his before

we took ten steps. Look, I don't like this either, but I have to go and find him. You can stay here if you like."

"I'm not leaving you alone with him again," said Edgar. "From now on, where you go, I go. Even if you are insane."

The two of them headed out into the corridor together, took the stairs up to the ground floor, and found Silas in the main hall, kicking away piles of bones, wood, and fallen wire. He had already cleared a wide space and was beginning to tear up floorboards in the very center of the hall.

"You're no use to me standing there," he said without looking up. "Get working."

Kate and Edgar tugged at the floorboards, using broken boards to lever others up and push them aside. It was easier than it looked. The museum hall was ancient, but the floor was false and had been recently laid. Beneath those boards was the real museum floor and on it—being uncovered piece by piece—was a circle of symbols carved deeply into the stone. Kate stopped work, not daring to go any further, and Edgar did the same soon after.

"Whoa! Is this what I think it is?" he said.

Kate touched one of the symbols. There were dozens of them, each one intricately carved and as wide as her palm. The floor reminded her a little of the spirit wheel, only these symbols were very different. They looked more like letters than pictures, and if that was true, she was looking at a language she had never seen before.

Even though she had only read about places like this, there was no mistaking what it was. "It's a listening circle," she said.

For generations people had told stories about the listening circles, about the Skilled who had first created them, and of the madness said to claim people who dared to use them more than once. Most people did not know if they really existed or not, but as with any good story, the more gruesome the details, the more quickly it spread, and when it came to the listening circles there were plenty of gruesome stories to go around.

Some said the circles allowed the restless souls of the dead to enter a body and take physical form. Others said that by standing within one of the circles, people opened their minds to the voices of the dead, which would follow them until the day that they died. And a few even speculated that the circles had somehow been responsible for the bonemen's disappearance, through a death ritual that had gone horribly wrong.

The only aspect of the circles that most people agreed upon was that they were carved in places where the veil between life and death was at its thinnest, and that they were made to pierce through the veil and let the Skilled see deeper into the world of death itself. Standing next to a real one for the very first time, Kate sincerely hoped that every story she had ever heard about them was untrue.

If she had known what they were uncovering she would never have begun, but most of the work was already done. Many of the floorboards were heaped up against the walls, revealing the full span of the circle, which looked completely intact. It was at least thirty feet wide, with four narrow lines radiating out from it at the points of the compass, and where the lines reached the walls a further row of smaller symbols circled around the edges of the room. Kate did not know what those outer symbols were for, but she stepped into the central circle and read a curve of words carved neatly along its northern edge.

A Circle Made of Blood and Stone,
To Bind the Worlds of Soul and Bone.
A Meeting Place for Those Who Seek
The Spirit Sleeping Underneath.

Wintercraft suddenly felt heavy in her pocket, as if the circle was trying to pull it down toward the floor. Kate pressed her hand against it and a gentle vibration thrummed along her palm.

"I don't like this," said Edgar. "I don't like this at all."

"This is Da'ru's work," said Silas, standing on the other side of the circle. "She found this circle, restored it, and put it to use in some of her earliest experiments. You are going to finish what she started in this room."

"What is he talking about?" Edgar whispered, as Kate pulled the book out into the light. "Is that . . . ? That's the book Da'ru's after, isn't it? It's *Wintercraft*!"

Kate did not answer him.

"This is bad, Kate. Silas being part of some experiment

definitely explains a few things, but that book is serious trouble. Da'ru talked about it all of the time. It should be kept hidden. If the wardens, or even the Skilled, find us with it, and Silas here too—"

"They won't," said Kate, opening the book.

"How do you know?"

"Because that's why I'm here. Silas wants me to kill him."

"You!" Edgar tried to keep his voice down. "Silas could stand in front of the Night Train going at full speed and it would come off worst!"

Kate did not know what she was looking for, but she was drawn to *Wintercraft*'s final section, the only part she had not yet read, and she looked at Edgar with the same cold expression he knew from Silas's face. Her eyes were no longer the bright blue he knew so well. A thin shadow of black lay across them as the effects of the veil started to close in around her, magnified by the presence of the circle.

"Maybe I can't do it," she said, feeling the energies tingling in the air around her. "But *Wintercraft* will."

"Oh n-no. That can't be good," said Edgar, backing away and pointing to her eyes. "What just happened there? What's going on?"

"The spirit has to be sent back. Just stay out of my way."

"The spirit *what*? Listen to me, Kate. This is a very bad plan. Maybe you should think about this. You're not yourself. I don't think you know what you're doing!"

Silas squeezed Edgar's shoulder, silencing him at once. "If anyone comes through that door, shout a warning *before* they kill you," he said. "You do remember how to take orders, don't you, servant?"

"Kate, please don't do this." Edgar had heard enough about the veil to be glad that he had never shown even the slightest hint of being able to see into any world other than his own. He had enough to contend with in life without worrying about what came after it. But as much as he wanted to avoid the listening circle, he needed Kate to stay clear of it as well. Somehow he doubted that was going to happen.

Kate was already standing in the center of the room, reading the book while Silas prowled around her like a stalking cat. She was biting her bottom lip, the way she always did when she was concentrating. Edgar didn't know if she had even noticed Silas, but Silas was not taking his eyes off her. Edgar retreated so he was nowhere near the carved symbols, and Kate looked up.

"I think I know what to do," she said.

Silas took off his sword and coat and joined her in the circle. "Then do it."

Kate nodded and a brief flash of anxiety crossed her face. The look lasted only a second, but Edgar saw it and it gave him hope. He knew Kate well enough to know something was not right. She was hiding something.

Kate read one of the green-inked pages again. The

experiments written in those pages were more rushed and random, as if the Walkers had tried to squeeze in as much as possible in a short space of time. If the main sections were daunting, the last section looked almost impossible and the warnings accompanying each technique were very clear.

One warning was written in small letters tracing around the edges of the current page, where someone had slipped a thin black feather next to an experiment called the "Most Dangerous and Permanent Binding of a Soul."

The warning read in tiny green letters:

BEWARE THIS BINDING MOST OF ALL. FOR ONCE THIS DEED IS DONE THERE CAN BE NO REVERSAL. THE SOUL SHALL REMAIN EVERMORE TAINTED AND BROKEN, UNABLE TO WALK FULLY THE PATH INTO DEATH. TRAPPED IN PERPETUITY, HALF WITHIN THE VEIL, HALF WITHOUT, BOUND AND SUBJECT TO THEE AND THY BLOOD.

NO ENDEAVOR YET ATTEMPTED HAS RELEASED A SOUL BOUND IN THIS WAY.

THERE EXISTS NO METHOD TO APPLY.

Kate did not know what to do. She had never considered that the book would not tell her what she needed to help Silas. She tried to look confident, and if Silas knew she was lying to him, he showed no sign of it.

If what the book said was true, there was no way anyone

could end Silas's life. He was a creation outside the usual laws of the veil. Even if she managed to open a pathway through the veil, it would never accept him. And if she could not send him into death, what was to stop him ending her life and Edgar's instead?

She couldn't give up. She had to do something.

She turned back to the section called "Life & Death," taking care not to let Silas see. If she could at least try to help him, maybe he would accept that she had done her best. Maybe then he wouldn't—

"Wardens!" cried Edgar, pointing to the broken door and six black-robed men who had just reached the top of the museum steps.

Silas turned to face them, leaving his sword on the ground.

The patrol leader spotted him from the doorway and immediately gave his men the order to attack. Silas tightened his scarred hand into a fist. "Now, Miss Winters."

The wardens spilled into the hall all at once, daggers out, but Silas stood his ground, ready to take them one by one. Two of the wardens headed right for Edgar, who ran into the circle to protect Kate.

She was out of time.

Kate concentrated hard, summoning up every ounce of will left in her. Frost glittered on her skin as the chill of the veil spread around her and, with a feeling that was a mixture between hope and dread, she reached out into the veil.

↢ 18 ↣
THE
HALF-LIFE

Kate felt the floor shudder beneath her as the symbols around the circle began to glow. The floor was shrouded in a soft blue light that seemed to rise up out of nowhere, and any of the Skilled nearby would have felt the pulse of energy swell outward as the lines spreading across it throbbed into life.

Edgar cried out in fright as frost whipped up his arms and face, and Silas's gray eyes shone as the circle fed from Kate, infusing her energy into its carved symbols and spreading its own ancient power into her. He had seen this happen before during Da'ru's many experiments into the veil and he held out his scarred palm and traced its burning pattern: the place where Da'ru had once burned her blood into his.

Da'ru thought that the knowledge written in the pages of *Wintercraft* would give her exactly what she had wanted: the perfect protector, as much a slave to her as any that was bound by a chain, but Silas could no longer be controlled by someone who had stolen his freedom and torn apart his soul. Da'ru's blood had forged an unnatural bond between them. Now that bond was about to be broken.

Kate struggled to keep control of the energy around her. The veil descended across the entire hall, hanging like white mist that gathered upon the ceiling and crept slowly downward, smothering everything in the room and making the outer symbols around the walls flare into life, marking the boundary beyond which it could not pass. The wardens stopped their advance and lowered their weapons, too busy staring upward to do anything else. Silas smiled. He knew what to expect, so when the circle's energy reached its peak, he was prepared.

Kate, Edgar, and the wardens were not.

The blue light beneath the floor intensified, making the mist glow brighter until it flared suddenly into an immense burst of dazzling silver light. A shockwave of energy blazed out from the central circle, striking the wardens hard enough to slam them against the wall, knocking them into unconsciousness, while Kate and Edgar covered their eyes with their arms, shielding themselves from a glare so powerful it was like looking into the sun. Then the light began to dissipate, fading slowly back to a transparent ripple that hung in the air.

Kate checked the book. Everything was exactly as it was meant to be. According to what was written, everything within that room was about to be exposed to the unpredictable realm of the half-life, and only people who were standing inside the central circle would be protected from its full effects. The protected area was marked by the blue light that was still rising from the floor, forcing the mist back until it was moving gently around them like a gathering storm. The mist hung like a soft wall just a few feet from their faces and Edgar stared at it with fascination, reaching out to see what it felt like.

"Don't touch it!" shouted Kate.

Edgar snatched his hand back at once. "What is it?" he asked.

"It is the veil," said Silas, standing perfectly still as the strange cold sank into his skin, trailing through his fingers until they were bristling with ice. "This is as substantial as it can appear to the human eye. Beyond this room, the world no longer exists. We are standing in a place outside the laws of time."

"Kate?" Edgar said warily. "What is he talking about?"

"The book says that this circle acts as a gateway to the half-life," said Kate, reading as she spoke. "It's like we're standing in a viewing room. The circle on the floor will keep us safe so long as we stay in the middle of it. Out there is a different story. The veil drains life out of anyone who doesn't have enough Skill to resist it. Without a physical connection to someone grounded to the circle, any normal person—even a Skilled—would be vulnerable out there. According to this, the spirit could become trapped and the body would die."

Edgar took a step back, keeping his hands well away from the mist. "So, what happens now?" he asked. "I know Da'ru used to be obsessed with circles like these but I never saw her actually use one."

"That should be obvious," said Silas. "The circle has been opened. The shades are coming."

Kate and Edgar followed Silas's eyes up to where the mist was thickening quickly, spreading out as if it were being kept from their heads by a clear glass dome. Then, like a silent wave gathering speed, the room flooded with moving shadows as the veil opened and the shades poured in. There were hundreds of them, all massing together until the mist was filled with twisting wisps of black and gray. They swept around the circle, moving in quick short bursts, speeding around desperately like insects caught in a jar.

"What are they doing?" asked Kate.

"The half-life is filled with lost souls," said Silas. "Their spirits are trapped here inside the veil. Part of them is still bound to the living world so they are unable to pass fully into death. They know you are in control of the circle. They are waiting to see if you intend to help them or harm them."

"What should I do?"

"Exactly what you came here to do," said Silas.

The shades moved together like dark fish, shifting in one writhing mass.

"The circle is ready," said Silas. "It is time to finish this."

Kate realized that she could not just stand there. She had to take control. So, with the book in one hand she ignored her own warning and stepped forward, reaching out to touch the misty surface of the veil. It felt like pressing her palm into a bank of snow, cold and soft. There was no resistance and, as she stepped across the protective line, the shades gathered close to her hand.

"Kate, don't!" Edgar tried to grab her, but Silas held him back.

The half-life claimed Kate's senses and nothing could have prepared her for what she felt in that place. It was not cold or warm, dark or bright. There was no feeling of any kind. No smell of bone dust that usually hung in the hall. No sound beyond her own nervous breathing. The shades moved around her, existing in a silence so complete that Kate found it disorientating. She had no real sense of there being a floor beneath her feet, the air was still and dead, and the mist that had seemed so dense before had now lightened enough that she could see Silas and Edgar clearly inside the circle. Her heart felt hollow, her mind detached and slow. This was not the same place she had entered when Da'ru had forced her to return Kalen's spirit to life. Using the circle had opened her to a far deeper level of the veil. It was not peaceful, it was not frightening. It just was.

The shades swarmed gently, pushing past each other and

brushing softly against her skin. Each touch carried with it a burst of half-forgotten memories, tiny glimpses into the lives of each shade that came close enough, along with something else. Fear.

Every one of those souls was afraid of her.

"... *help us* ..." they whispered.

"... *release us* ..."

Kate tried not to listen. This was not what she had come to do. She couldn't help them. She didn't know how. She looked back at the central circle, and beyond it—just a few feet behind Silas—she sensed what she was looking for. She could not see it yet, but its energy was unmistakable. The invisible current that threaded through the half-life. The path leading directly into death.

The shades drew back from her and parted as she walked between them. Silas stayed perfectly still, his eyes following her. Standing where they were, Silas could do anything to Edgar if Kate let him down. She had to give him something and she still had no idea what.

The shades' whispers became louder the closer Kate got to the surging current. She held out her hand to feel for the shift in energy, not wanting to wander into it herself, then a rush of movement ran across her fingertips and she stopped walking, knowing she was close.

Kate kept her fingers inside the current and with one perfect wave of clarity she sensed the presence of every shade still bound in Fume. There were spirits everywhere, wandering the streets of the Cities Above and Below, many of them clinging so strongly to their old lives that they could not leave the houses they had once known, or the graves of loved ones they had mourned but never truly let go. Some of them did not know they were dead, others were confused, not knowing what was meant to happen to them next, and some were sealed away, their names lost forever, never to be spoken of again. Those were the souls trapped in the spirit wheels, the souls time had truly forgotten, and she heard their voices distantly upon the veil, sad voices, speaking words she could not understand.

The shades were prisoners, trapped between life and death by the powerful energies of the ancient city. Some were there because of Da'ru and her experiments, but many more had become bound there through neglect. Without the bonemen to see their souls safely through the veil, most of them had simply lost their way.

Somewhere in Albion's history something had gone very wrong.

Kate stepped back from death's current and felt the shades' tug of desperation as she reluctantly closed her mind to them. She looked back at Silas, seeing the expectation in his eyes. He wanted death even more powerfully than the shades. He *needed* it and she still did not know why. She walked back to the central circle, stood in front of Silas and held her hand out to him through the mist. Edgar was shouting something, but the silence of the veil swallowed his words before they could reach her. Silas held his head high, took her hand and let her lead him into the half-life.

The veil reacted to him as strongly as it had before. A void of darkness gathered around him and the shades backed away, not daring to come close. Silas was much taller than Kate and the darkness made him look even more intimidating, making it difficult for her to do what she was about to do next.

She reached up and pressed her fingers on either side of his head, just as he had done to her the first time he had taken her into the veil. She let his void surround her and then she listened, searching out the memory that would tell her why Silas wanted death so badly. He did not resist her. Their thoughts merged into one, and the memory she was looking for played out.

Kate was Silas, walking into the museum's main hall as it had been twelve years before. He was a soldier then, but in the reflection of the glass door, he did not look a day younger than he did now. His blue blade marked him as a warden of the highest rank and he had risen quickly to a position of responsibility by proving his worth in countless battles against the Continent's men. Da'ru had summoned him to the old museum, but he had no reason to be suspicious. She was new to the High Council and known to be a Skilled of some ability. Meeting in unusual places was often their way.

Kate saw Da'ru standing in the center of the circle with Kalen at her side, and she felt Silas's hand twitch instinctively toward his blade. Kalen was well armed, too well armed for a simple meeting, no matter whom he was protecting. Something was wrong.

Silas was suddenly wary of the new councilwoman and her guard, but to put his hand upon a weapon in her presence would be seen as treason. Da'ru greeted him in the formal way and he did the same, dropping to one knee to show respect. But when he lowered his head, Kate felt the cold stab of metal as a needle sank deep into Silas's neck, his hand closed weakly around the hilt of his sword and a flood of poison pulsed swiftly through his veins.

The rest of the memory came in patches. The blaze of light as Da'ru opened the circle to the veil, the cries of the shades swarming overhead and the confusion Silas felt when the current of death drew close to him. Kate had assumed that Silas had participated willingly in the experiment that had altered his life forever, but now she saw how wrong she had been. Silas had not even been one of the Skilled when he had entered that circle. The veil was as new and impossible to him then as it had been to Kate the first time she had looked into it. And despite his nature, despite a life spent defending Albion against its enemies, Silas was afraid.

Da'ru had the book, Wintercraft, with her in the circle and she used its knowledge to bind Silas's spirit to her blood. He was to be her greatest achievement. One that would secure her place in Albion's history forever.

Kate felt Silas's fear rise into rage as Da'ru dripped her blood onto his palm and seared it with a red-hot blade, blending it with his own. The current of death retreated from Silas, but his soul was broken. Kate felt the tearing emptiness as part of his spirit was dragged back to his body, leaving a greater part of it behind, trapped forever inside the half-life at the very edges of the veil. Silas's lungs breathed again, his hand burned with pain, and Kate shared the moment when he looked through his dead gray eyes for the first time to witness the cold look of triumph on Da'ru's face.

After that, the memory shifted. Kate saw the stone walls of a tiny prison cell and sensed the cutting bite of chains gripping Silas's wrists. Da'ru was standing in front of him, and Kate saw the countless flashes of a green glass dagger, sending cut after cut searing across Silas's bare chest. Da'ru tested his resilience, burned his skin with flames, and forced him to drink vials of venomous bloodbane just to witness its effects. Silas's muscles twitched with pain, and Kate watched it all, feeling his hate for the councilwoman growing deeper with every strike.

Kate pulled back from the memory.

Da'ru was Silas's enemy. The bond she had created between them on that night had condemned him to a life with only a fraction of a soul. For two years he had been a subject of her experiments, and since then he had suffered constant pain as his spirit struggled and failed to rejoin its two halves.

Silas had learned to endure that suffering over time but

the rituals in *Wintercraft* had bound him to Da'ru, letting her cruelty and hate drip into him day after day. He could sense her spirit inside him, even when she was not there. He could feel her anger and taste the venom of her thoughts, as if an echo was traveling through the veil, feeding directly from her spirit into what was left of his.

This connection had become Da'ru's greatest power over him. She had made Silas believe that to turn against her would condemn him to even greater suffering than he already faced. She had used his early ignorance of the veil to deceive him. He had no reason to doubt her threats, but Kate knew now that there was no truth behind them. That bond had been Silas's greatest torment. Da'ru had infected his life, forcing him to endure years in the service of his torturer, and that was something he could not bear.

Kate might not be able to send Silas into death as he had asked, but Da'ru's link with him had been created by the circle and that circle was under Kate's control now. If there was even a chance she could break it, it had to be worth a try.

Kate lowered her hands and held one of them against Silas's palm-scar. Now that she was looking for it, she could see a silver thread of light trailing out of it like a spider's web, binding what was left of his spirit to Da'ru. All she had to do was sever it. But how?

The circle answered.

Blue light from one of the inner symbols struck out like a

bolt of lightning, infusing the thread with blinding light. The shades stayed well back as the entire hall began to shudder and shake, and faint cracks spread across the listening circle, crumbling many of its carvings into dust. Kate did not know what was happening. The energy spreading up through her feet was too powerful. She couldn't stop it. Light burst through her hand, the silver thread ignited in pure white fire and the flames leaped into Silas's palm, making his body buckle as the fire spread through his blood.

Kate closed her eyes—all she could do was let it happen— then the thread snapped in two and the two halves crumbled to the floor like fallen ash, returning its energy to the circle that had created it. The white fire bled out through Silas's boots and down into the floor. The light faded, the mist cleared, and with one last scream of anguish the souls within the circle disappeared to be seen no more.

Kate looked around, confused. She had not meant for that to happen.

She snatched her hand quickly out of Silas's grip and he glared at her, exhausted, very angry and still very much alive.

"What . . . did you do?" he asked.

Moonlight bled in through the museum's windows. Night had fallen over Fume. They must have been in the circle for hours, but it felt like only a few minutes. Sweat covered every pore of Silas's skin, his breath coming in gasps as his body tried to recover.

"What did you *do?*" he asked again.

Kate dared to meet his eyes. "You wanted my help. I helped you," she said. "What Da'ru did to you can't just be undone. Maybe there is a way, but the book didn't tell me how. I did the only thing I could do. There was a link binding her to you. I broke it. You are free of her now."

Silas looked at her with suspicion, then touched the old scar on his palm. The heat that had smoldered within it was gone and the wound was already beginning to heal. Kate could not tell if he was pleased about that or not.

"Da'ru shouldn't have tried to bind your soul," continued Kate. "She knew she wouldn't be able to fix it. The book warned her not to do it. *She* is your enemy, not I."

"I know what she is," growled Silas.

"What Da'ru told you about the link between you . . . it wasn't true," said Kate. She was not sure if it was a good idea to tell Silas the truth, but decided that he deserved to hear it anyway. "If she had died, you would have lived on. You would have been free of her. She had to lie to you. She had to protect herself. She knew you would kill her if you knew the truth."

Silas's jaw twitched and he turned on Edgar, who was still staring up at the ceiling, shocked by what he had just seen.

"Give me my sword, boy." His voice was cold and black with hidden anger.

Edgar did not dare to disobey, and he scrambled quickly over to where the blue sword lay. It was a lot heavier than he expected, and he needed both hands to pick it up. "What are you going to do with it?" he asked.

"Nothing that you need care about." Silas took his sword before Edgar even realized he had moved. "Now get out of my sight. Both of you. Go."

Silas grabbed his coat and pulled it on, heading past the unconscious wardens and out of the museum's front door. "That's it?" said Edgar, gladly watching him leave.

"No," said Kate. "It's not."

"What? Where are you going?"

Kate ran across the hall, following Silas, and Edgar raced after her, not wanting to be left alone. But he was not on his own.

Hundreds of shades filled the rooms and corridors of the old museum. Attracted by the energy of an active listening circle, they had drifted in from the streets of Fume and witnessed what Kate had done in that place. Severing a bond created by the knowledge written in *Wintercraft* required a level of Skill not seen since the book was first written, so when Edgar left the museum's hall he had more company than he could have imagined. The shades were with him, hidden safely within the thinnest level of the half-life. Hundreds of souls all moving as one, following Edgar and Kate out into the night.

THE NIGHT
OF SOULS

Edgar caught up with Silas and Kate on the front steps and the three of them stood there together, looking out across a city that was completely transformed.

Celebrations for the Night of Souls had begun.

Hundreds of people filled the streets, singing, dancing, and celebrating the lives of their ancestors, unaware of what had just taken place inside the old museum. Carriages hung with long colored ribbons trundled through the streets, winding between groups of women in fine dresses and men in hats and brightly striped cloaks.

There were storytellers on horseback, walking proudly along, with troops of listeners trailing behind them like a living cloak. Dancers weaved expertly through the crowd, and blue banners had been hung from the towers high above them, reflecting the light of the moon and imbuing the city with a strange, eerie glow. Some of the banners had been painted with large black eyes, as people wanted to believe that their ancestors were watching over them. Kate doubted any of them would really be ready to know the truth.

At ground level the streets flickered with moving candlelight. Many people were carrying candles to remember the lives of the dead, and they all wore feathered masks over their eyes, decorated with tiny crystals that sparkled in the flames. They moved together in one long procession, snaking their way toward the center of the city, where small bonfires were casting smoke and heat across the cold night sky.

Bright music filled the air and Kate spotted a group of musicians at the base of the museum steps, playing fiddles and flutes and thumping out a beat on a huge, deep drum. Three of them had painted their faces deathly white, were wearing tattered clothes, and had blackened their teeth; and other people in the crowd had dressed the same way to represent the dead rising up from their graves to join in the celebration.

Kate had always respected the Night of Souls, but standing there in a graveyard city overtaken by the rich and their slaves, it felt gruesome and ghoulish. The sound of other instruments echoed loudly from the towers and she could not help staring at the spectacle below her as the color and noise brought the ancient city to life.

Silas kept to the shadows and looked up at the rooftops, vainly searching for his lost crow. "I said you could go," he said absently. "Why are you still here?"

"You're going after Da'ru, aren't you?" said Kate.

"I have a promise to keep." Silas clenched his fists. "Da'ru will pay for what she has done."

"I want to go with you."

Silas looked down at her.

"I've done everything you ordered me to do," said Kate. "Now I need your help. You owe me that."

"I owe you nothing."

A stray firecracker streaked from the crowd and burst with an ear-splitting bang overhead. Three more followed. Silas headed down the center of the steps, pushing through the people as they danced and twirled their way along like a living river.

Kate ran to catch up to him.

"What are you doing?" shouted Edgar, struggling to be heard above the noise as he followed her down. "We should go!"

Kate was jostled, pushed, and squeezed between enormous dresses as the masked dancers swallowed her into their midst. She fought her way past pipe players, horses in black veils, and men on stilts wearing decorated blindfolds who were throwing handfuls of dead leaves over anyone they could reach. She ducked beneath one of the stilt walkers and a woman next to her cried out—a single red leaf had caught in Kate's hair.

"She's next!" the woman shouted, trying to grab Kate before she slipped away. "This girl will be the next to die!"

Kate ignored the woman and left the leaf flapping where

it was. She had no time for superstition. They had the same tradition in her own town but no one took it seriously anymore. The woman shouted something after her, but she was already too far away to hear. She had spotted Silas moving up ahead and she was closing in.

"I did everything you wanted," she shouted the moment she was close enough. "I need your help. I need you to help me find my uncle. He could have been up here, safe with us, and you just left him behind!"

"We *both* left him behind," said Silas, refusing to slow his pace. "I did not hear you complain about it until after the deed was done."

"I have to find him!" said Kate. "Edgar said those wardens went to the museum looking for you—*and* for *Wintercraft*. Artemis was the only other person who knew that you had it." She dodged the hot breath of a fire breather and people squealed excitedly away from the flames. "He wouldn't have told anyone about it unless someone forced him. I think Da'ru has him. I need you to help me get him back."

"Your family's problems are no concern of mine," said Silas. "I have spared your life and I spared his. That is payment enough."

Silas pushed his way on to a street lined with stalls selling every kind of food that Kate had ever known. Steam rose from hot ovens, soups bubbled in enormous pots, and water spat from open pans. The smells were intoxicating. Kate had not eaten since she had been locked in the Council's cell, and her stomach growled as she followed Silas through clouds of heat filled with the scent of spices, fried meats, and stewed fruits.

"You told me that you were honorable," she said, ducking beneath the outstretched arm of a biscuit seller. "That you never say things unless you intend to carry them out. You said that as long as I did what you told me, Artemis would live. I've tried to do everything you wanted and he is still in danger. You broke your word. I don't think you have any honor."

Silas stopped and spun around to face her. "You do not know me, Miss Winters. Do not pretend to."

A handful of masked people stared at Silas, recognizing him at once, and Kate heard them whispering together before they backed away. Word of his presence spread swiftly, the people parted around him, and he forced his way past a sausage seller, almost toppling the terrified man's cart as he made a sharp right turn down into an empty barrow alley.

"When those wardens don't report back, Da'ru will know something is wrong," shouted Kate, starting to get out of breath. "Her guards will be waiting for you. They will stop you before you even get close to her. You want Da'ru, and I want Artemis. If we work together . . . maybe we can both get what we want."

"You are a bookseller," said Silas. "Whatever plan you think you have, it will not work."

"Da'ru still wants me, doesn't she? What if we went to see

her together, with me as your prisoner? How close would the guards let you get to her then?"

That got Silas's attention. He stopped walking so suddenly that Kate almost bumped into him. "You would not suggest that if you knew the consequences," he said.

"I don't care about that."

"You should care. Da'ru is not the only one in the High Council who is interested in the workings of the veil. They know what you are now. They will never let you go once they have you. They will imprison you and experiment upon you, regardless of anything that happens to her."

"And what will they do to you for killing a councilwoman?"

Silas's eyes grew darker. "Whatever happens, it will be worth it to see the look on Da'ru's face when I send her into death."

"And your best chance of doing that is with my help."

"*Our* help," said Edgar, panting as he reappeared beside them. "Da'ru still has my brother. If there's a chance I can help him, I have to do it. I don't want to leave him behind again."

"I will not protect you. Either of you," said Silas. "It is of no interest to me if you live or die."

"We know that," said Kate.

"Then you are both fools. But you are right. Presenting you as my prisoner would certainly get Da'ru's attention."

A dog's fierce bark echoed above the music.

"The wardens must not find us," Silas said. "Follow me."

The barrow alley led into another part of the crowd and the flow of people carried them along so strongly that Kate lost sight of Silas as he raced ahead again, disappearing between a moving carriage and a masked juggler on horseback. She kept going, trying to spot him in the heaving crowd, and Edgar pushed his way along beside her.

"Can you see him?" he shouted.

Kate spotted him at last, walking through a wide stone archway that linked two towers together. Beneath it, tucked just inside an alleyway, was a two-horse carriage decorated with black ribbons and paper skulls. The carriage still had a driver, but he was more interested in watching the crowd than in anything else going on around him. Silas crept up beside him, grabbed the whip, and held it firmly to the man's throat. Kate was too far away to hear what was said, but Silas talked while the driver just nodded nervously. She was expecting the worst, until Silas lowered the whip and the driver leaped down from his seat, fleeing into the night.

Kate and Edgar ran to the carriage and climbed into the back while Silas snapped on the reins, guiding the horses swiftly into the busy streets. Kate looked out of the window at the leaning towers gathered around them, which looked much older and more decrepit than any she had seen before. "Is this the way to the council chambers?" she asked.

"We're not going to the chambers," said Edgar. "Da'ru won't be there tonight."

"Then where are we going?"

"The city square. The High Council go there every year. That's where Da'ru will be."

Silas took the carriage down through the narrowest streets of the city, dodging the busiest areas and driving the horses along at a steady pace. He could have gone faster, but he did not want to draw attention to himself. No amount of prisoners would do him any good if he was captured by a warden patrol. He kept his eyes fixed straight ahead, concentrating on the task before him, until the four round towers marking the corners of the city square rose slowly into sight.

Fume's main square was very different from the one in Morvane. It was edged by tall white-stoned buildings with arched roofs and high stained-glass windows, and instead of barrow alleys, the crowd entered through ornate stone tunnels that sloped gently upward, decorated with carvings that looked centuries old. Silas took the carriage into one of the tunnels and stopped it a short way inside. "We'll get out here," he said, speaking through the hatch behind his seat.

They abandoned the carriage behind another that had stopped in the same place and then they were part of the crowd again, squeezing along by candlelight into the bright fiery glow of the square.

Inside the straight edges of the outer buildings, Kate was surprised to see that the city square was not a square at all. It was a circle. The tunnel came out at the top of a long staircase, which led down to stepped galleries of wooden seats surrounding a sunken circle of stone. A huge bonfire was burning at one side of the circle, most of the seats were full, and the whole plaza rippled with noise as people began cheering and clapping at a line of polished black carriages that rolled into the circle through a pair of high arched doors. Kate remembered the vision of Da'ru she had seen in the council tower and knew that this was the night she had seen. The Night of Souls. It was actually happening.

"Time to go," said Silas, clipping the silver chain back on to Kate's wrist.

"This wasn't what we agreed!" she said.

"You are my prisoner, *exactly* as we agreed," said Silas. "Now walk."

Kate heard four thuds as wardens closed heavy wooden doors across the mouths of the entrance tunnels. The stairways between the galleries were packed with people trying to find a seat before whatever was about to happen began. Silas forced a path through them, pulling Kate along so fast that Edgar was soon left behind, his face lost among a sea of strangers.

Down in the circle, the carriages' passengers stepped out into the open air and twelve of the councilmen took their seats near the center, surrounded by twice as many of their own personal guards. The thirteenth council member, Da'ru, walked over to a large stone table, ready to address the crowd, and anyone who was still on the stairs stopped where they were to listen to what she had to say.

"Once again, we are together," she said, her voice carrying powerfully around the square as firelight reflected from a glass locket at her throat. "The war goes on, both outside our borders and now within, as those upon the Continent continue to challenge us for what is rightly ours. Our people fight to protect us, to defend our lives and preserve our history, but as we, the inhabitants of this ancient city, know only too well, no victory can be achieved without sacrifice."

Silas and Kate came up against a tight group of people blocking their way. Da'ru signaled to her carriage and Tom climbed out, carrying a cage with a large bird flapping angrily inside.

"Those upon the Continent think they can defeat us," said Da'ru. "But they have not yet seen our true strength. Our ancestors are always by our side. They guide us and watch us from a place beyond the veil. Once a year we ask them to reveal themselves, to lead us forward and show us our path. Tonight, I call upon them to honor us. To show us that they are here. To prove to us that Albion does not fight alone!"

Cheers exploded around the square. Many people stood up, and the few who had brought drums beat them to a rousing rhythm that grew faster as Da'ru thrust her hand inside the cage and pulled the bird out by its neck. It pecked and scratched, cutting her arm, but Da'ru took no notice. The councilmen watched as she pinned the flapping bird against the tabletop and held a shining glass dagger high above her head.

"Move!" demanded Silas, forcing his way through the crowd.

That was his bird! His crow!

"By the rite of black feather and red blood, I call to the ancestors. We are here. We are waiting. Show yourselves to us!" Da'ru brought the blade down and plunged it into the struggling bird's chest; with one last weak flap of its wings, it was dead.

The crowd fell silent. The drums slowed to a deep low beat, and Da'ru held the crow's limp body up for all to see. A drop of blood fell onto her necklace, and the bonfire flared suddenly in a gust of strong wind. The flames rose, died a little, and then rose again. It must have happened a hundred times since the fire had been lit, but the crowd cheered again even louder than before, taking it as a sign that their ancestors had answered Da'ru's call.

"The proof is given!" she shouted. "We are protected!"

"Councilwoman Da'ru!" Silas's voice thundered over the sounds of celebration as he reached the edge of the circle. Wardens closed in around him, but Da'ru, noticing that he had a prisoner, signaled for them to move away.

"Let him through," she said.

People in the lowest seats fell quiet immediately and

frightened whispers spread swiftly around the square. Every one of them knew the face and deeds of Silas Dane.

Kate followed Silas into the circle, and halfway across it she felt something change. The air was different there. Dead and thin, like the air inside a tomb.

"What are you doing here, Silas?" Da'ru's voice was calm and threatening. The crowd was too far away to hear her words, but the councilmen were listening with interest.

"I have brought you what you asked for," said Silas. "The girl and the book."

"You have *Wintercraft*? Here, with you now?"

"The girl has it." Silas pulled Kate forward. "Show her."

Kate pulled *Wintercraft* slowly out of her coat pocket, and Silas took the precious book, handing it formally to the councilwoman.

"I believed you had turned against me, Silas," said Da'ru. "I will admit, I did not expect to see any loyalty from you tonight."

"You command the circles," said Silas. "With *Wintercraft*, you can conduct the ritual of souls the way it was meant to be done. That is what you want, after all."

"I never should have let this out of my sight," said Da'ru. "And I should have kept a far closer eye on you from the beginning. Two mistakes that I shall not make again."

Silas glanced at the dead crow on the table and his eyes narrowed, just for a second. Kate sensed his anger, but Da'ru was too busy turning through *Wintercraft*'s pages, making sure they were all intact. Once satisfied, she closed the book and spoke loud enough for everyone in the square to hear.

"As many of you know, Silas Dane is one of Albion's most loyal sons," she said. "He was once our greatest warrior and now he is our finest collector, ensuring that this country is kept safe from the few unwanted elements who still lurk within our midst. For generations the Skilled have chosen to hide in fear rather than stand at your side, yet I stepped forward, the only one among them willing to use the veil to help our country survive. Many of those cowards have since been hunted and captured because of Silas's efforts. He has proven himself a hero to us many times over, but what you do not know is that Silas is far more than any ordinary man. He is unique." Da'ru walked right up to Silas, and Kate was sure he would take that chance to strike, but still he held back. "Silas has seen the very depths of the veil for himself. He has walked the path into death and he has survived."

Half the crowd cheered again, thinking that Da'ru's speech was all part of the festivities, while the other half stayed quiet.

"Twelve years ago, I witnessed Silas's death. And, using knowledge passed down to me by our ancestors themselves, I changed his fate. I reached out to his spirit and returned it to our world."

That was a lie. Kate watched Silas, waiting for him to say something.

"Many of you may not believe me. But here, tonight, I shall prove it." Da'ru signaled to Tom, who ran along to the rear black carriage and opened its door. "You are all gathered here to see proof of life enduring beyond death. Proof which I, and the rest of the High Council, fully intend to provide."

Two wardens stepped out of the carriage carrying someone awkwardly between them: someone slung in a blanket with a bloodied leg swinging out over the side.

"This prisoner is a traitor," said Da'ru. "He has been found guilty of theft and of conspiracy against the High Council. For that, he deserves death. All traitors must face their executioner and this man shall be no different. But tonight, I intend to show mercy to this criminal. I have restored life to the dead once before and, once his rightful sentence has been carried out, to prove Albion's strength beyond any doubt, I shall do it again."

The crowd chanted together as the wardens rolled the prisoner out of the blanket and onto the table. "Traitor. Traitor. Traitor."

His wrists were bound and he wriggled painfully as the wardens tied him down, leaving him powerless to do anything except look nervously around at the people surrounding him.

"Artemis," whispered Kate.

Da'ru was already cleaning the crow's blood from her blade. "Prepare him," she said.

∻ 20 ↦

BLOOD

Kate tried to run to Artemis but Silas kept her chain held tight. She was about to shout at him to let her go, when Silas's eyes met hers and he glanced at the floor.

Kate looked down. The ground she was standing on was carved with thousands of tiny symbols, some of them so small that they looked like little scratches in the stone, all written in the same language she had seen on the floor of the museum. Together they made up a circle far bigger than the one she had seen there, and this one was not just surrounded by a ring of symbols, it was covered with them. The four staircases leading up from it matched the points of a compass perfectly and Kate was willing to guess that the upper level had its own row of smaller symbols running around its edge, just like the ones that she had seen around the perimeter of the museum's hall.

Silas nodded to her secretly.

They were standing in the heart of an enormous listening circle.

The crowd was still chanting ominously. If any were against the idea of a public execution on a day meant for celebrating the dead, none spoke up. A few people were trying to slip quietly toward the tunnels, but the doors were locked and wardens stood guard, refusing to let them out. Da'ru clearly wanted witnesses to what she was about to do, whether they wanted to witness it or not.

Artemis struggled against the guards as they tied him tightly to the table. Da'ru opened *Wintercraft* and an icy wind swept around the circle as she began opening it to the veil. The carved symbols closest to her feet began to flicker and glow, the horses harnessed to the carriages whinnied and stamped, and blue light spread out across the ground, flooding the circle and creeping steadily up the staircases, parting the crowds as it went.

Then Kate had a terrifying thought.

She, Silas, Da'ru, Artemis, the wardens, and the councilmen were all inside the central circle, a place of protection. If this circle behaved in the same way as the one in the museum, in a few moments the entire city square would shift into the half-life and the mist of the veil would spread around the galleries, exposing hundreds of living people to a place they were not meant to see. Every one of their souls would be vulnerable to the pull of the half-life, and Edgar was nowhere to be seen.

"This circle will not open fully for Da'ru," said Silas, speaking quietly beside her. "This is the oldest and most powerful listening circle in Albion, capable of channeling many thousands of souls. Da'ru does not have the ability to command it herself. She will need you to complete it."

"But, those people . . ."

"Are about to see what the Night of Souls is truly about," said Silas. "Do what Da'ru says, and leave the rest to me."

"You, girl," said Da'ru. "Here."

Silas allowed Kate enough loose chain for her to walk over to the councilwoman, who was standing beside Artemis with her glass dagger by her side.

"I am told this man means something to you," she said. "If you want me to restore his life, you will do exactly as I say. If all goes well, *Wintercraft* will confer upon him a life free from injury and death. He will be the first of many soldiers and will serve Albion faithfully, as every man and woman should. If you choose to do nothing, his death will be permanent and you will never see him again. Do you understand?"

One of the wardens had tied a cloth gag over Artemis's mouth but he tried to shout through it, glaring at Kate and shaking his head.

"Answer!"

Kate did not want to watch Artemis die, but she could not let his spirit be torn apart, cursing him to live a life of pain at the hands of the High Council. Even death would be better than that. She looked away from him as she made her choice. Silas had a plan. She had to trust him to do his part. "Yes," she said. "I understand."

Da'ru clasped hold of Kate's hand. "A wise decision," she said quietly. "Together, the two of us are about to create history."

Kate felt Da'ru's energies connect with her own. It was a sickening feeling that began at her fingertips and felt as if spiders were crawling inside her, burrowing beneath her skin. She let it happen, allowing the cold grip of the veil to creep over her as the mist descended and moonlight streamed down across the square. Da'ru's eyes were bloodshot, her body quickly becoming exhausted by the effort of opening the circle, but Kate found it easy this time. She knew what to expect, she knew what she had to do, and when the blue light blazed into silver across the square, she and Silas were the only ones who did not close their eyes.

The blaze of energy surged into the crowd, slamming them all back in their seats. The high walls of the surrounding buildings absorbed the greater force of it, shuddering in their foundations as the energy of the circle took hold, the light sank back slowly into the symbols on the ground, and the air filled with blue. Nervous talk spread around the galleries as the mist settled. And then, from a shadowy place high above the crowd, the shades rushed in.

There were many more than Kate had seen before.

Thousands of them, traveling through the mist, all moving together as one. The bonfire crackled and died in a cough of black smoke, and every candle in the galleries blew out at once. The crowd did not know what to do and most just sat, transfixed by the eerie sight of the spirits swirling around them.

Da'ru smiled in triumph, laid *Wintercraft* open on the table and held her dagger high above Artemis's chest, shouting out so everyone around her could hear. "With the blood of a traitor," she cried, "I shall conquer death!"

Kate felt movement behind her and saw a flash of blue as Silas drew his blade and swept its edge up against Da'ru's neck. He held it there, perfectly still, savoring the look of surprise on her face.

"You will not do anything here tonight," he said. "The girl has already told you your fate. You should have listened to her, Da'ru."

The wardens swarmed around Silas, then they hesitated, caught between their duty to the councilwoman and their fear of the man standing before them. Da'ru signaled to them to stand back, then lowered her dagger and pressed her throat up against the sword, deliberately making a tiny thread of blood appear on her skin.

"You cannot harm me, Silas," she said smoothly. "You have just made a very grave mistake."

Silas turned to Kate, his face fierce and cold as the wardens backed away. "Unlock your chain," he said, throwing a tiny key toward her. "Take the book."

Kate freed herself quickly and snatched *Wintercraft* from the table beside Artemis.

"As you can see," Silas said to Da'ru, "our situation has changed."

"You will rot in the darkest cell for this," said Da'ru, her face seared with anger at his betrayal. "When I am finished here, history will remember me as Albion's greatest protector. But you? You are nothing, Silas. Even death does not want you. I could have used *Wintercraft* to give you peace, but I shall make you suffer for what you have done."

"More lies," said Silas. "Your words mean nothing to me. They are poison. Venom. You have used them as weapons against me for too long, Da'ru. I know the truth. I know what you have done. Your words are worthless. Just like you."

"Seize the girl!" Da'ru shouted to her guards. "Seize her and take this traitor away!"

Faced with a direct order, the wardens had no choice but to obey.

Four of them rounded the table at once, heading straight for Kate; she ducked beneath the slab of stone, crawling quickly over to the other side. Artemis tried to squirm free to help her, but he was bound fast. When another warden blocked Kate's escape, Silas snatched Da'ru's dagger and ended the man's life with one perfect throw to the heart. The warden was dead before he touched the ground. Kate stared at the body for a moment, then clutched *Wintercraft* to her chest and pushed past him. More wardens were closing in.

Any doubts the wardens had about attacking Silas vanished completely with the death of their first man. They fell upon Silas like ants. His sword flashed and swung. Bodies fell and Da'ru backed away, untouched by it all, her eyes set firmly on Kate.

People in the galleries shouted and screamed at the sight of a battle being fought below them. Some were cheering for Silas, others were backing the wardens, but most of them had left their seats and were busy fighting their way to the exits. Some tripped on the steps and no one stopped to help them up. All any of them could care about was escape. The four upper doors being guarded by wardens were swiftly overrun, but they were all sealed fast by the circle's outer boundary. The doors would not open. No one could get out.

A wave of panic rolled like thunder across the crowd and Kate ran toward the black carriages that were gathered together within the circle of protection. She ducked behind a pair of frightened horses and ran past five carriages lined up behind them, until a door swung open farther down and a head of wild black hair leaned out.

"Edgar?"

"Quick!" Edgar shouted, reaching out an arm to help her up. "Get in."

Kate grabbed his hand and climbed inside. Tom was in there with them, huddled on one of the seats with his knees pulled up to his chest, trying to block out everything that was going on.

"He'll be okay," Edgar said quickly. "What about Artemis? What's happening?"

The gruesome sounds of Silas's battle carried into the carriage and Kate let the horror of what they were hearing speak for itself.

"I have to close the circle," she said, opening *Wintercraft* and turning desperately through its pages. "There are wardens behind me. Da'ru too. I don't have much time."

"Wait . . . wait!" said Edgar. "Think about this. You closed that circle in the museum, you can just do it again."

"I don't know how I did that!"

"But you still *did* it." Edgar put his hands on the book, stopping Kate from looking any further. "Look, I don't know much about this stuff, but I know what I've seen and I don't think this book is all it's cracked up to be. I saw you help Silas at the museum. You *helped* him, Kate! And I bet this book didn't tell you how, did it?"

"Let go," demanded Kate, trying to pull *Wintercraft* away from him, but Edgar held on tight.

"This book can't make people do things," he said. "It just points them in the right direction. The people who wrote it didn't need it to do what they did. They just wrote about it all afterward. Think about it, Kate. I don't know *how* it all works, but it does. I think you already know what to do. You just need to trust yourself. And you definitely don't need this."

Kate did not want to let go of *Wintercraft*. There was too much at stake to simply give in and trust that everything would be all right, but she felt her fingers weaken and Edgar slid the book away.

"All right," he said carefully. "That crowd is going to start trampling one another out there soon. If you're going to do something, now's the time."

"But it's not my circle," said Kate. "I don't know how to stop it. Da'ru made it, not me."

"Da'ru can't do what you do. She used to spend hours trying to get a good circle going. With you standing next to her it took seconds. What do you think that means?"

Edgar ducked suddenly as glass splintered across the carriage floor and the window exploded against the force of a warden's fist. A thick arm reached in to grab hold of his neck and Edgar used the book as a weapon, hitting it against the warden's head to fend him off while Tom leaped to his aid, punching and biting whatever part of the attacker he could reach.

"Run, Kate!" Edgar shouted. "Run!"

Kate burst out of the carriage's opposite door and saw Silas still locked in battle on the other side of the circle. He had taken at least ten of his attackers down already, leaving the ground around him stained with blood, but not all of that blood belonged to the wardens. Silas was wounded. His injuries were coming too quickly for his body to heal itself before others took their place. The wardens were brutal, surrounding him like a pack of dogs and challenging him all at once, their daggers flashing in the night. Kate could see the pain of every blow written across Silas's tortured face. He would not be able to keep them away for long.

Two of the wardens tried to restrain Silas with ropes and chains, but he claimed the chain as a new weapon and strangled them with it before they could get close. His face was bloodied and twisted with rage, and Kate was worried that this was a battle he would not win. Then Da'ru rounded the front of the carriage just a few steps away from her. She had hesitated too long.

"Give me the book," Da'ru said, as Kate backed toward the edge of the protected circle. "Give it to me!"

Da'ru grabbed hold of Kate's arm before she could move, and Kate felt the veil's energy crackle and snap beneath her skin. She sank into Da'ru's memories, unable to break the link the circle had created between them, and the veil carried her back through time, letting Kate witness firsthand what Da'ru had done.

Her life was filled with blood and anger, torture and death. Kate saw the glass dagger and the faces of those whose lives it had claimed. She saw Edgar as a boy, half-drowned in the testing room water tank as she tested him for signs of the Skill, and then a barred door slamming shut as she locked him in an underground cell. Then she was outside Fume, joining the wardens in their harvests as she hunted the Skilled just as she had tried to hunt Kate. In every town Da'ru left her own trail of death. Informants and whisperers fell to her blade. The Skilled she discovered died within days, and then there was Kalen. . . .

Kate saw Kalen in one of Da'ru's tower rooms, retreating from her as she raged about Wintercraft, ordering him to find the book and punish those who had stolen it from him. Da'ru had been with him on the night Kate's parents were taken away, watching from the other side of the street as they were forced into a warden's cage. She had searched the bookshop herself, desperate to find Wintercraft and unaware of the girl hiding in the cellar beneath her feet. When she could not find it, Kalen was the one to suffer next. A poisoned blade tainted with bloodbane gave him the scar across his face that Kate had seen, along with a dose of the poison large enough to drive him into madness forever.

Kate watched the experiment Da'ru had conducted upon Silas through her own eyes, and she saw the dozens more who had died before him in the museum's listening circle. She witnessed the moment Da'ru found Wintercraft, reaching down to lift it out of an open grave, and then the years rolled back even further, to a meeting Da'ru had with the Skilled, long before her time with the High Council. The Skilled had offered to help her and protect her as one of their own, but Da'ru had no intention of living her life below ground, hiding from the world. She had turned them away and chosen to experiment upon the veil herself.

Finally, the memories carried Kate to a time when Da'ru was only a few years younger than Kate was now, to the moment she first recognized that she had the Skill. She was in a sunlit room, lifting a dead mouse from the claws of a black cat. When the little creature squirmed back to life within her hands Kate heard Da'ru laugh as if she had found a new toy. The mouse tried to wriggle its way to freedom, but Da'ru threw it back into the cat's jaws, waiting for it to die so she could revive it again.

Silas may have been a killer, but Da'ru was something worse. Kate could feel something dark inside that woman. She did not care about Albion or anything else. She enjoyed the destruction and uncertainty of endless war. She wanted to damage people. She wanted to see them suffer, using her position on the High Council to wield the ultimate power of life and death.

Kate broke from Da'ru's memories, not wanting to see any more. It had all happened in an instant. Da'ru had felt nothing, and she twisted Kate's arm cruelly, dragging her out of the safety of the central circle, deep into the wall of churning mist.

Silas watched the two of them cross into the veil as he ended a warden's life, then another, and another. He watched the shades move apart to let the two women pass through and then close behind them, swallowing them completely into the darkness of the veil.

With the last man lying dead at his feet, Silas turned to the councilmen, blood smeared across his skin and dripping from his blade. "This is what you all deserve," he said, his words breaking a little as a handful of damaged ribs cracked suddenly back into place. "You let this happen. This night rests on your heads, not mine."

Silas fell to his knees, all energy spent, but slowly and steadily his body healed. His wounds sealed themselves, his bones reset and his torn muscles knitted together again. The effort of it exhausted him. Pain clouded his mind and so he did not notice a trickle of strange blood creeping slowly down his injured chest.

The vial of Kate's blood that he had stolen from the testing room had smashed during the battle, slicing his skin and spreading some of her blood into his own. A thread of warmth raced through Silas's veins and he slid his hand into his coat, pulling out thin slivers of bloodstained glass. There had been no ritual. Silas had never intended for it to happen and yet he could sense Kate's energy within him—a distant echo reflected somewhere deep inside. Her blood had been bound to his within the energies of an open listening circle. It connected them. The pulse of Kate's life reverberated alongside his own, and Silas could feel the potent rush of Kate's fear as she walked within the veil.

For ten years, echoes of Da'ru's spirit had crept inside him. She was arrogant, fearless, and malicious. Her influence had stripped away parts of Silas that he had since learned to live without, and he had fought against it every day, holding back the overwhelming force that threatened to engulf his identity fully in the dark. Silas had become used to restraining the worst of Da'ru's nature deep within himself, but it had been a long time since he had felt true fear. Kate's spirit did not overwhelm him as Da'ru's had done for so long; it glowed like a hidden flame within his blood, and the fear he sensed from her was not for herself, but for the foolish uncle she had come to save: the man who was wriggling futilely against his bonds upon the stone table, incapable of doing anything for himself.

The glass dagger still sat inside the chest of Silas's first kill. He struggled to his feet and limped toward it, unsheathing it from the man's ribs while Artemis fought against his ropes.

"Where is she?" Artemis asked despairingly. "Where is Kate?"

Silas left him bound and turned away, carrying a blade in each hand. "Stay here, bookseller," he said. "It will be over soon."

The shades gathered around Kate as Da'ru pushed her into the veil. They were screeching and screaming, their voices filling the half-life with desperate words.

"...free us! ..."

"... help us! ..."

"... release us! ..."

The shades moved gently around Kate, but when Da'ru stepped among them, everything changed. The air filled with a low hiss. The shades' hatred spread like fire, and Kate knew that Da'ru's connection with the circle was all that was protecting her from their wrath.

"I did not believe what Silas told me about you at first," said Da'ru, forcing Kate deeper into the mist with strength Kate would not have guessed she had. "Now I can see that he did not tell me everything. I had heard about the Walkers, of course, but I never imagined that I would meet one outside the pages of *Wintercraft*."

Da'ru looked at the shades in wonder, mesmerized by the presence of so many pressing closely against her skin. She closed her eyes, absorbing the experience of being able to step physically into the veil for the very first time, and her fingernails scratched deeply into Kate's skin. Kate realized that she was holding on to her far too tightly. Da'ru was afraid of something.

As a Walker, Kate was able to step into the veil without danger, but Da'ru did not possess the level of ability to allow her to walk safely on her own. She needed Kate beside her. Without a physical link to a Walker, she risked endangering her spirit if she stayed within that mist for too long.

The shades swirled anxiously around them. Kate's hair whipped up in the current made by their frenzied movements, and she looked through the mist toward the frightened crowd. Every one of those people was in danger, and she had no idea what she was supposed to do to help them. The circle belonged to Da'ru. Kate could not close it. Da'ru was its master and she was completely in control.

"Forget them," said Da'ru, following her gaze. "Those people do not see the world the way we do, Kate. They never truly believed in the veil. The Night of Souls is just a joke to them, another excuse for a mindless celebration. They have never once dared to try and understand it. Now they can see the truth for themselves."

Kate glanced back at the central circle. She could see Silas standing at the very edge, but he wasn't doing anything. He was just standing there, watching her. Da'ru's hand went up suddenly to Kate's throat, and Kate could feel her own energy draining down into the circle as Da'ru channeled it out of her, weakening her. Soon it was hard to move . . . hard to breathe.

"Listen to me," demanded Da'ru. "Your life belongs to me now. Those people are going to die, and when they do, you will use my blood and bind every one of their souls to me. The council is watching. It is time for me to claim my place in history, and you are going to do exactly as I say."

Da'ru saw her looking over to Silas, and she smiled darkly. "Silas is not your ally, Kate. Men like him have no need for allies. You have witnessed the terror he can create and the respect he commands. With an army of people like Silas by my side, Albion will no longer need to hide in the dark. We shall conquer our enemies, make every one of them suffer, and then we shall crush them one by one. You will help me do this, Kate. Together we will make this country live again."

Kate's eyes felt heavy and the screams of the dead spun deafeningly around her. She could see Da'ru's madness in her face, and struggling to take one last full breath, Kate spoke as firmly as she could. "I won't do anything for you," she said. "Albion doesn't need more soldiers or more war. It needs to be protected from people like *you*."

Da'ru's face darkened and she threw Kate to the ground.

Kate's head struck stone and pain exploded behind her eyes. Then, like a match being struck inside her mind, her instincts took over. The mist of the half-life lifted as her eyes were suddenly able to filter it out and she saw something within it that Da'ru had not seen: the current of death moving swiftly toward them, like a silvery reflection flickering through the air.

"You have two paths ahead of you," said Da'ru, standing over Kate, oblivious to the danger so close by. "You will join me. Or you will join them."

The shades screamed again. Something moved behind Da'ru, and a pair of solid, living arms wrapped firmly around her neck.

"Get away from her!"

Edgar had left the safety of the inner circle and was pulling on Da'ru as hard as he could, trying to drag her away from Kate. He knew about the dangers of the veil, but he was there anyway, refusing to let Kate fight alone. The shades circled above him as Da'ru grabbed his hand and twisted him away. Then she forced him to the ground and bent over him, drawing a slim silver blade from her sleeve and pressing it against his neck.

"That is the last time you will disturb me, boy," she said.

The current of death was closing in. It was just a few inches away from Kate when she gathered the very last of her weakening strength and grabbed hold of Da'ru's dress, pulling her from Edgar long enough for him to roll out of her reach and back into the safety of the inner circle. She dragged as hard as she could until Da'ru turned to face her, and she managed to catch hold of her wrist instead.

"What are you doing?" cried Da'ru, but it was too late.

Her eyes widened as the current of death washed over Kate and then came straight for Da'ru, spreading through her body and rippling against her face. Kate took one last look at Edgar as the warm touch of death spread into her, making her body feel light, safe, and free. Then she closed her eyes and, with one final breath, she let the current take her.

←· 21 ·→

DEATH

Kate felt warm and peaceful. Time stretched and sounds faded into silence as her thoughts traveled deep into the veil, slowly leaving her life behind. She could feel the gentle emptiness of the current spreading around her, but there was no pain, no struggle, no thought beyond the certainty that what was happening was right. The current could have carried her forever and she would have been completely at peace.

But there, in the midst of it all, something distracted her.

Da'ru was beside her, battling against death, fighting against it with all her strength, so desperate was she to return to life. Kate tried to forget her and let her mind become empty once again, but then something happened that she did not expect. Something moved close by: a dark shape surrounded by an empty void of black. Death drew back from it as it forced its way into the flow, and Silas stepped into the current, as immovable as a rock in the face of a storm.

"Silas!" Da'ru reached out when she saw him. "Help me, Silas!"

Silas looked at the glass locket hanging from her neck, its surface stained with his dead crow's drying blood. "After everything you have done," he said. "You still think I would help you?"

"You have no choice!"

"Yes," said Silas. "I do." He grabbed the locket and snapped the chain from around Da'ru's neck.

"No!" she cried. "Stop!"

Something moved beside Kate. A shade, darker than the rest, crept past her and started wrapping itself around Da'ru, holding her like a spider binding a fly.

"Life is too good to waste on you," said Silas. "Your life is over and death is a pleasure you will never know."

Da'ru struggled to free herself as the shade clung tight, gaining clearer form whenever it moved close to Silas. For one brief moment, Kate was sure she saw gray eyes within its darkness and then she knew what she was looking at. Silas's broken spirit—the part of him that had been left behind within the half-life—had joined them in the current.

"Silas!" Da'ru cried, her voice echoing out across the city square. "You cannot do this! You are bound to me, Silas!"

"The ways of death are familiar to me now," said Silas. "Because of you, I can never know the peace of it. You betrayed me, as you have betrayed hundreds more."

He held the locket in his scarred hand. The fire in his palm had burned away, but the old mark left by Da'ru's blade was still deep and dark.

"Twelve years ago, you made a mistake," he said. "You made an enemy of me, and now you will feel the emptiness I have known for yourself. Your soul will scream and no one will hear you. It is over, Da'ru. I will make the half-life your prison for as long as I live. And as you said: immortality lasts a long, long time."

The shade smothered Da'ru like an oily web, capturing her spirit and dragging it out into the empty void of the half-life. Silas watched Da'ru's body release its final breath, and the shade pulled her spirit down through the stony ground, into a deep level of the veil that the circle could not reach.

The last few members of the crowd who had dared to stay in their seats now fled with the rest, pushing themselves up against the outer divide, desperate to escape before they faced the same fate, and Kate felt her connection to her own body start to weaken and break. The sudden feeling of separation took her by surprise. Her spirit caught upon the gentle flow of the current and her body fell to the ground, detached, empty, and still.

Silas saw Kate fall and he crouched down beside her, brushing a strand of hair from her half-closed eyes. It looked as if all life had left her, but he knew better. Da'ru was gone, yet the circle was still active. Kate's spirit was not lost yet.

Silas lifted Kate up in his arms. Every step was a struggle and with every inch he gained, death willed him more powerfully to turn back. Its promise of peace overwhelmed his thoughts and smothered his senses, but still he walked forward, knowing better than to listen to something that could never be his. Da'ru was right. No matter how much he longed for it, death did not want him.

With one last immense effort, Silas broke out of the current and into the half-life, carrying Kate's body through the veil and hesitating on the edge of the central circle just long enough to hear Da'ru's screams echo distantly upon the air. For twelve years he had longed to hear that sound, to finally be able to repay her for what she had done to him. He had always known it would be worth it. He had been right.

Silas closed his eyes, allowing the call of death to tempt him one last time, then he opened his hand and let Da'ru's glass locket fall to the ground. The little sphere fell slowly, as if all those years of waiting had been crushed into those last few moments and, with the quietest of tiny sounds, it smashed.

A patch of blood stained the ground among the broken shards and a thin trail of white rose out of it, twisting and splitting into many separate threads, snaking up to link with some of the shades around Silas before each thread snapped and faded away. His may have been the only spirit Da'ru had bound into a cursed life, but it was not the only one who had been denied the path into death. Whatever bond that blood had created between Da'ru and them, it was broken now.

Shouts of surprise spread around the crowd as the candles in their hands illuminated one by one. Each one had been carried there to remember a life that had been lost, and the spirits who had lived those lives drew closer to those who were remembering them, relighting the flames and showing them that there was no reason to be afraid.

Many in the crowd stopped trying to run and reached out to the spirits of their ancestors, to lost parents, children, and friends. The current of death continued its journey through the half-life, shining with inner light as the freed souls drifted peacefully into it, completing their journeys at last. And for a short time the Night of Souls was what it was always meant to be: a time of peace, remembrance, and joy.

Kate's skin was deathly cold and her lips touched with blue as Silas carried her out of the mist and into the central circle. The call of death severed from him at once as his feet touched the symbols, and the pressure of the living world returned to him like an iron weight dropped upon his shoulders. Kate's energy spread through his blood like hot needles, connecting with the circle until its light faded and died. The circle's energies collapsed, reconnecting the city square with its rightful place in time. The mist dispersed and the bonfire blazed suddenly back to life.

With the shades gone, the crowd overran the few remaining wardens, tearing open the upper doors and pouring out into the city like ants. One of the councilmen stood up to speak to the fleeing people, but his voice was lost among the frenzy of stampeding bodies, and Silas caught only three words of what he had said. Three words that were set to shape his future.

Silas Dane. Traitor.

Silas laid Kate carefully on the ground. There was movement around the table as Edgar and Tom ran to free Artemis from his ropes, and he turned toward Kate, sending Silas's hand instinctively to his blade.

"Stay back!" said Silas. "This is no time for you."

Artemis stopped, not daring to move any closer. "Don't touch her!" he cried.

Silas ignored him, pulled a bloodstained cloak from the shoulders of a dead warden, and covered Kate with it. Artemis stood painfully, and limped over to the spot where Kate was laid.

"Why couldn't you just leave her alone?" demanded Artemis. "This shouldn't have happened. What have you done to her?"

Silas glared up at him in fury. "If you want this girl to die, keep asking foolish questions. If not, get out of my sight."

Artemis faltered, stunned by Silas's anger, and Edgar stepped forward, holding *Wintercraft* out for Silas to take. "I don't know if it'll help," he said quietly. "But . . . here."

Silas took the book from him, and Edgar took hold of Artemis's arm.

"What is he doing?" asked Artemis.

"It's all right," said Edgar. "We have to trust him."

"Trust him? After everything that's happened? Why should we trust him?"

There were many things Silas could have said to a man who had allowed himself to be taken prisoner, relied upon his niece to help him escape, and then dared to complain at her not being unscathed at the end of it. Instead he shot Artemis a look that would have made anyone wither. Edgar led the limping man away.

"You did well, Miss Winters," said Silas, as he pressed a hand against her forehead, using the veil's energy to call her spirit back into life. "There are few people who could have done what you did tonight. Your idiot uncle will never understand it, but you should be proud of yourself. You did many souls a great service today."

Silas looked over at what was left of the High Council. They were talking among themselves, no doubt discussing how best to make a dignified retreat. Some of them were smiling deviously, despite the gruesome scene of death around them, and Silas realized that it would be so easy for him to end them all right there. In just a few moments he could rid Albion of its greatest threat.

He considered it carefully, noticing the thinly disguised fear in the men's eyes as they made their way out of the circle.

No, he decided. Now was not the time.

Gradually, the color started to return to Kate's skin. She opened her eyes, and Silas lifted his hand gently from her head.

"Silas?"

"It appears I am not the only one who can look into the face of death and survive," he said. "I was starting to believe you had gone too far."

"Where's Artemis?" asked Kate, sitting up. "And Edgar?"

"They are here. We have both done as we promised. I may not be dead, but I am free of Da'ru and your uncle is still alive. My honor is satisfied, as is yours. As of this moment, we owe each other nothing."

Silas held *Wintercraft* tightly. The book's ancient leather felt rough against his fingertips as he passed it to Kate, and he felt a warm flood of energy rush across his skin as the new blood within him reacted to her being close by. "This book is as much responsible for my situation as Da'ru herself," he said. "It has made me what I am, and I do not want anything more to do with it. It belongs with you now. Keep it safe. Let no one know that you have it, and do not be afraid. You will become used to the veil in time."

Kate looked down at the book, not knowing what to say.

"Many souls are free because of what you have done tonight," said Silas. "Da'ru never could have opened this circle on her own. If it had truly belonged to her, it would have died when she did, but she was not in command of it. You were. Your energy created this circle, and your link to it acted as a beacon when you fell into death, allowing lost souls to pass freely into death's current and letting them finally find peace. You have a rare gift, Miss Winters. Do not turn your back upon it."

Silas stood up. "There is no place for me in this city anymore," he said. "I suggest you leave here as soon as you can. Hundreds of people saw your face today. Many of them will fear you, and there are those who will hunt you for what you can do. You must disappear. Do not let them find you, and more than anything else, be careful whom you trust."

Silas turned to walk away, and Kate called after him.

"Good-bye," she said. "And thank you . . . for what you did."

Silas looked back and nodded once. "Good-bye, Kate."

Then he stepped out of sight behind one of the council carriages, and was gone.

"Kate!" Edgar ran up to her, with Artemis and Tom close behind, and Artemis pulled her into a crushing hug.

"You're alive!" he said, almost squeezing the life out of her again. "I thought you were gone. I thought . . ."

Edgar waited awkwardly as Artemis took his time, and when he finally let her go, Kate hid *Wintercraft* under her coat before letting Edgar help her up.

"Silas is gone," Edgar said, but his smile faded when he looked into Kate's face. "What happened to your eyes?"

"Why?" said Kate. "What's wrong with them?"

"Nothing's *wrong*, exactly. They're just a bit . . . different."

Kate headed to the nearest carriage and looked at her reflection in the dark window. Her eyes were a completely different color; her irises were rings of deep black, edged with blue, and her pupils were glazed with a sheen of silver that could only be seen when the light caught them a certain way.

"Most of the Skilled spend years looking into the veil before it affects them like that," said Edgar. "But I've never seen silver in anyone's eyes before."

Kate looked toward one of the lower gates just in time to see Silas riding a stolen carriage horse out of the square.

"Do you feel all right?" asked Edgar.

"I'm fine," said Kate, not wanting to admit that her eyes felt like she had been staring too long at the sun. When she looked down at the ground the symbols closest to her feet still looked like they were glowing with gentle light.

"The wardens won't just let us go, not after all of this," said Artemis nervously. "Edgar, can you drive a carriage?"

"Tom's a better driver than I am. Why?"

"I think we should take a carriage and find somewhere safe before the council send their men back here to find us."

"If we need a place to hide, we should go to the Skilled," said Edgar. "Tom and I know the way. They trust us."

"No!" said Kate. "I can't go back there. Silas killed two people while I was with them. They'll think I did it!"

"Then we'll just have to put them right, won't we? Those

eyes of yours will definitely give them something to think about. They won't turn us away."

"The Skilled it is, then," said Artemis, nodding with the wariness of someone not used to making big decisions.

"Kate?" Edgar said carefully. "Are you sure you're okay?"

Kate was looking up at the galleries as the last few people trickled out of the city square. Even though it was no longer active, she could see the symbols around the edge of the enormous listening circle as clearly as when it was linked to the veil. She could see traces of hidden energy sealed within its central stones and as she walked over the symbols she could feel it, too, like gentle vibrations beneath her feet. If this was what Silas had been talking about, he was right, it was definitely going to take some getting used to.

The moon hid briefly behind a bank of purple clouds and the stars shone down upon the glowing circle. The energy was so clear, Kate did not know how she could have missed it before. And she was not the only one attracted to its light. A large black bird flew smoothly across the empty square, soaring powerfully over her head and swooping down to land upon the bloodstained table.

"Can you see that?" she asked, as the bird perched beside the body of the dead crow.

"See what?" asked Edgar.

Kate walked slowly up to the bird, not wanting to scare it away, and when she got closer she realized that she could see right through it. Its feathers had no substance, and it flickered in and out of her sight, watching her all the time.

"It's Silas's bird," she said.

"Yeah, I know," said Edgar, thinking she was talking about the body on the table. "It's a shame, I suppose. Who wouldn't want a crazy feathered thing flying around taking orders from a madman? If you ask me, it got off lightly. Who'd want to spend all their time with someone like Silas? It's probably relieved to be free of him. I know I am."

Kate stood beside the crow's body and watched its bloodied feathers ruffling in the wind. Silas had saved her life. He had spared Edgar and saved Artemis, and that bird meant something to him. If its spirit was there, maybe it had not yet gone fully over into death. If there was any way to thank Silas for what he had done, surely this was it.

Gently, she picked up the body—it was lighter than she had expected—and balanced it carefully between her hands, concentrating upon healing the wound, just as she had done with the man in the river. Nothing happened, and she was worried the bird might have been dead too long. But then, like a subtle heat growing from her bones, she felt the energy of the veil pass softly through her hands, spread into the crow's delicate body and out across its skin, healing the muscles and binding the flesh until the faint throb of a heartbeat fluttered against her palm.

The crow's spirit gathered into a thin gray wisp and sank

like smoke back down into its body. Kate waited, hoping that the heartbeat would last . . . until one limp wing flapped back into life, then the other, striking the air and sending the crow tumbling out of her hands and onto the table. It scrabbled drunkenly up onto its feet and shook its feathers before screeching out a call that echoed loudly across the city square.

"Go to your master," said Kate, picking up the crow and holding it high in the air. "Go to Silas!"

The bird took flight, swooping across the square and soaring out over the city, calling out victoriously into the night.

"It's more than he deserves," said Artemis, climbing into a carriage as everyone else watched the bird fly away. "Come on. We're wasting time here."

With everyone safely on board, Tom steered the horses expertly through the square's lower doors and out into the streets. The roads outside were littered with the remains of the night's celebrations, and despite what had happened in the city square, there were still hundreds of people dancing together, sharing stories of what they had seen, determined to keep celebrating until the sun rose again.

Edgar sat next to Kate, his hands and face cut by the broken window during the warden attack, and Artemis sat opposite them, his injured leg stretched on the seat beside him, his forehead wrinkled with thought. Kate wanted to heal them both, but she knew she did not have the strength. Using the circles had left her weak and tired, and healing the bird had taken the very last piece of energy she had. All she could do was sit there, watching the city pass by, feeling the secret weight of *Wintercraft* hidden safely beneath her coat.

"Don't worry," said Edgar. "The Skilled will help us. I'm sure everything will be all right."

After what had happened, Kate wasn't so sure about that. All she had at that moment was the brief safety of the carriage and the rhythmic rumble of its wheels as it carried her on toward an uncertain future in an unfamiliar city.

"I hope you're right," she said.

Halfway across the city Silas and his stolen horse thundered along the streets, racing toward the southern gate and the freedom of the wild counties beyond. Silas knew every inch of that city and most of the City Below, but Fume was no longer his home. To him, its walls had been a cage for too long. Now he was free.

The gate guards saw him coming long before he reached them, his gray eyes gleaming fiercely in the dark. They unbolted the gate without waiting for his command, letting the horse and its rider gallop out into the wilds, leaving Fume and all its history behind. Silas carried with him questions the city could never answer and an ambition it could never help him reach. As a traitor he would be a hunted man, so he would find a ship and travel to the Continent, far away from Albion and the High Council, its laws, and its men. Kate Winters had allowed him to take revenge against his greatest enemy, and she had given him his freedom. The rest he was going to find on his own.

Silas followed a gravel road running alongside the red train's tracks, and he came across an old signpost marking a trader's path that was long overgrown. There, sitting on top of the sign, was a crow exactly like his own, except for a short line of white feathers running right down the center of its chest. A spark of familiar intelligence shone in its eyes, and Silas slowed his horse to a stop beneath it.

"Crow?"

The bird sat still, its eyes fixed upon the path.

Silas was about to snap the reins, cursing his mistake, when the crow looked at him, spread its wings, and circled him once before flying down to take its place upon his shoulder. Silas ran his fingers down the bird's white feathers where the wound from Da'ru's blade would have been.

"Well, Miss Winters," he said, looking back at the city one last time. "It seems I do owe you something, after all."